MEET ME IN ANOTHER LIFE

MEET ME IN ANOTHER LIFE

A Novel

○ ✺ ◉

CATRIONA SILVEY

𝓌𝓂

WILLIAM MORROW
An Imprint of HarperCollins Publishers

Map © Nicolette Caven.

HarperCollins books may be purchased for educational, business,
or sales promotional use. For information, please email the Special
Markets Department at SPsales@harpercollins.com.

FIRST EDITION

Designed by Leah Carlson-Stanisic

Library of Congress Cataloging-in-Publication Data has been applied for.

ISBN 978-0-06-302020-7

21 22 23 24 25   LSC   10 9 8 7 6 5 4 3 2 1

To Mum and Dad,
for this life

MEET ME IN ANOTHER LIFE

Part 1

WELCOME TO FOREVER

○ ✳ ◉

Thora wishes she could start again.

She wishes she hadn't dyed her hair blue, or worn the clashing orange pinafore dress that screams trying-too-hard-to-be-interesting. Above all, she wishes she hadn't come here, to the thudding crush of the international students' welcome party. The music rises another notch, obscuring what the boy in front of her is shouting.

"What?" she yells.

He leans close to her ear. *"I said, I really feel like we've met before!"*

She gives him a weak smile and throws back the rest of her half-empty red wine. Shaking the glass in explanation, she slips past him through the dark, strobing space, pushing the bar on the fire escape Out, she thinks with sudden desperation, *let me out*—to emerge into the cold wind outside.

"Whose idea was this?" she asks the cobbled square, the reconstructed façade of Cologne's old town. "Who holds a 'get to know you' event where no one can hear what anyone's saying?"

The city doesn't offer an answer. But Thora knows the noise wasn't really the problem. The problem was her. Since she stepped out of the Hauptbahnhof three days ago, she has felt a wall between her and everyone else, impenetrable and invisible as glass. She came to this party hoping the music and the drink would blast through it. Instead, she feels like she has spent the night screaming at her own reflection. Nothing from the other side came through. *What are you studying? Physics, no way! Where are you from?* Echo after echo of the same question, each leaving her more alone than the last.

She walks, not knowing where she's going. A breeze blows her hair back, cools her heated face. To her right, the square leaks out through narrow alleyways to the flat silk of the Rhine. To her left, past a grassy courtyard, a ruined clock tower points toward the sky, hands frozen at seven minutes to twelve.

Thora doesn't believe in fate. Still, she thinks some paths are better than others. Here, in her first week of university, on the threshold of so many futures, she feels a sick sense of vertigo. This is supposed to be where her life begins, and already she's taken a wrong turn. Why can't she be happy with one party, one city, one planet? What made her this way, gave her this ghost at the corner of her eye?

At the courtyard gate, she stops. Ignoring the padlock and chain, she vaults the railings and drops into the grass, following her shadow until it disappears. Ten steps bring her into a new world, quiet and roofed by stars. Thora breathes in like a swimmer surfacing from a long dive. She's about to lie down on the grass when she sees someone has beaten her to it: a boy, spread-eagled, head thrown back like he's trying to inhale the universe.

Someone else might thrill at encountering a kindred spirit. Thora only resents him: this space was hers, and he has taken it from her. She hovers on the grass, orbiting two possible worlds. She's alone, and it's dark: she should keep her distance. He's drunk, maybe passed out: she should check on him. She sucks in a breath and takes a bet on the second world. "Hallo?" she says. "Um—ist alles okay?"

The boy scrambles to his feet. Thora takes him in. Wide eyes and curly black hair, good-looking in a way that puts her on edge in case he knows it. Short, even accounting for the fact that most people are short from Thora's five-foot-eleven perspective.

"Englisch?" he says hopefully.

"Oh. Yeah. Please." She laughs. "As you may have noticed, my German is basically English in a German accent."

He looks over his shoulder at where he was lying, as if he owes her an explanation. "I was just—" He cuts himself off. "Santiago López. Santi." The accent matches the name. It takes Thora a moment to register that he's actually put his hand out for her to shake.

She takes it. "I thought you were passed out. I was coming to check on you."

"You kidding me? The beers in that club were five euros. I couldn't afford to pass out." He looks like he's laughing at her. "Do you have a name?"

"Of course. Introductions, that's how they work." She continues absurdly shaking his hand. "Thora Lišková."

He lets go of her hand to point at her. "You sound like you're from England. But your name doesn't."

One blessing of the loud party: it kept this conversation from happening. *Explain your existence!* Thora sighs, hoping to keep it short. "My dad's Czech and my mum's from Iceland, but I grew up in the UK." She shrugs. "Academics. You know how it is."

He runs a hand self-consciously through his hair. "Well, my father is a bus driver and my mother works in a shop, so—no, I don't."

"Oh, I'm sorry. I mean—I'm not sorry they're—" Every word pushes her on to a worse path. What right does he have to do this to her? She laughs under her breath. "Shit. You know what, I'm just going to start introducing myself as Jane Smith from now on."

Santi throws his hands up in mock-apology. "Sorry for trying to start a conversation."

"I didn't ask for a conversation." She hugs herself, looking up at the stars. "I just wanted to come outside and be alone."

"Of course. I'm sorry I trespassed in your private city." He bows mockingly and walks away.

Thora cringes. "Wait."

Santi turns.

"I'm sorry," she says. "This whole night—I've spent it failing to get through to anyone. I thought it was the noise, or everyone else, but I guess it's just me. And now—"

He's staring at her, caught between amusement and irritation. "Now what?"

Thora clicks her fingers. "I know. Do you mind lying back down? Just there, where you were. Like I was never here."

She expects him to walk away. But he shrugs and laughs and lies back down, and she has learned something about him.

"Okay. Wait there." Thora walks back the way she came. In the dark by the railings she counts to three, considers leaving, thinks God-what-am-I-doing, and sweeps back onto the grass, holding out her hand to a bewildered Santi. He takes it, letting her pull him to his feet.

"Hi," she says brightly. "I'm Thora Lišková. Nice to meet you for absolutely the first time."

A beat passes. A grin lights him up. "Santiago López Romero," he says, shaking her hand vigorously. "Please, call me Santi."

"Delighted." Thora lets go of his hand; with nothing to hold on to, hers drifts self-consciously to her hip. "So, um, if you weren't passed out, what were you doing?"

"Stargazing," he says, like it's a perfectly normal thing to admit to.

Thora's heart leaps. She squints up through the haze of city lights. "Can't see much from here."

"No. But maybe from up there." Santi points to the top of the clock tower.

Thora blinks. "You're suggesting we climb it?"

Santi shrugs. "Unless you have a jetpack handy."

Thora looks up at the tower, its brickwork a mess of holes. Something in her rings at the sight, a bell struck the right way at last. She feels it: the itch in her heart that goes away only when she's somewhere she shouldn't be, somewhere no one in their right mind would want to go. She wishes she'd suggested climbing the tower herself. Now, it will look like she's just doing it to impress him. "I'm not climbing a half-ruined tower with you! I don't even know you."

He is already crossing the grass. "How well can you ever really know someone?"

"Better than this," she says, catching up with him.

"Really?" he says. "I think we are all forever a mystery to each other."

Thora wonders how he pulled this sleight of hand, turning a joke into an earnest discussion. Part of her doesn't care. For the first time tonight, something is coming through. "Where's your evidence?" she demands.

"My parents. They've been married thirty years, but my father still discovers things about my mother that shock him."

"Really," Thora drawls. "Does your mum say the same thing about your dad?"

He looks confused, then wary. "Why?"

"Because that's a classic thing men say when they don't want to engage with women as people. *Oh, she's such a mystery*, when she's been telling you for the past thirty years what she wants and you just haven't been listening."

Santi smiles, but there's an edge to it. "Maybe your parents are like that."

"Oh, no. My parents have learned all there is to know about each other." Thora pulls her scarf tighter against the cold. "Forget finishing each other's sentences. These days they can skip entire conversations because they already know how they would end."

Santi vaults the railing and offers her his hand. "But that doesn't mean they know everything about each other. Sure, they know their relationship, but they still only know each other from one—I don't know how to say it. From one side."

Thora ignores his hand and climbs the railing herself. "What do you mean?"

"I mean, they only know each other as husband and wife. They might say things, do things, with their friends, even with you, that they'd never show to each other." He shrugs. "You can't ever know someone completely. You'd have to be everything to them, and that's impossible."

They're at the foot of the tower, where the stones bloom with graffiti: layers of words in pen and paint, an unreadable palimpsest in a dozen languages. Thora looks up. The tower is higher than she thought. Santi gives her a look like he's expecting her to back out. It's that, more than anything, that makes her step through the jagged gap in the wall.

Out of one world, into another. She expects to have lost Santi on the way, but he's with her, his breath the only sound in the universe. They look up into darkness studded with points of light. Through the hole at the top, the surviving roof tiles mask a glimpse of stars.

Thora steps onto the half-crumbled stairway that winds up the inside wall. She looks back at Santi. "So we're doing this."

He grins. "Why not?"

Thora ponders his words as she reaches the first gap in the stairs. Why not risk your life for curiosity? For her, it's a question that has never needed an answer. She jumps across, a thrill running from her scalp to the tips of her toes. As she climbs higher and the gaps get wider, she hunts for hand- and footholds in the wall, using the holes in the brickwork as stepping stones to take her higher. Before long, she's absorbed. The party, the terrible first impression she made on Santi, her fear of stepping onto the wrong path, all fall away. Now, the only path is vertical, and it leads her to the top of the tower, chasing the shrouded stars. She doesn't think about the drop, not even when the gaps in the wall show her night sky veiled with wisps of cloud. The wind whistles through, flicking her hair over her eyes. When her feet find the steps again, she turns to watch Santi climb across after her. It's much scarier to watch than it is to do. Music rises on the air: a melody whose source she's not sure of until she sees Santi's lips moving.

"Are you *singing*?" she says in disbelief.

He leaps to the other edge of the gap, dusting off his hands. "Yeah." He continues past her, up the final twist of the spiral. Thora thinks about what it means: he's not afraid. Not of falling, not of making a wrong choice. For a moment, her envy of him is absolute.

She follows him up through a hatch onto a wooden platform. Arches on three sides give onto views of the city. On the fourth side is the back of the clock, gears clogged with rust. Heated by the climb, Thora unwinds her scarf and hangs it on a rusty nail. At the edge, she sits down and tilts her head back. Cleared of the city lights, stars spray across the sky like blood-splatter from a god's violent death. "Isn't it weird how reality sometimes looks unrealistic?" she muses. "That shouldn't be possible. I mean, what are we comparing it to?"

"Something more real that we can't remember," Santi says, sitting down beside her. He follows her gaze upward. "When I was a kid, I used to think the stars were holes in the wall between us and heaven."

Thora smiles. "I thought they were stuck on the inside of the sky. Like the glow-in-the-dark ones I had on my bedroom ceiling."

"I had those too!" Santi grins. "Did you bring yours here?"

Thora looks at him warily, wondering if he's trying to catch her out. She takes a risk. "No. But I got new ones from the Odysseum." She points to the floodlit glass of the adventure museum across the river. "It's amazing. The gift shop has European Space Agency badges. You should go." She laughs. "If you don't mind being the oldest person in there by like—ten years."

"We're supposed to grow out of all that." Santi speaks quietly. "Little kids all love the stars. They all want to be astronauts. Explore the universe, see what no one else has ever seen. But then we get older and—we stop looking up. We keep our eyes on the ground and decide to be something realistic."

"I never did." Thora can't believe she's telling her biggest secret, the tender heart of her, to this boy she just met. She runs through his likely responses: laughter, fake interest, well-meaning advice to let go of what's never going to happen.

"Me neither." He tilts his head to the stars. "I want to go up there. It's all I've ever wanted."

For the first time since she arrived in the city, Thora relaxes into a genuine smile. "Why do you want to go?"

He looks at her like it's obvious. "I want to see God."

Thora laughs, because of course he's joking. He looks back at her calmly, not offended but not laughing along either.

She frowns. "You think God lives in space?" He cracks a smile. She pursues it. "You know all that stuff about heaven being up, it's—probably a metaphor."

"There is no up in space," he says seriously.

"So in space, you wouldn't be short? That's convenient," she says without thinking.

He looks hurt. She wants to go back, to try again, but in this universe, time only moves one way, tumbling her with it. "As for me," she says, "I want to go to space because in space, no one can hear me say the first stupid thing that comes into my head."

He doesn't exactly smile. "Why do you really want to go?"

She sighs. "I want to get as far away as possible from—all this." She gestures vaguely at the tower, the city, the planet.

"All this?" He stands up, swaying—she reaches out, but he catches himself on the arch. "What's wrong with all this?"

"Nothing." She shrugs. "It's fine. It's here. I've just always wanted—elsewhere."

"I know what you mean." Santi looks out at the city. "Still, here is pretty amazing."

For the first time since she climbed up, Thora looks down. Santi is right: the city by night is a marvel, a planet riven by glowing fissures. Directly below, the cobbled square gleams, the fountain in the center a puff of silver mist. To her left, the twin spires of the cathedral point like Gothic rockets to heaven. From the square at its feet, mismatched buildings trail down toward the river. Thora breathes out a smoke-cold breath and inhales the city, bomb-scarred and rebuilt, endlessly under construction. Her eyes follow the Hohenzollernbrücke stretching across the Rhine, lights reflected in the water like another version of it lies there drowned.

She points down at the bridge. "You know that whole thing's covered in padlocks?"

"Yeah, I walked across. It's impressive."

Thora snorts. "It's stupid, is what it is. What couple says, *Hey, let's celebrate the uniqueness of our love by doing the exact same thing thousands of other couples have done?*"

"Not just couples," Santi says. "I read the messages. There are locks there with the names of parents, children, friends."

"That's even worse! Great, let's make every human relationship equally trite!"

He throws her a teasing look. "You don't think that's beautiful? How universal it is?"

"Two tons. That's how much extra weight everyone's universal gestures add up to." She shakes her head. "One of these days the whole bridge is going to fall into the river."

"But think about the symbolism," Santi says in an awestruck tone. "A miracle of engineering, borne down by the weight of human love."

He's definitely teasing her. "I'm sure the people who symbolically die when the bridge symbolically collapses underneath them will appreciate it."

He laughs, high and exultant: the kind of laugh a boy might be mocked for. That he kept on laughing it anyway tells her something important about him.

Thora has been sitting still for too long: there is more to explore here, more to discover. She gets to her feet and steps around the opening in the floor to examine the rusted mechanism of the clock.

Santi stands up. "Need some light?"

"No, I've got it." She pulls out her lighter and flicks it on.

"You smoke?" Santi sounds surprised.

"God, no. My mum chain-smoked my whole childhood. That leaves a mark."

Santi steps closer as she holds the light up to the gears. "Think we can fix it?"

Thora puts her weight to one of the gears and tries to shove it backward. "No," she says, after a few seconds. "I'm afraid time has stopped."

Santi tries to push the gear in the other direction. Giving up, he steps back. "I guess it has." He smiles at her sideways in the flickering light. "Welcome to forever."

It's a pretentious thing to say. But Thora has to admit that's exactly how this feels: a moment taken out of time, with no beginning or end.

"So we have to commemorate this, right?" Santi says.

Thora blinks. "What do you mean?"

He reaches into his jacket and brings out something made of dark wood. It's only when he unfolds the tapered steel blade that Thora realizes it's a knife.

She stares. "Are you suggesting some kind of blood ceremony?"

"No! Wow, you Czech-Icelandic-British people are so intense."

Thora throws her head back in a laugh. "Congratulations on remembering all the nationalities. Most people have to be told a hundred times before they get it right."

He darts her a look. "I pay attention."

She holds out her hand for the knife. He gives it to her, and she examines it, turning the blade to the light. "Wow. You could stab someone to death with this."

"Why is that the first place your mind goes?" Santi shakes his head. "It was my grandfather's."

Thora looks at him suspiciously. "Why do you have a knife if you don't want to stab anyone?"

"Why do you have a lighter if you don't smoke?"

Thora shrugs. "You never know when you might need to set something on fire."

"And you never know when you might need to carve something into a wall." He takes the knife back from her and goes to one of the pillars between the arches.

She watches over his shoulder as he cuts into the stone. "Santiago López Romero," she reads.

He hands the knife to her. "I don't know how to spell your name." He leans over her shoulder to watch her work. "I hate to tell you, but that's not a letter."

She brushes the brick dust off the Þ that begins her first name. "Yes it is. It's a thorn. We still use it in Icelandic. It used to be in the English alphabet too."

"So what you're saying is, I *really* didn't know how to spell it."

Their two names sit stark on the wall: no ampersand, no heart, nothing but shared space holding them together. That's right, Thora decides. "I'm glad I left the party," she tells him.

"Of course," Santi says. "I mean, this was fate, right?"

Thora blinks. "'Scuse me?"

"Fate. Us meeting each other. Climbing the tower."

She laughs. "Really? You're a determinist? Free will is an illusion, the universe is a ball rolling down a hill, et cetera?"

He shakes his head. "I'm not talking about determinism. I'm talking about fate."

"What's the difference?"

He sits down again on the edge of the platform. "Determinism means everything's meaningless but we can't change it. Fate means there's a plan that God is working through us."

"Right," Thora says slowly. "So the only reason we climbed this tower was because God wanted us to?"

Santi stays irritatingly serene. "That's not how it works. He didn't make us do it directly. He made us the kind of people who would choose to climb a ruined tower just to see the stars."

Thora pushes her hair back. "Where to even start. What made me the kind of person I am?" She frowns at the echo of her thought as she left the club. "Maybe there's something genetic there. God knows my parents are weird. But it also has a lot to do with my childhood, with the things I've experienced in my life." The buzz of the argument makes her feel drunk, even though she only had one glass of wine and that was an hour ago. "Think about it. What if your parents had moved to Cologne before you were born? If you'd grown up here? What if mine had stayed in the Netherlands where they met? What if—I don't know, something tragic had happened when we were children? We'd be completely different people."

Santi shakes his head. "I don't accept that. We are who we are. We would be the same people whatever happened to us."

"Okay. Let's do a thought experiment. Tonight, did you make a series of decisions that led to you lying on the grass and staring at the stars?"

He hesitates. "It felt like I did," he concedes. "But I made those decisions because of the person I am."

"And you weren't even close to deciding something else?"

She's animated now, turned toward him, the city and the stars forgotten. "I can tell you I was. I nearly went down to the river. I nearly went back into the club, God help me. And if I had done either of those things, we wouldn't be having this conversation."

He grins. "So you think this conversation will radically change who we are?"

"Stop twisting my argument!" She's angry at him, his security in who he is, when she feels like a bundle of contradictory ideas clumsily woven into a person. "No, maybe not this conversation. But if we—see each other again, become part of each other's lives—"

His grin intensifies. "You want to become part of my life? Thora, I don't even *know* you!"

She hits him on the shoulder. "*Friends* change each other's lives all the time." She rolls up her sleeve to reveal the tattoo she got two days ago in the Belgian Quarter, the skin of her wrist still reddened around a cluster of faint stars. "Take this. My friend Lily said we should get tattoos to commemorate starting uni. So if I hadn't met Lily ten years ago, I would literally be physically different right now."

Santi takes her arm, turns it to the light. "What is it?"

"It's a constellation. Vulpecula. The fox. That's what my surname means." She picks at the edges where it's starting to scab. "I guess—it sounds stupid, but I got it to remind me who I am. That I belong up there."

Santi flicks a leaf off the edge, watches it make its erratic way down. "Why would you need a tattoo to remember that?"

He probably doesn't mean it as an insult. But Thora feels it as one, like he's seen through her affectations to the incoherence at her core.

The cathedral bells toll. It's two in the morning. Thora feels a waver of decision, the only evidence she has that Santi is wrong: she did have the choice to climb up here, and she has the choice now to climb back down. "I should go," she says.

Santi grins at her. "I knew you were going to say that."

She rolls her eyes at him. "Fine. Just to prove you and God wrong, I'll stay."

"Okay. Enjoy yourself. I'm going," he says, and disappears through the hole in the floor.

Thora meant to stay, to steal some time alone with the stars. But sooner than she expected, she starts to feel lonely. As she lowers herself onto the stairs, she makes the mistake of looking down. The tower drops into darkness, shot with shards of light like Santi's childish idea of heaven. Except what's beyond is solid ground, and Thora doesn't believe she's going anywhere else if she falls to her death tonight. Her palms sweat. Wedging her foot into a dent in the brickwork, she feels for the next foothold as her hands start to slip. Lunging wildly, she grabs for a protruding brick and pulls herself into the wall.

She hangs, staring through a gap in the bricks. She knows what she should see: the starry sky above the city. Instead, she sees herself, endlessly refracted. An infinity of Thoras stare back at her with fear in their eyes.

She almost loses her grip. Squeezing her eyes shut, she swings herself to the safety of the steps and collapses.

"Thora?" Santi climbs back up to her. "Are you okay? What happened?"

"Nothing. I just—I thought I saw—" She trails off. She knows exactly what she saw. Her nightmares come to life: endless versions of herself spiraling out from every decision she makes, all but one of them lost forever.

"What?"

She meets Santi's worried gaze. "God," she says mockingly.

Santi shakes his head, smiling. "I guess we are pretty high up."

By the time Thora reaches the ground, her limbs are shaking. "I can't believe we just did that."

Santi is grinning. "I can."

"As we've established, you'll believe anything." Something's missing. Thora's hands go to her neck. "Fuck! I left my scarf up there."

Santi is already stepping back through the gap. "I'll get it."

"No! Don't worry. It was—a cheap thing, it doesn't matter." Her father knitted it as a good luck present for her new start. Thora thinks of how they parted: the angry words they threw at each other after he couldn't resist criticizing her choices one last time. She straightens her shoulders. She didn't want the scarf anyway. Better to think of it as her flag, planted at the top of the city she's claiming for her own.

"You sure?"

"Sure."

"Okay." He looks over his shoulder. "You walking back to Lindenthal?"

Thora weighs up her options before she answers. She doesn't want this conversation to end. But on the long walk home, there are so many ways it could go wrong: she might insult him again, or he might expect her to kiss him goodbye. Better to walk away while something's still perfect. "No, I—left my friend Lily in the club," she improvises. "I should go and check on her. See if she's okay."

"All right." He hesitates. "Can I get your number?"

"Sure."

He watches for her missed call on his screen. Then he steps back, like he doesn't know how to end this. "Well. Good night."

"Good night," she says.

They walk away in opposite directions. Thora doesn't look back.

She puts off calling him. She's worried he'll think she wants something romantic, and she's almost sure she's not interested in him that way. She has a crush on Jules, a girl in her dormitory, and is starting to think it might be reciprocated. The last thing she needs is a misunderstanding with a boy as intense and unpredictable as Santi. Still, she looks up at the glowing lights on her ceiling and thinks about the snap of magnets, the mutual orbit of binary stars. She wishes ardently that there was a way in this world for a girl to tell a boy she wants to be his best friend. She would take any form—a boy his age, an old woman, a brain in a vat—anything to guarantee that he would get past the surface and engage with the truth of her.

Weeks later, she's mulling it over when she walks past a noticeboard in the dormitory and sees his face, surrounded by flowers.

She stops short. Three words on the wall, stark as graffiti. REST IN PEACE. The picture and the words are two incompatible languages shoved into a sentence.

Jules stops next to her. "Did you hear? It's awful. They found him under the clock tower in the old town. People are saying he jumped."

"He didn't jump." Thora sees it more vividly than she can bear: her scarf, billowing out from the top of the tower. Santi climbing, eyes lifted past it to the stars. So sure of himself, of his one God-guided path through the world, that the possibility of falling would never have entered his mind.

She wanted to win the argument. She didn't want this, the

darkest proof of her victory: she has had an impact on his life, the worst and most permanent of all. She flashes back to her hands slipping, almost falling. Why does this feel like an exchange? As if Santi has taken her death, fallen in her place?

She quakes with anger at the person she was a few weeks ago. *Better to walk away while something's still perfect.* What kind of idiot thinks like that? Who chooses perfection that doesn't exist over messiness and complication that does?

"Did you know him?" Jules asks.

She opens her mouth. *No one ever really knows anyone*, she wants to say, like his ghost is at her lips. "Yes," she says instead. Because the whole of him is inside her, prismed through that one night at the top of the tower: Santi, who wanted to reach the stars so he could see the face of God.

Jules hugs her, leaning her head on Thora's shoulder. Jules is only seventeen, a year younger than the rest of her class, but there is something about her that makes Thora feel looked-after, safe. Relaxing into her embrace, Thora sees the future as clearly as if Santi's ghost were speaking her fate into her ear. She will go to the bar with Jules for a consolatory drink. They will talk, and later they will kiss. She will go back to Jules's room, three doors down from her own. It will be everything she wanted, but for a long time, she will be too numb with grief to feel it.

The next morning, she leaves Jules's room without waking her. She goes down to the hall where Santi's memorial has collected flowers and cards. She reads the messages, looking for any that understood him. *Miss you, man. You were a good guy. God bless.* Each one could have been written by a machine. The desperate loneliness of it hits her: to die in the first few weeks of university, when all someone knows of you is that you smiled at them in the library, or bought them a drink at the bar. But she knows him better.

She leaves him the European Space Agency badge she got at the Odysseum, the one she didn't wear the night they met because she was afraid what people might think of her. She puts it at the back of the table, turned toward his face. She is sure, now, that she will never reach the stars. If she was on the right path, Santi would still be here, and he would be coming with her.

"I hope you found what you were looking for," she says.

Two nights later, she buys a can of spray paint and walks to the old town at three in the morning. Over the faded words at the base of the tower she writes, for him, WELCOME TO FOREVER.

OPEN YOUR EYES

○ ✸ ◎

Santi is late.

It's not unusual: lateness is a trait in him, unchangeable as the curl in his hair. Still, there are better times for it to manifest than on the first day of a new school year. Bad enough if he was still a student: unforgivable in a teacher with twenty-five years' experience. He hurries past the fountain in the center of the cobbled square, dodging the crowds. As he passes the ruined clock tower, he looks up to check the time, forgetting that the hands are stuck as always at eight minutes past eleven.

This morning, he woke sprawled across his bed as if he'd fallen there from an unfathomable height. It's a dream he's had before. This time, it took thirty minutes of walking around his apartment, examining the evidence of his life—his cat Félicette meowing for her breakfast, the tablecloth crocheted by his mother, the picture of Héloïse on the balcony, looking apprehensively at the approaching rain—until he felt like it was his own again. Now, he steps from the busy market into the quiet courtyard of the international school and tries to gather himself into coherence. Unconsciously, his hand reaches into his jacket to touch the smooth wood of his grandfather's knife.

He enters the classroom under the gaze of thirty assembled seven-year-olds. The faces are different, but everything else is the same. The lonely déjà vu of being a teacher: living the same year over and over, surrounded by children for whom this is the only version that matters.

"Hello," he says. "I'm Mr. López. I'm your science teacher. In this room, you'll be learning about the world and how it works. About the things we know, and the things we're still figuring out." He scans the room, meeting their eyes. "If there's one thing I hope you learn this year, it's to pay attention to everything around you. Don't take anything for granted. That's what science is all about." He's been working on this speech for years, dropping a word here, refining a phrase there, but he doubts the children are listening. They're sizing him up in other ways: his accent, his gestures, his clothes. Deciding, as unconsciously as animals, whether or not he is part of their pack. "I thought we'd start by getting to know each other," he says. "Raise your hand. When I call on you, tell me your name, and what you want to be when you grow up. I'll write it on the board, so we can all learn something about each other." A flurry of hands shoot up; most stay down. "If you don't put your hand up now, I will call on you later. But there'll be less space left on the board, so you'll have to be smaller. Hands up if you don't want to be small."

The number of hands increases slightly. He smiles and picks a boy on the right. "You were first. What's your name?"

"Ben," the boy says.

"And what do you want to be when you grow up, Ben?"

"A footballer."

A predictable start. "Great. What's your team?" As the boy starts to answer, Santi cuts him off. "Real Madrid, same as me! Cool." Laughter from the other children. He turns to the board and draws a cartoon boy heading a football. When he steps back, some of the kids giggle. It's not exactly a work of art. He always meant to spend more time on his drawing, to take his skills from adequate to impressive. But his doodles are enough to keep the children's attention.

"Next." He looks over the sea of hands. His eye is drawn to a girl with mid-brown hair, tall for her age, with stark blue eyes that look older than the rest of her. "You," he says. "What's your name?"

She lowers her hand. "Thora Lišková."

"*Lish*-ko-va," he repeats, copying her stress on the first syllable. "How do you spell that?"

She tells him. "It means Fox," she adds with somber pride.

"Really? My name means Wolf."

She smiles back, a goofy grin that makes the boy next to her snigger. Santi's heart hurts. One of those kids the world hasn't yet closed down, her joy like a target on her back. *Stay how you are, Thora Lišková*, he prays silently, although he knows it's no use. He gives it a year before she starts caring more about what people think of her than what makes her happy. "And what do you want to be?" he asks.

She doesn't hesitate. "An astronaut."

Santi manages to smile. He has no problem with the ones who want to be footballers or vets or racing drivers. *Go on*, he tells them. *Chase your dreams.* Even though, statistically, they will end up working in call centers. But the ones who want to be astronauts are harder.

He swallows down half a lifetime of regret. "That's a tough choice," he says. "But worthwhile." He draws her in blue: a tiny, relentless figure in a space helmet, planting a flag on a miniature planet. When he turns back, her face is pink and she won't meet his eyes.

He goes through the class until the board is full of rappers, cake decorators, doctors. Thora floats at the edge, as if she's about to step off into the untrammeled world beyond. "Now," Santi says, handing out lined paper, "I want you to write and illustrate a story about your future self. Imagine you are what you told me you want to be. Show me what it's like." He sits down, ready for fifteen minutes of relative peace.

A hand waves at the corner of his eye.

"Yes?"

"What about you, Mr. López?" Thora, her face bright. "What did you want to be?"

He lies without hesitation. He can't show her a living example of someone who wanted the same thing and failed. "Obviously, I wanted to be a science teacher," he says. "And here I am."

Scattered laughs and groans. None of the children he's drawn on the board are teachers.

Her hand goes up again.

He sighs. "Yes, Thora."

"You should draw yourself."

Other voices join in. "Yeah." "Go on, sir." The only space left is at the edge, next to Thora. He draws himself there, smaller than any of them, hair a mad-scientist frizz, bald spot a full monk's tonsure. First rule of working with children: stab yourself in your own weak points before they can find them. *Mr. López*, he writes underneath, to gratifying giggles.

He bows and sits down. He can tell without looking that Thora's hand is still up. "Last question, then I want you to get on with your writing."

"You should give yourself a space helmet," she says. "Or you won't be able to breathe."

He looks back at the board. He was imagining each drawing

as its own separate universe. Now she's pulled him into hers, into the orbit of the tiny planet she's exploring.

"You're absolutely right." He draws a quick bubble around his head. "Now, I mean it. Silent working."

He sits down, oddly touched by Thora's generosity. He's still pondering it at the end of the day as he passes through the empty playground onto the cobbled street, the buildings of Cologne's old town pressing in on him under lowering clouds.

Santi wants his life to make sense. Usually, his faith carries him through when the world sends him nothing but static and noise. But moments like this, clear as a voice speaking in his ear, are what he lives for. If he couldn't do it, perhaps Thora can. And perhaps he can be her first step on a pathway that leads to the stars.

He knows this is a terrible idea. It's one reason he never had children of his own, so he wouldn't project his frustrated ambitions onto them. (The other is that Héloïse divorced him and moved back to France.) But this, he argues with himself as he passes under the golden sign of the centaur and sits down at the bar, is different. Thora already told him her ambition: his job is to let her know it's possible.

Brigitta the barmaid places a slim glass of local lager in front of him. Santi raises it to her and drinks, taking in the reflected version of Der Zentaur that exists in the mirror behind the bar. Conversations in half a dozen languages wash over him: thick Kölsch dialect, standard German, English, Russian, Spanish. Those he understands, he can almost mouth along to: familiar complaints about the traffic on the Ring, the new crop of university students crowding the bars of the old town. He remembers when he was one of those students, stumbling into Der Zentaur with no idea of the resentment he was causing to the old-timers at the bar. It feels impossible that he should be one of them now.

Usually, he meets his friend Jaime here and stays for a few drinks, but Jaime is back in Spain visiting family. Alone, Santi finishes his one beer and leaves. Out of habit, he looks up, but the stars are shrouded by the city lights. As he walks the night-lit shopping streets of Neumarkt, he sings to himself, a wordless, familiar tune. He should feel at home here by now, in this city with its many names. Köln to the locals, Cologne to the teachers of the international school, Colonia to his family, when they call to ask him when he's coming back. Only the Spanish preserves the meaning of the colony it once was, named and founded by foreigners. He steps over the invisible line of the old Roman wall: another foreigner, not conquering but passing through.

His phone rings. His sister, Aurelia. "Lita," he says as he crosses the broad, tree-lined Ring into the Belgian Quarter.

"Is this a good time?" she asks, her voice compressed by distance. The couple of thousand kilometers between them might as well be light-years.

"Yeah. Just walking home from work." A passing man shoots Santi a look and spits into the gutter. Because he's speaking Spanish, or for some other reason, or for no reason at all? His brain whirls in the exhausting mental dance of not belonging.

"How are the new kids?" Aurelia asks.

"Same as always." He corrects himself. Thora, the anomaly. "One of them wants to be an astronaut."

His sister makes a sympathetic noise. "What are you going to tell her?"

"To try her best."

Aurelia is quiet for a moment. "Is that kind?"

Santi wonders how to answer. *It's what I wish I'd been told.* "She's a rich kid at an international school," he says instead. "She has more chance than I ever did." Before Aurelia can argue, he changes the subject. "How's my niece?"

Aurelia sounds exasperated. "God knows. She calls me once every six weeks to tell me she's not dead."

Santi smiles as he turns onto his street. "Tell her to come visit me sometime."

"She wouldn't need to visit if you were closer. Mama wants to know if you applied for that job in Almuñécar."

He should have known Aurelia would seize the opportunity to return to her favorite subject. He sighs. "I'm thinking about it."

"That means no." He leaves a gap for her to continue. "Santi. You tell me all the time you don't feel right there."

"I know," he says. But the truth is, he hasn't told them the half of it. How after almost thirty years, he's still sometimes so home-sick he can't breathe. How the daily texture of life here, among these cold, hurried strangers, is alien in a way that keeps him constantly on edge. He switches the phone to his left hand, fumbles with the keys to his apartment building. "I'm just—I'm not ready to leave yet."

It's not quite true. But what is true, he doesn't know how to tell her: that going home feels like the wrong direction.

Aurelia sighs. "I know what your problem is. You don't want to live on this planet."

He laughs as he climbs the stairs. "You know me so well."

"Look, I have to go. But think about the job, okay?"

He promises her and hangs up, unlocking his door and switching on the lights. He waters the twisted, overgrown shrub Héloïse left behind—her abortive attempt at a bonsai tree—and sits down heavily on the sofa. He's tired, but in an enervated way that doesn't let him rest. Félicette stalks across the floor, disappears into the kitchen, then reappears suddenly by his shoulder. He strokes her chin, pours himself another beer, and starts marking the students' essays. When he gets to Thora's, he saves it at the bottom of the pile for a treat.

Finally, he's through the rest of the stack. He clears them aside and leans over Thora's. She's drawn the tiny planet he made for her, with her own additions: purple lakes, outlandish trees, aliens with eyes in their toes. Her imagination has overflowed to the point where he can barely tell what's happening. He squints at a figure sticking out from the side of the planet.

"Dr. Lišková, I presume," he murmurs.

Seen through her own eyes, Thora is gangly and awkward, sticks of hair spilling out of her space helmet. In her hand, she triumphantly clutches a bottle of some red substance. Santi consults the text to find it's a "sample." She's a good writer for her age, if a little prone to using long words without fully understanding what they mean.

He's starting to write his comment when he spots himself. A tiny figure on the planet's opposite side, barely more than a crayon smudge. He wouldn't have recognized himself if she hadn't labeled him, in lettering twice the size of his diminutive shape.

"That better not be a comment on my height," he mutters, taking a swig of his beer.

Good work, he writes. *Thanks for inviting me along.*

He puts her work with the rest of the pile and leans back, amusement mixed now with melancholy. He envies Thora: not the small miseries of life at her age, but the illusion of infinite potential. He lists again the things that held him back: lack of money, failing his physics exam, his family telling him to settle for something reliable. He asks himself how many of those were just excuses. Perhaps he sabotaged himself: brought down the failure he feared so he wouldn't have to wait for it anymore. Or perhaps God wanted him for something different.

He dozes off on the sofa, thinking about miracles: about the man he once saw floating five inches above the cobbles, perfectly still, his face expressionless and his hands spread wide.

At the parents' evening, Santi meets them for the first time: Thora's mother, a comparative mythologist, and her father, a philosopher built like a prizefighter.

"Mr. and Mrs. Lišková," he says, putting out his hand.

"Actually, it's Dr. Liška," says the father. His handshake is slightly too firm. "My daughter has the feminine form of my surname."

"Dr. Rasmusdottir," says the mother.

"My wife preferred not to take my name in any form," says the father with a too-loud laugh.

The mother's English has no discernible accent. Santi suspects expensive international schools, like the one he teaches in. He gets the whiff of alcoholism from the father: the trembling hand, an overly enthusiastic demeanor, fragile like the casing of a bomb.

"Your daughter is very bright," he says.

"We know that," says her father, laughing again.

"Her problem is she doesn't apply herself," says her mother.

"She applies herself where she's interested," Santi points out. He doesn't know why he's defending Thora: he is supposed to be on the other side. Everything about this is upside down. He feels like a child catapulted into the body of a middle-aged man, expected somehow to know what he is doing.

"I see," says Dr. Liška. "You are the science teacher, yes?"

"I am."

"Yes. We see Thora's true strengths as being more in the arena of the humanities. Writing, history, and so forth."

"Her writing is very good," Santi agrees. "But that's a skill she can continue to develop in many contexts. Studying the sciences would allow her to pursue what she's interested in, as well as opening up other opportunities."

The parents exchange a look. Dr. Rasmusdottir looks back at Santi. "You mean her ridiculous obsession with space."

Santi feels a quiver of disbelief. The scornful tone, the rolling eyes: it's cartoonish, a seven-year-old's version of parents who don't understand. When Thora described them to him, he assumed she was exaggerating.

"It's not ridiculous." He's not supposed to contradict the parents directly. He revises. "What I mean is, an interest like that is an important motivator. I would advise encouraging it. Or at least not actively discouraging it."

He can tell they aren't convinced. They nod, though, and thank him before moving on. Santi watches them go. He reminds himself: if God's test were easy, it would be meaningless.

At morning break the next day, Santi brings his coffee back to his classroom and finds Thora at her desk, drawing. He watches her pause to delineate a cluster of faint dots on the inside of her wrist.

"Thora, it's break time."

She doesn't look up.

He tries again. "You're supposed to be outside."

"I want to stay here."

Officially, he should send her out: he can't shelter a child from the natural order of things. The lions take down the gazelle and it lies twitching and eviscerated. But, fresh from his anger with her parents, he rebels. When he sits down next to her, she flinches in surprise. She bows her head and starts violently coloring in.

"What are you drawing?" Santi asks.

She looks up, a flash of blue like a shy tropical fish. "Hades."

"Wow." Santi looks at her drawing: a lot of black, with fragments of exploded buildings and what looks like a rabbit with a baby's head. "You like the Greek myths?"

Her expression is noncommittal. "My mum and dad got me a book about them."

First blood to her parents and the classical education. "They're good stories," Santi says. "It's interesting to see how people used to explain the world, before they had scientific ways of figuring out what was really happening." Second blood to Santi and the stars.

"Yeah," Thora says. "Like, in ancient Greek times, they thought people went on after they died."

Santi frowns. "You don't think they do?"

She gives him a look of flat scorn. "You're a *science* teacher," she says, and goes back to drawing her hellscape.

Santi leans back, weighing his words carefully. "Science can't tell us much about what happens to people after they die."

She looks up at him in challenge. "Yes, it can. We go moldy and decompose, like in the bread experiment we did last week. And then we're skeletons."

"You're right," he acknowledges. "But that's just what we can observe. How do we know there isn't some other part of a person that goes on? A part we can't observe?"

Thora chews her pencil. "I guess we don't," she says, looking annoyed. "Unless we could talk to someone who had died and ask."

"Well, I'll probably die before you," Santi says. "I promise, if there's anything after, I'll try to come back and tell you about it."

"Thanks." She grins, all suggestion of shyness gone. At this age, she seems to transform from moment to moment. But it's an illusion: the person Thora will come to be is in there. All he can do is help her emerge.

He stands up. "In the meantime, I was planning a class trip to the Odysseum."

Thora looks up, breathless. "The adventure museum?"

He nods. "What do you think?"

The joy on her face is almost enough.

The Odysseum is on the other side of the river, tied up in a knot of conference centers and autobahns. As Santi leads a straggling group of children across the Hohenzollern bridge to the boom of the cathedral bells, he reminds himself why he is doing this. *For Thora*, he thinks with determination, as two children try to pry one of the padlocks from the fence and a third hangs back to poke at a dead pigeon.

"Keep up!" he yells, clapping his hands. By the grace of God, he shepherds them safely down the steps, through the playground scattered with fiberglass models of the planets, into the humming lobby of the museum. He pays for admission and ushers them one by one through the turnstile. "Meet in the cafeteria at three," he manages to tell them before they scatter like loose marbles. Among them he sees Thora in a mustard-yellow scarf, running off on her own. Part of him wants to trail her through the museum, be there to answer her questions, but he knows nothing would be so likely to put her off. He needs to let her find her own way.

Instead, he wanders on his own hyperbolic path through the exhibits. He has been here so many times that if a bomb hit the museum, he could reconstruct it room by room: the curving walls of the faux-planetarium, dotted with lights that correspond to no Earthly constellations; the empty spacesuits lined up like celestial knights. He catches his distorted reflection in the mirror of an astronaut's helmet. Thinking of Thora's drawing, he smiles. Behind him, made tiny by the curve of the gold-coated plastic, an alien figure appears.

"Hello, Thora." He turns. "I like your scarf."

"It's itchy." She tugs at it discontentedly. "My dad knitted it."

Santi tries to imagine the trembling, muscular philosopher knitting. He blinks. "My mother does crochet," he offers.

Thora looks baffled.

"Ah yes, I should have explained. Scientifically speaking, it's necessary even for ancient people like myself to have mothers." He gives her a tired smile. "Don't you want to explore the museum?"

"I already have."

He looks at her in surprise. "That didn't take you very long."

She shrugs. "I wish there was more of it."

Her curiosity, scraping against the limits of her world, hurts his heart. "Did you have any questions?"

She stares at their reflections in the space helmet, brow wrinkling. "Is it true that if you were in a spacesuit and it got a hole in, your blood would boil and your lungs would explode?"

Santi considers her worried face and thinks about how to answer. "Depends," he says. "If it was a small hole, the suit would decompress slowly. You'd just run out of air and fall asleep." He gives her a reassuring smile. "Any other questions?"

"Yes, actually. I wanted to ask you about windows."

"Windows?"

She nods enthusiastically.

Santi has no idea where this is going. At least he can expose her to the museum a second time while she finds her point. He leads her back through the hall of spacesuits toward the planetarium.

"So there's a window in my attic that looks out into the garden," she begins. "Or, it should look into the garden, because it's on that side of the house. But it doesn't. It looks into somewhere else."

"Somewhere else?" He's half-listening, half-concentrating on the exhibits scattered through the ground floor of the planetarium, trying to guess which one might spark her interest. He pauses in front of a display titled "PROXIMA B: EARTH'S CLOSEST EXOPLANET." He wonders wryly if the word "closest" might put Thora off.

"Yes," says Thora, ignoring him and walking on. "I know because it doesn't have the bush that should be under that window, the one with the white flowers. Instead there's this building, but it doesn't look like a real building. More like—a dream of one."

"That sounds very strange." Santi slows down as they come out of the planetarium into a dead end. Ahead of them is a closed-off room hung with a yellow sign reading "im Bau/Under Construction." Santi goes up to the barrier, trying to peer through, but the space beyond is dark.

"Excuse me," someone says in English.

Santi turns. A tall man with long hair, wearing a bright blue coat. The apparel suggests museum staff, some kind of educational entertainer for the children, but the expression doesn't match: he looks anxious, like there is something he needs to say but he doesn't know how. The way Héloïse used to look, before she left.

"I'm afraid that room isn't ready yet," the man says. "However, we do have another room you might like to see." He points to the right, where Santi remembers a wall papered with an image from the Kepler telescope. Now, a door hangs open.

The man looks back and forth between them with a nervous smile. He probably thinks Thora is Santi's daughter. His stomach twists, thinking of the children he and Héloïse never had. He smiles. "Sure, we'll check it out."

The room is small and bare, home to a cardboard cut-out of the Moon and a push-button game called Rocket Mission. Santi walks up to the game, hands in his pockets. "Wow. They really spared no expense."

Thora joins him, still absorbed in her story. "I was thinking of climbing out of my window. To see what it's like out there," she says, as she punches in a launch sequence with the casual competence of the young.

"You probably shouldn't," says Santi, wondering whether he ever had dreams this vivid; certain that if he did, he never told his teachers about them. "Remember what we learned about gravity last week?"

Thora rolls her eyes as their imaginary craft reaches the mesosphere, solid rocket boosters falling back like spent candles. "I wouldn't fall," she says. "But I guess if I did, I'd find out if it was really somewhere else or not."

A scientist at heart. Santi imagines Thora's parents finding her flat on her back in the garden. *Mr. López told me not to take anything for granted.*

"So. What I wanted to ask was," Thora says, "can windows take you to other places?"

He frowns. "I'm not sure I understand. I'm guessing you don't mean places like your garden?"

"No," she says firmly. "I mean like—*other* places."

Santi watches the blip of their craft curve across the screen. "You mean other worlds?"

She lights up. "Yes. Other worlds."

Santi smiles. The kind of conversation he'd imagined being a science teacher was all about. "Probably not. At least not on Earth. In space, there might be holes that could take you from one part of the universe to a different, faraway part."

She frowns. "But my window couldn't be one of those holes?"

"No. What you saw was probably just a trick of the light." She looks so disappointed that he adds, "That doesn't mean it's boring! It's very interesting, how what we see turns into what we think we see."

"I know what I saw," Thora insists.

The machine emits a strangled bleep. The screen flashes, prompting them for input.

"Look," Santi says, glad for the distraction. "We have to decide whether to go through the debris field or reroute to avoid it."

Thora, suddenly focused, stands on her tiptoes, squinting at the screen. "I suppose rerouting would be safer. But it says if we do that, it'll take us longer to get there."

Santi considers his words carefully. He knows what the right answer is, or at least the answer the machine wants. But he doesn't want to teach Thora to be cautious, to always choose the safer path.

"We have shields," he points out. "They might not catch everything, but they give us some protection. And going the long way would use up more fuel. But—you're the captain. You should decide."

Thora ponders it, her furrowed brow making her look older than she is. "I think we should go through the debris field." Her finger hovers over the button. Santi feels her indecision like a vibration in the air. "If it goes wrong, we can always just play again," she says with a nervous laugh.

"That seems like cheating to me," Santi says. "I think we should make a choice and stick to it."

Thora looks up at him, appalled. "But what if we make the wrong choice?"

"There's no wrong choice," Santi says. "There's just what happens."

"Bet you won't say that if we die," she mutters, and presses the appropriate button. The ship blurts forward, then the screen goes dark.

Santi taps the screen, thumps the console. Nothing happens. Thora kneels down and jiggles the cable. "I think it's broken." Standing up, she looks for the man in the blue coat. "Hello? Mr.—museum person?" But when they go back into the corridor, he is nowhere to be found.

Santi checks his watch. "Come on. We're out of time."

On the last day of the school year, Thora comes to see him in his classroom. Her parents are transferring her to a school with an intensive humanities program. Santi tried to argue them out of it, throwing himself against the machinery of the world, but they were immovable. He has given up, gracefully, accepting that his time in Thora's life is done.

She slides a card across his desk. "I got this for you."

"Thank you." He doesn't open it; he doesn't trust himself not to get emotional, and that doesn't fit with who Thora needs him to be.

"I don't want to go to a new school," she says.

Santi experiences one of those rare moments he can count on the fingers of one hand, of seeing her as the person she will one day be: tall, awkward, angry but focused, capable of anything. "You'll be fine." He gives her what she deserves: an undoubting smile. "You're going to make an amazing astronaut one day."

She twists her hands together. "I don't think I want to be one anymore."

He feels it like a blow to the heart. "Oh?"

"I want to be a teacher like you."

She will not chase the dream he gave up, and it's his fault. God's hand has made him the instrument of his own failure. *This should teach me*, he thinks, but he's not sure what.

"Bye," Thora says in a strangled voice, and flees.

He opens the card. He expects one last drawing, but there are only words.

Mr. Wolf,
Thank you for being my favorite teacher.
I hope I see you again.
Love,

Thora

Santi tucks the card into his desk drawer. He's been round this track too many times: students and their goodbyes, a fuzz of static cutting out to radio silence. Thora may miss him now, but he'll soon fade into the background of her life, just as she will fade into the forgotten hundreds who have passed through this classroom. If she sees him on the street in ten years' time, she will double back to avoid him, rather than face the awkward retreading of a relationship long since expired. *I hope I see you again.* He already knows he never will.

NO GOING BACK

○ ✻ ◎

Thora sits at a corner table in Der Zentaur, waiting for Brigitta to bring her a glass of wine. The wiring diagrams she brought as a gesture toward the social acceptability of solitary daytime drinking are out on the table, but she knows she won't give them more than a glance. These days, most of her is lost in space. What's left rattles around Cologne, oscillating between her flat in Ehrenfeld and her job at an engineering firm across the river: a distance so small that from the perspective of the universe she might as well be standing still.

Watching dust fall through a sunbeam, she runs through her excuses. The ones she gave her parents: not realistic, not smart enough. The real one: her paralysis in the face of important choices. Each time life puts her at a crossroads, she doubles back, terrified at the thought of trapping herself on a single path. It's driven away everyone she's ever tried to have a relationship with. And it's kept her from her ambition as effectively as a wall across the sky.

Brigitta thunks a glass onto the table.

"Danke," Thora says without looking up. She's surprised

when her fingers touch cold. A slim glass of Kölsch, the local lager, not what she ordered.

"Entschuldigung," someone says from across the room.

A man about her age, mid-twenties, with dark curly hair, holds up a glass of red wine. Cautiously, Thora nods. As he comes over, smiling, she feels a tremor that is something like dread.

His accent wasn't German; she makes a safe bet and switches to English. "I don't have to talk to you just because you have my drink."

"What about because you have *my* drink?" Spanish, she guesses, but his English is confident.

"Here you go." Thora slides the Kölsch across the table. "Interaction complete."

He places her wine on a mat and pushes it closer to her, sitting down on the other side of the table. "Really? Why not turn a mistake into an opportunity?"

"Brigitta doesn't make mistakes." Thora eyes the barmaid over her glass, but she is conveniently serving another customer.

"Hmm. So it wasn't a mistake," the man muses, tapping his chin. "What other theories do you have?"

Damn. It has been the weakness of Thora's life that she can't resist a scientist. "She might be trying to ruin my day."

"We need more data." He leans forward, lowering his voice as he looks sideways at the bar. "Have you ever gotten the sense that Brigitta doesn't like you?"

His murmur actually makes Thora shiver. Ridiculous. "No, she's been nothing but pleasant to me."

He sits back, triumphant. "Then why not assume she's trying to improve your day, rather than ruin it?"

Thora tries as hard as she can not to smile. "You're very sure of yourself."

He is smiling for the both of them. "Are you an engineer?"

Thora gives him a deadpan look.

He frowns in confusion. "Is that a no?"

"Oh, I'm sorry. I thought that was the start of a chat-up line. *Are you an engineer? Because . . .*" Thora tails off. "Shit, I don't know. Something about screws."

He laughs, sudden and loud. "No, I just—I saw the wiring diagrams." He taps the papers under her elbow. "But, that's a good one. I'll definitely use that in future."

Thora smiles despite herself. Their eyes meet, and something passes between them, something she didn't think she believed in. "Who are you, anyway?" she demands, almost angry.

"Santi," he says, holding out his hand.

She takes it. "I'm giving you until we finish this drink. Then I'm going back to my original plan of morosely drinking alone. Deal?"

He throws up his hands. "Seems like I don't have a choice."

They talk, starting with how long they have lived in Cologne— Santi since he came to study for his master's, Thora since her parents moved here from England when she was ten. Within an hour, they are deep in conversation about where they've come from and where they long to go. "There's so much *out there*," Santi declares, pounding the table for emphasis. "I don't understand people who can look at this"—he gestures vaguely at the bar, the other drinkers, the square outside "as if it's all there is."

Thora's mind is made up. She takes his hand and gets to her feet.

Santi looks up at her like she's pulled him out of one world and into another. "What are you doing?"

"Leaving," she says. "With you."

He gets up, startled but delighted. He tries to insist on settling the bill, but she orders him out to wait for her in the square. As Brigitta goes to the till to get her change, Thora faces her reflection in the mirror behind the bar. She looks flushed, self-conscious. She doesn't want to meet her own eyes. She turns away, shifting around the corner of the bar until she's standing on the wrong side. In the mirror, something shimmers. Thora turns to look, and freezes, trying to understand what she's seeing: an aerial view of the square outside, the fountain a wisp of smoke, the cobbles the shining scales of a dragon. She can even see Santi waiting for her, his tiny, dark-headed figure a study in expectation.

"Excuse me?"

Thora jumps, refocuses. Brigitta stands in front of her, looking pointedly at Thora's feet on her side of the bar.

Thora steps back. "Sorry." As Brigitta hands over her change, she looks again at the mirror. All she sees is her own reflection.

She pockets her change and steps slowly outside. Santi is standing where she saw him from above, lit by a ray of sun like a pointing finger. A shiver settles across her shoulders.

"What's wrong?" he asks.

"Nothing." She can't tell him what she thought she saw. He would only try and make it mean something. She lets him take her hand. "Where are we going?"

"God knows," he says with a smile.

God brings a tram that takes them to the Belgian Quarter, then guides their steps through an unlocked green door onto concrete stairs.

"Why do you have to live on the bloody roof?" Thora protests after the third flight.

Santi grins back at her. "I see things more clearly from up here."

His door is set with green glass, framed by wildly overgrown plants. Thora, still dislocated, feels the threshold as more than a doorway, a humming portal to another world. Staring through it, she retraces the chain of causality that led her here. She went to Der Zentaur and ordered a glass of wine. Brigitta delivered it to the wrong table. Now, she orbits her way into Santi's living room. A blue sofa, a coffee table, a star map on the wall. A black shape streaks past, and Thora yelps. "Jesus!"

"That's Félicette. She doesn't really obey the laws of physics." Santi runs his hand self-consciously through his hair. "My current theory is she lives in a pocket dimension that happens to open into my apartment."

"Félicette," Thora says. "The first cat in space."

Santi grins. "You're the only person who's ever got that reference."

Thora takes him in. He's familiar and all new. Where has he been all her life?

He's looking at her with a caution she understands. "Do you, ah—can I get you a coffee?"

She shakes her head. She's sure. Thora isn't used to being sure. She can't help mistrusting the feeling, wondering where it comes from.

"This is embarrassing," Santi says. "But—I don't know your name."

Thora looks back over the bright, urgent moments since they met. She knows his name; how can he not know hers? She sees herself suddenly from his perspective: a nameless woman with purple hair and a leather jacket, a bundle of cryptic signifiers. "Guess," she says.

He frowns, like it's a test he doesn't want to fail. "You said you were born in England?"

She nods, holding back a smile.

"Jane Smith," he says.

She bursts out laughing. "Statistically, a good guess. But no. It's Thora. Thora Lišková. Is Santi short for something?"

"Santiago López Romero," he says: every syllable exactly right. "Nice to meet you." He holds out his hand for her to shake.

Thora doesn't take it. Instead, she steps into his space and kisses him.

He doesn't draw back, but he doesn't exactly respond. When Thora starts to feel like she's applying mouth-to-mouth resuscitation, she breaks off. "Are you—is this—"

"Thora Lišková," he says breathlessly, and kisses her back.

They kiss like they're starved for each other. Thora walks him backward into the bedroom, shrugging off her jacket. He's already undoing the buttons on her shirt. As he turns his attention to her neck, Thora tilts her head back and laughs and laughs and laughs.

Afterward, she lies in Santi's bed. It's afternoon: no darkness to cover her escape. Damn him, he should have fallen asleep like every ex-boyfriend she's ever had, but he's looking across at her with an irritating smile. He reaches for her hand, turns it over to trace the dots of the tattoo on her wrist. "What does this mean?"

"It's a constellation. Vulpecula, the fox." She gives him a look. "I don't do this, by the way."

"What?"

"Jump into bed with men I've just met."

Santi shrugs. "That's okay. Neither do I."

"With men?"

"Men or women." He looks uncertain. "Why, is it different for you with women?"

"Yes."

He looks at her to check if she's joking.

"I'm not joking," she says, to help him out.

Mild surprise, but no judgment. "I'm honored to be the exception."

"You're just lucky I happened to watch that movie about the hot mariachi at a formative age," Thora says with a teasing smile. "In a universe where I hadn't, I probably wouldn't even be interested."

Santi moves closer to her. "Please don't kick me out of my own bed for what I am about to say." He curls a strand of her purple hair between his fingers.

"I make no promises," she says.

He looks at her earnestly. "It really doesn't feel like I just met you."

The thump when he hits the floor is immensely satisfying.

"Tips on dating women," Thora says, "from someone who knows. You're supposed to come out with that bullshit in an attempt to get me *into* bed."

His tousled head appears over the horizon, followed by the rest of him. She admires the view as he climbs on top of her, one arm propped on either side of her head. "What if I want to get you into bed *again?*"

She looks left and right, pretending to notice for the first time the pillows, the headboard, the bedside table stacked with Borges and sci-fi.

"Well," she says, looking up into his amused brown eyes. "You seem to have succeeded."

The next morning, Thora wakes in an existential panic. It's not that she doesn't know where she is. She knows exactly where: she is in Santi's flat.

All her life, she has fled from anything that felt significant. Now, everything is so significant it hurts: from the black cat curled up between them, to the crochet rug where her clothes lie scattered, to the way Santi breathes unevenly in his sleep. It is as terrifying as looking up at the stars and seeing her name written there.

Her breath hitches. She has to get out. She slides out of bed and tries to dress silently, but Santi is a light sleeper. He opens his eyes and reaches across the bed, startling Félicette into flight. "Where are you going?"

"Out to get coffee," she says. "What kind do you want?"

"Just black."

"Okay. Back in a bit," she says brightly. She pulls on her boots and walks out, down the stairs, through the green door onto the tree-lined streets of the Belgian Quarter. She keeps walking, across the park where feral parakeets swoop between the trees in the slanting sunshine, past the mosque into her own neighborhood of Ehrenfeld. She doesn't stop until she passes the lighthouse, relic of an electric company's whimsy, rising above the city roofs two hundred kilometers from the nearest sea. Safe inside her flat across the street, she closes the door and slumps against it, breathing hard as if she just escaped a fire. Her eyes move across her familiar mess: the television she only uses for re-watching *Contact*; the scarf her dad gave her, balled up in the window to block a draft; the scented candles Jules left behind that she can't bear to burn or give away. She thinks of Santi lying awake in his flat half an hour away, waiting for her to come back.

"It's okay," she tells herself under her breath. "I don't ever have to see him again."

She stops going to Der Zentaur. It's a wrench—she likes the wine and Brigitta treats her like a local—but she can't face the idea of finding him there again, waiting for her to fall in with the universe's plan. Fuck the universe's plan. She finds a new bar on the other side of the old town to sit and drink her wine alone.

Three weeks later, she is with Lily in the Turkish café down the road from her flat. She must have been staring out of the window too long, because Lily clicks her fingers by her ear, startling her back to the present.

"Girl trouble?" Lily asks knowingly.

Thora sighs. "Not this time."

Lily frowns. "Boy trouble? It's been a while."

Thora considers telling her about Santi, about why she walked away. *He was perfect. That was the problem.* Lily would, quite reasonably, tell her that was insane.

Lily pours an unconscionable amount of honey into her mint tea. "Has there been anyone since Jules?"

Her name is still painful, a reminder of all the ways she was good to Thora and all the ways Thora failed her. "Not really."

Lily stares at her piercingly. "Okay, so you're obviously in a cryptic mood, and I can't be arsed to play detective. Call me if you ever want to talk about it. In the meantime, can we make a plan for the sci-fi festival? If we don't book soon, the whole thing's going to sell out."

As the days pass, Thora waits, at first warily and then with something like longing, for the universe to throw Santi back into her path. She crosses and recrosses the park between Ehrenfeld and the Belgian Quarter, waiting for running steps and a hand on her shoulder. At the sci-fi festival, she remembers the books on his bedside table and turns, searching the darkened cinema for his face. Finally, one weekend afternoon, she steels herself and walks into Der Zentaur, fully expecting him to be at the table where she first saw him. But there is only Holger, the morose local who always sits at the bar, and a couple talking in whispers in the window.

She sits down at her usual table and orders a glass of red wine. As she waits, she brings out the wiring diagrams and places them carefully under her elbow. She has tried to make everything the same, but differences beyond her control keep intruding: the whispering couple, the new arrangement of the tables, each detail breaking the mad magic she's trying to weave.

When Brigitta brings her drink, Thora looks at it with a despair so profound that the barmaid hesitates. "You wanted wine, yes?"

Thora nods and takes a sip. "Brigitta," she says. "Do you remember the man I ended up talking to in here after you swapped our drinks? Dark-haired, Spanish, kind of short."

"Oh, yes. Santi." Brigitta shrugs. "He hasn't been here for a long time. He stopped coming about the same time you did."

Thora slumps in her seat as Brigitta goes back behind the bar. So much for her attempt to start again, to make a different choice this time. She ran away because she felt like the universe was pushing her into something. Now, it is pushing her the opposite way, and she resents it all the more.

"Fuck it," she says, downs the rest of her wine, catches a tram to the Belgian Quarter, and climbs the stairs of Santi's building to knock on his door.

It opens a crack. "Félicette, *no*," she hears him say, and her heart goes supernova. When he finally opens the door and sees her, he doesn't speak. He just exhales, a sound that could be relief or disappointment, and lets her inside. "You want some coffee?"

"Tea, if you have it," says Thora, following him into the kitchen.

Santi opens cupboards, looks through neatly stacked boxes and tins. "I think Héloïse left some before she moved out."

Thora notes the name. Flatmate? Ex-girlfriend? She pulls out a barstool and sits down. "So you're probably wondering why I left to get coffee and never came back."

Santi folds his arms, leaning back against the worktop. "I mean, I had a theory. But that theory doesn't explain why you're here now."

"What was your theory?"

He shrugs. "You didn't like me enough."

"No. That's not it."

Santi's brow furrows. "Then I go to theory two, which is that the coffee shop got sucked into another dimension, and you only just now managed to escape and find your way back."

"Close." She smiles. "But no. The problem was I liked you too much."

The kettle boils. Santi goes to pour the water. "You're going to have to explain that to me."

Thora bites her lip, searching for the words. "Do you ever feel like the universe is trying to push you into something? Like it's what's supposed to happen, and you're just meant to let it?"

Santi takes out the teabag, smiling. "Not often enough."

"I felt that. As soon as I met you, almost." She crosses her arms. "And that's exactly why I left. Because I didn't trust that feeling. Not one bit. I hate being told what to do."

He crosses to her, hands her the cup of tea. "Even by fate?"

"Especially by fate." From where she's sitting, he's taller than her. She looks up into his eyes. "But now, I've decided. The universe isn't pushing me into this. I'm choosing it."

Santi looks troubled. Thora realizes what it means, and the

ground falls out from underneath her. "Oh, shit. I'm an idiot. I'm completely assuming you're still interested. You've probably got a girlfriend now, or you've become a monk, or—"

He shakes his head, still serious. "It's okay. I can quit monk training anytime."

Thora nods slowly. She takes one sip of the tea. Then she puts it down on the worktop and pulls him into her arms.

She moves in immediately: another first. She tells her parents over dinner. Her father says nothing. Her mother asks if she's thought this through.

"No," she says cheerfully. "Not at all. Isn't that great? You know, once in your lives, maybe you should try not thinking something through. Not interrogating it from multiple angles. Not figuring out the deeper connotations. Just—letting it happen. How about it?"

No answer. Thora wishes for a heartfelt second that she had a sibling to soak up some of their patient, dissolving regard.

She blinks. "Well," she says, getting up and gathering the dishes. "Good talk."

"How was dinner?" Santi asks as she comes home, tripping over Félicette at the door.

She blows a raspberry and sits down on the sofa. "Trying to tell my parents anything is like—I don't know. Confessing to a skeptical wall."

Santi smiles and brings her a glass of wine. "I feel like I know them already."

Thora leans into him, resting her head against his. "This'll never work, you know," she says conversationally.

Santi frowns at her. "Who says?"

"All my exes. Most recently, my ex-girlfriend Jules. She told me when we broke up what my problem is."

"What's your problem?"

"I always want somewhere else. I'm never just—content to be where I am."

He shrugs. "Neither am I."

She gives him a look. "What do you mean? You're, like, Mr. Serenity."

A smile cracks his face. "That may be what it looks like on the outside. But inside, I'm always searching." He strokes her cheek, tucks her hair behind her ear. "We're the same, that way."

Thora thinks of her loneliness, of Jules and the girlfriends and boyfriends who came before her, all of them feeling like ghosts in the end. She looks now for the same transparency in Santi, but he is solid: a thing that proves its existence by blocking the light. "So, what's the plan?" she asks, half-laughing. "We'll be discontent together?"

He smiles. "Better than being discontent alone."

When he proposes to her, she's angry.

He doesn't understand. "I thought this was what you wanted," he says, getting up from his knees.

She opens her mouth. "It is."

"Then why do you look like I just slapped you?"

"I don't know." She crosses her arms. "It just feels—strange."

"Strange," he says, his voice tense with patience. He's still holding the ring.

"Put that away," Thora says. "You look like a ringmaster in a flea circus."

He looks down, confused, then laughs. He pockets the ring

and comes to her, taking her hands. "Please," he says. "Help me understand."

Thora sighs. "How did we meet?"

"You're telling me you don't remember?"

"Not every question needs a straight answer, Santi."

He frowns. "You're saying there's something wrong with the way we met?"

"No. I mean—yes. What if Brigitta hadn't sent my wine to the wrong table? What if she had mixed your drink up with someone else's instead of mine?"

"Then I'd be proposing to Holger right now." Thora doesn't laugh. He stares at her, the beginnings of panic in his eyes. "But she didn't."

"Right!" Thora exclaims, like he's proved her point. "And our whole lives, down to—this," she says, gesturing hugely at the ring, "hinge on that. Something so stupid, so arbitrary."

Santi folds his arms. "You know I don't think it was arbitrary."

Thora casts her eyes upward. "So you're proposing to me because you think God wants you to? That just makes it worse. How can you not see how that makes it worse?"

He is unflappable, relentless, a lake that absorbs every stone. "I feel like I've spent my life waiting for a sign," he says. "For something I could be sure of."

"Please don't," Thora says, but he goes on.

"Nothing made sense until you. And then you disappeared, and I—" He laughs, with a desperate edge. "I felt like a crazy person. Being so sure something was right, and then being wrong, I—I felt like God was playing a trick on me." The fear in his eyes is exactly what Thora has been running from. "You're afraid because you don't feel the same," he says.

"No. I'm afraid because I do." To his baffled look, she says,

"But I don't think that should be possible! That's why I don't trust it."

"I—" Santi stops. "Let's forget about fate for a second. Deal?"

She nods. "Deal."

He comes to her. Sometimes, in their arguments, words no longer reach her: what she needs is his hands, and his attention, and his eyes looking into hers. It slows time to a manageable pace, makes her feel less like a careening top on the verge of falling.

"I am proposing," he says, "because I love you. I love your mind, I love your body, I love your infuriating skepticism and your need for space. I love the way you throw your head back when you laugh. And I don't want to ever be without you."

She blinks. "Right," she says. "Well, I can certainly get behind that."

They get married in Great St. Martin's, the church that looks like a fairy-tale castle tucked behind the pastel-colored houses of the waterfront. Jaime, Santi's friend from work, is his best man; Lily is Thora's maid of honor. As they come out of the church, the bells in the tower are ringing. Thora feels like she's ringing too, picking up a vibration and humming with it until it threatens to shatter her. She lets it spill out of her in bursts of laughter.

They have their reception at the Odysseum. Their guests roam the pretend planetarium, eating freeze-dried canapes under the glassy gazes of ghostly astronauts. It's as funny as Thora hoped it would be, especially when the dancing starts. She spins with Lily, throwing her head back as she laughs. In one corner, her father is trying to talk to Santi's father in Latin, and in another, Aurelia is laughing at them both, and in another, Santi is watching her, his whole heart in his eyes.

The next day, Thora slips out of the flat early without waking him. He's still a light sleeper, but the hangover has sent him deep enough that he doesn't stir. She walks in the opposite direction she walked the last time she left him, into the heart of the city. At the ruined clock tower, opposite the place where they met for the first time, she takes a permanent marker from her pocket. NO GOING BACK, she writes on the wall. She has made her choice. She's still afraid.

She never expected what being happy would do to time. It speeds up, sliding away under her fingers, distorting into fantastic shapes. She tries to cling to every moment. Coming home after the sci-fi festival and arguing so loudly about the ending of the last film that the neighbors call the police. Santi singing to himself in the kitchen, doodling tiny versions of the two of them on the table until it forms an imperfect record of their lives. Her Spanish getting hesitantly better, until she manages a joke that makes his father laugh for half an hour. Santi bringing her cookies at Christmas as she sits watching the snow fall, pregnant and lazy.

"My love," he says.

She just stares at him, the impossibility of him. "There shouldn't have been room for this," she says.

"What?"

"In the time we've known each other. There shouldn't have been—this shouldn't be possible."

"What?" he says again, with a smile.

For me to love you this much. It frustrates her, as his proposal frustrated her, triggering a deep sense of not understanding. Thora likes to understand. But she can't say it. He knows. He has to know.

"Nothing." She grabs a cookie and stuffs it in her mouth.

Estela is born in January, on a long night that pain stretches into forever. Santi yells at the doctors—*she's hurting, can't you see, aren't you supposed to stop it?* Thora screams every swear word she can remember in Czech and Icelandic and English. Finally, all words are gone and she's nothing but a stretched arc of agony. She loses sight of him then, even as he's gripping her hand. He comes back to her in waves, after they've taken the baby away to clean her up: his hands first, then his eyes, warm and so afraid.

"Not fair," she murmurs.

He leans close. "What's not fair?"

"For you to see me like that. I'm never going to see you in that much pain."

He smiles, worry still in his eyes. "Not like you to give up before you've tried."

She crushes his hand weakly. Then they bring Estela back to her, and everything is different forever.

Thora never thought of herself as motherly. She worried she wouldn't be able to love a child the way she's supposed to. She's surprised to find the love part comes easily. What's difficult is everything else: keeping Estela alive and happy; snatching moments of sleep between feeding her and changing her and worrying over every sound she makes.

Things don't get easier. Hard just becomes normal. Santi's sister Aurelia comes to visit, and Estela becomes obsessed with her, following her around the flat with earnest cooing sounds. Then, with no time in between, Estela is five, full of tumbled sentences of half-English, half-Spanish, and Thora has never loved anything so much in her life, and then they get a call from the hospital.

It was a routine blood test. They have been thinking about

having another child, and so they both went in for a checkup. Now they sit in the hospital waiting room. Santi holds Thora's hand, as if it's her results that were the problem. His thumb strokes her knuckle until she can't bear the repetition. She pulls her hand away.

"Thora," he starts.

"Don't," she says. "I don't need one of your speeches about accepting God's plan. I can't—"

"Santiago López?" calls the nurse.

Thora follows him into the small clinic room. The nurse closes the door behind them.

Afterward, she leaves him in the lobby, pretending she has to go to the toilet. *Feel something,* she screams at herself as she climbs the endless stairs. But all she feels is justified, her fear finally coming home to roost. She finds a fire escape on the ninth floor and smokes, as she hasn't done in six years, the symbolic pack of stale cigarettes at the bottom of her handbag. Through a gap in the buildings, under the clock that reads a quarter to eleven forever, she can see her old graffiti on the ruined tower. NO GOING BACK. She broke her rule: she made a choice. Now, here she is, exactly where she didn't want to be. Santi will die before her, and the one solid thing in her world will be gone. The city will collapse, the towers boil away; a great hole will open in the fabric of everything, pulling her inside.

Unaware, Santi stands below her in the spitting rain, playing with his grandfather's knife. Damn him, he looks serene. This is what he's wanted his whole life: a real test of his faith.

When she goes down to join him, he smells the cigarette smoke in her hair. "Oh, cariña," he says, and folds her in his arms.

Life slows down, decompresses from glimmering fragments to afternoons in the oncology ward that drag forever. One night, she wakes at his bedside with a crick in her neck and a sense of complete dislocation. *Estela*, she thinks in panic, but no: she's safe with Santi's mother.

He's awake, looking at her with loving exhaustion. "Are you okay?"

She almost laughs in his face. *No. I'm falling apart. I want to get up and run out of the hospital, out of the city, out of the world.* But there are some things she can't say to him. Things Estela can say, things his mother can say, things Jaime can say, that from her would be stabs to the heart. It's part of the unspoken pact they made under the spoken vows, a host of small print Thora didn't know she was agreeing to. She sits by his bedside and holds his hand, furious at the limitation of it. She doesn't want to be his wife. She wants to be something else, something elemental and boundless. Another thing she can't say.

She squeezes his hand. "I'm fine. I love you. Go back to sleep."

Santi doesn't respond to the treatment. Thora isn't surprised. She saw all this coming, the whole sorry trajectory. She wishes she'd walked away as soon as he sat down at her table. She breaks the rules and tells Santi this, and he laughs, and she loves him, and how dare he keep on making it worse?

On Estela's sixth birthday, he dies.

Thora didn't realize how much she counted on his unwavering faith until, at the last, it wavers. He clings to her hand, as if he doesn't want to go where his God is waiting for him. Afterward, she waits for the better part of a year, insanely and sincerely, for him to come back. She doesn't tell anyone: they're already watching her. Lily, her parents, Aurelia, who has moved to Cologne to help with Estela. If they knew that every time she hears footsteps on the stairs, she thinks it's Santi coming home, they would move in, frighten his ghost away. So she bites down on her grief and stays silent.

They had ten years. It wasn't enough. Even if sometimes, it felt like eternities; even if the time expanded as it turned, like the spiral arm of a galaxy.

She thinks about leaving. Once, she even takes Estela to the Hauptbahnhof, standing in the long arcade as trains to elsewhere flash up on the screens. She walks out without buying a ticket. The time to leave was before she met him. Now, she has too much tying her here: her job, Estela's school, the way Aurelia uprooted her life to come and support her. She doesn't admit to herself that none of that really matters. What makes her stay is one mad thought: if she leaves, Santi won't know where to find her.

Estela changes, as if the part of her that was Santi's daughter died when he did. Gradually, she becomes someone new, not like him and not like Thora either. Someone they made up out of bits of themselves, like mad inventors. It has never seemed more miraculous, or more cruel. Thora tucks her daughter in, kisses her forehead. She wonders when she consented to have a spear driven into her chest, on the understanding that the wound would stay open forever: that through the whole procedure, she would remain impossibly alive.

"Where's Papa?" Estela asks.

A little more blood lost. "Sweetheart, Papa died," Thora says.

"I know," says Estela seriously. "But where is he?"

Thora's head swims. She wonders if Estela has talked about this with her grandparents. One set would have told her Santi is in heaven. The other would have told her what they told Thora at the same age, after her uncle died: that he just didn't exist any-more.

"Where do you think?" she asks.

Estela casts her eyes to the ceiling, covered in glow-in-the-dark stars since before she was born. A memory snags Thora like barbed wire: Santi up a ladder, laying out a universe for his daughter.

"I think he's somewhere else," says Estela. "Waiting."

Thora's breath catches. It's so strange, hearing her own inex-plicable conviction from her daughter's mouth, that she's afraid to ask her what she means. "Waiting for what?" she finally says.

But Estela doesn't answer. She rolls over, and Thora is left to pour herself a glass of wine and sit on the sofa with Félicette, old now and almost blind, her rattling purr a bare threnody of mourning.

Thora goes on, out of spite and habit and love for her daughter. Estela grows up, all her quirks and silliness transmuted into the best person Thora knows: an alchemy she will never understand. Thora stays in the top-floor flat in the Belgian Quarter, not lis-tening when Estela tells her it's too many stairs, not caring when she becomes a shuffling old woman who takes fifteen minutes to climb them. Lily, when she comes around, tells her she feels time speeding up, that the moments slip through her hands too fast. Thora disagrees. For her, time stretches like the universe is being poured into a funnel, leaving great vacancies behind.

Lily gives her a knowing smile. "You think you're going to see him again."

"No!" It comes out automatically: she is a skeptic, has been since before she knew the word to describe it. She is an accident of atoms, and when life is done with her, she will disperse. But Lily is right. Deeper than thought, deeper than her deepest principles, is that irritating conviction, like his faith is a virus that has been incubating silently inside her. It is unthinkable that she won't see him again.

Her lip curls, not with sadness but with anger. How dare he do this to her? She could have been different without him: a whole person, as she was meant to be, not pathetically waiting for a dead man to return. All it would have taken was one choice. "I could have walked away," she says, defiant.

Lily squeezes her shoulder and goes to make more tea.

When it comes, finally—pneumonia, racking her lungs until each cough shakes her apart—it feels like it's happened before. She assumes it's her brain shutting down, déjà vu as an epiphenomenon of dying consciousness. She wishes Santi were here so she could argue with him about it.

Estela is there, in the blurred region where her awareness fades. She's crying, and her sorrow hurts, tears salting the wound that still hasn't killed her. With the last of her strength, Thora squeezes her daughter's hand.

"I made the wrong choice," she tells her. "I take it back. I want to start again."

LOVE IS WAR

○ ✳ ◎

Santi meets his daughter for the first time when she is eleven. She's tall for her age, with straight eyebrows and lank hair scraped into a high ponytail. Her long sleeves hide her hands.

"This is Thora," says the social worker. "Thora, this is Mr. and Mrs. López."

"Santi," he says, holding out his hand. She takes it without meeting his eyes.

"Héloïse," says his wife. She's dressed for the social worker rather than for Thora, patterned dress swapped for a gray suit, braids bound back in a bun. It makes her look stiff, nervous, nothing like herself. Then she smiles, and her warmth shines through. Instead of shaking hands, she waves. Thora, surprised, looks up with a smile that's almost a laugh.

They sit down at a table outside the Kinderheim. It's not much of a garden: dying grass, a shallow pond, straggling trees ineptly screening the main road that leads back to the city center. Thora sits with her hands between her knees, answering their questions without making eye contact. Santi doesn't have much experience with kids; he can't help reading her as if she is a client visiting his office, rather than his prospective child. Smart, withdrawn, deeply hurt in a way that she pushes outward. A sense of humor that bites.

"What's your favorite thing to do here?" Héloïse leans forward, trying to get under Thora's guard.

Thora meets her eyes. "Watching the grass grow," she says, deadpan. "That's pretty fun."

Santi's laugh jumps out of him. An answering smile quirks the edge of Thora's mouth before it disappears.

After the visit, the social worker escorts them back to their car. They watch through the windshield as a boy chips away at the balustrade of the Kinderheim with a rusty nail.

"What do you think?" Héloïse asks.

Santi looks across at her. "She's ours," he says simply.

Héloïse nods, tears shining in her eyes. "Yeah," she says in a whisper. "Yeah, I thought so too."

They fill out a hundred forms, attend a dozen interviews. They answer questions about their marriage, their daily routine, how long they have lived in Cologne. They bear it all, if not with patience, then with determination. Finally, they get their prize: a file containing Thora's history, laid out year by year with accompanying photos. A baby with her eyes, blue and desperate, as if the sullen girl they met is trapped in there. Santi turns the page to meet her parents: a mother who left when she was two, a father who lost his position at the university after funding cuts and slowly succumbed to alcoholism, until social services battered down the door to find a trail of empty bottles and Thora screaming with a toddler's rage. He reads of her being passed on to a neglectful uncle—a picture of her in a sweater knitted for a much smaller child, with a design of a badger who looks almost as angry as she does—then to a string of foster families until she wound up at the Kinderheim.

Where she would have stayed, labeled a lost cause, had Santi and Héloïse not shown up with their empty nursery and their long-dried tears.

Santi's crying by the time he finishes reading. He passes the tablet to Héloïse. "You're going to need a drink." He goes to make her one, leaving her with their daughter's life story.

They repaint the room they've already started calling Thora's from light green to purple. Santi buys glow-in-the-dark paint and brushes careful stars onto the ceiling in patterns that mimic real constellations.

It's late spring by the time they're allowed to bring her home. When Santi unlocks the door, Félicette startles into flight. Thora pauses on the threshold, uncertain.

"Your room's upstairs," says Héloïse. "The door's open. Want to go and look?"

Thora nods and creaks warily up the stairs. The two of them follow, expectant and afraid.

"No *way*!" Thora yells in delight. "Stars!"

Once, back in Spain, Santi's sister Aurelia brought home a street cat with a torn ear. For the first few weeks, it barely left the upstairs room where she kept it, afraid to encounter the unfamiliar giants who roamed the halls. Thora, too, keeps to her starry room, emerging only for meals, which she eats in silence. Santi tries to bring her out, cracking bad jokes and showing her silly doodles, but she barely responds. Only Héloïse is favored with her rare smiles.

"What happened to her?" Santi asks Héloïse after Thora slinks upstairs. "That funny girl? That girl who loved her room so much she yelled?"

"She's not here to entertain us," Héloïse points out as she clears the plates. "She hasn't even decided if she likes us or not."

"She likes *you*," Santi says. "It's only me she has a problem with."

Héloïse shrugs. "That's because I'm better than you."

She's trying to make him laugh. It almost works. But it still hurts that Thora's indifference has a focus, and it is him.

Santi sighs and wraps his arms around his wife. He moves her braids aside to kiss the back of her neck.

Héloïse twists around in his arms, strokes his face. "Patience," she says. "We have to give her meaning before she can give it back to us."

Santi stays in the kitchen after she leaves, pondering her words. He thought they were adopting Thora to provide her with the stability she needs. But maybe it's not really about what she needs. Maybe this troubled girl is nothing but a distraction, a consolation prize for his own discarded dreams.

That night, he dreams of drowning in a hospital bed. He wakes, heart pounding, staring at his blank ceiling as if someone has taken the universe away. On his way back from the bathroom, he's passing Thora's room when he hears her voice.

He goes closer. "Thora? Did you say something?"

After a pause, she pulls the door open with her foot. She's lying on the bed, Félicette purring beside her. Thora stares up at her ceiling, fingers braced on her wrist. "The stars," she says. "They match the ones in the sky."

Santi feels a glow of approval: his daughter is a scientist. "Yes! I wanted them to make real constellations."

She tilts her head. "Do they look like that from space?"

"No. No, they would look completely different. Someone from a different planet probably wouldn't even put the same stars in constellations with each other."

Thora frowns. "Don't they belong together?"

"Not really. Ancient people just thought they did because they made pictures." He shrugs. "That's what humans do, I guess. Look up at the sky and see reflections of themselves."

"Themselves?" she says with a snort. "You mean ourselves? Or are you saying you're not human?"

"Blorgle fnarg," he replies.

Thora laughs, too loud to suppress. Santi feels a brief, intense high.

"It's like us," she says.

"What?" he asks with a smile.

"You and me and Héloïse. From far away we look like a family, but really we have nothing to do with each other."

The high crashes. Santi thinks of the three of them, he and Héloïse tightly bound binary stars, Thora drifting somewhere light-years away.

"The truth is, perspective is everything," he says finally. "We choose how we want to look at things." He taps the doorframe and leaves before she can see him crying.

The season changes. The bonsai tree Héloïse has been trying to train overspills its pot, growing out of control and wild. It brings a matching change in Thora. Or the change happens, the tree grows, and neither of these has anything to do with the other. Santi has always scanned the world this way, reading it for symbols. It means he is not surprised the day he comes home to find his mother's crochet blanket on the living-room floor, a black hole burned in its center.

Héloïse isn't home yet; two trams collided today in the old town, and the emergency-room staff are working overtime. Santi picks up the blanket and walks slowly up the stairs. *Calm*, he says to himself, remembering what the social worker told him. *Always try and deal with her calmly*. His thoughts wander away from the script. *She's the sea; she needs a rock to crash against*.

He knocks on Thora's door. She doesn't tell him to come in. She just nudges the door with her foot, watches him push it all the way open.

Santi sits down at her desk chair, holding the blanket between his hands. He thinks about his mother patiently making it, the love in every centimeter. Rage rises up, but he controls it. "My mother made this," he says.

Thora doesn't meet his eyes. "I know," she says. "That's why I did it."

He stares at her, uncomprehending. He wants to scream at her, to ask her why. Who takes offered love and burns it? The social worker's voice again. *She will try and test your boundaries.*

"You're lucky you didn't burn the house down," he says.

"Or unlucky," she shoots back. "Perspective is everything."

There have to be consequences. Otherwise, she will think there is nothing she can't do. And that won't help her become who she needs to be. Another breath. "You will learn how to crochet, and you will fix this. I don't care how long it takes. When you get home from school tomorrow, we start."

She snorts. "I can't make something like that."

"Is that why you did it? Because you don't think you can make something beautiful?"

"No. I told you why."

Santi feels like he is drowning, like he can't get enough air into his lungs. "You will learn. Starting tomorrow." He goes to the door. It's imperative he not give her the last word.

"I hate you," she says, with a venom lifetimes older than her years.

He does a lousy job keeping his expression neutral. "Well, that's a shame, because I love you."

"How? How do you love me?" Her face screws up. "You don't even know me. I just—arrived in your house, and now it's your job to pretend to be my dad. It's okay. I understand. You probably thought you'd get some sweet little girl who'd be easy to love. But you don't have to lie."

"I'm not lying." He can't keep the emotion out of his voice. *Calm*, he thinks, but it's useless, like trying to pin down a hurricane. "I don't say things I don't mean. I loved you before I met you."

She stares at him. "That's impossible."

He shrugs. "I don't care. It's true."

She gropes for words, her fingers digging into the bedcover. "That's not how love works. You don't just love someone for no reason. You love them for who they are, or what they do, or how they look. They have to deserve it."

A minor epiphany: this is what she wants, an argument. "And then you stop loving them if they stop being that way? If they stop deserving it?"

Thora looks like she's finally on solid ground. "Yes," she says defiantly.

Santi shakes his head. "Thora, no. If love was something we had to deserve, we would all be loveless. No, love is what the world owes us." He gives her an apologetic smile. "Sometimes, it doesn't pay up, that's all."

She looks at him in abject fury. For a blistering instant, Santi feels her fury move into him, become his own. He believes God has given him this purpose: that on some level, he is here to save her. But what does it mean that his purpose depends on Thora's misery? If love is what she is owed, how can he make up the world-heavy weight of the unpaid balance?

He chooses that moment to retreat to the kitchen. He doesn't feel like he's won. He feels like he's limping away from a skirmish, lucky to escape with his life.

Héloïse comes in, still in her hospital scrubs. She pauses, keys in her hand. "You're biting your nails again." Santi looks down at his fingers. A habit he thought he'd beaten thirty years ago, creeping back like a ghost. Héloïse closes the door behind her. "You shouldn't do that in front of Thora."

He laughs under his breath. "You really think I can influence anything she does?"

Héloïse shrugs off her coat, opens the fridge on her way to the table, and deposits a beer in front of Santi.

He opens the beer and takes a swig. "How did you know?" he asks.

"Because I know you. You live your whole life like you're being tested. And you want to pass with flying colors." She kisses his forehead, smooths his unruly hair. "But this isn't an exam. There's no pass mark. All we can do is fail her less badly than she's been failed before."

He starts teaching Thora crochet the next day. She's deliberately clumsy with it; after ten minutes, she refuses to do any more. Santi measures their progress not in the square she's working on, which grows by slow centimeters and shrinks at almost the same rate as she unpicks wrong stitches. He measures it instead in words hurled, points scored. Even if all they're building is a war, they're building it together.

Before she's even close to being able to fix the blanket, she starts sneaking food from the kitchen. Héloïse and Santi stand in Thora's room like detectives at a crime scene, looking down at the evidence stashed in a tin under the bed. Biscuits, bags of crisps, a wrinkled apple, a chocolate bar divided into individually wrapped pieces. Santi can't help seeing them as military rations. Along the window-sill, he counts thirteen glasses of water in various states of half-full. He flicks them in sequence, freeing an eccentric tune.

"She's living like a hunted animal," says Héloïse quietly, although they are safe: Thora is out with Lily, the only friend she's made so far. "Should we take all this away?"

Santi closes the tin and pushes it back under the bed. "No. We need her to know she's safe." He carefully puts back the papers he found next to it, hand-drawn maps of impossible worlds.

Héloïse chews on her lip, an old habit that's gotten worse in recent weeks. "Maybe she'll never feel safe, not completely. Maybe everything that's happened to her took that part of her away."

There is nothing Santi hates more than hopelessness. "Time," he says. "That's what she needs."

He calls his mother. He sits on the tree stump at the end of the garden, because Thora doesn't like hearing him talk in Spanish.

"Why?" he asked her the first time she got upset.

"You could be talking about me and I wouldn't even know."

He rolled his eyes. "Thora, I'm not constantly discussing you."

Now, the summer dark is heavy. A night bird he can't identify makes soft sounds in the trees.

"Bring her here," says his mother. "Why don't you bring her? I want to meet my granddaughter."

Santi rubs his forehead. He hasn't been back home since he moved to Cologne. Instead, he's waited for his family to come to him. There's always too much happening here: Héloïse, his job, now Thora. "We'll come, when the little magpie is more settled." The nickname is only for these phone calls. Nothing would feed Thora's paranoia more than conversations sprinkled with her name in a language she doesn't understand.

His mother doesn't tell him what she's thinking, but he hears it anyway. That his little magpie will never settle. That she will batter herself bloody against the bars of the cage he has built to keep her safe.

Later that week, he comes home from Der Zentaur and sets his keys down on the kitchen table. Félicette jumps up and rubs against his hand. "Thora?" he calls up the stairs.

The house vibrates with unnatural quiet. He goes to knock on the door of her room. "I'm coming in," he says, and pushes it open. Her usual mess: the panpipe of water glasses on the windowsill, the crochet square abandoned on her bed. He checks the bathroom—empty—and finally his and Héloïse's room, although he doesn't seriously expect to find her there. Santi reads what the world tells him, and right now it is spelling out disaster. He decides to call the police.

Then he hears something shuffle in the ceiling.

He opens the attic door. She's pulled the ladder up after herself, an outlaw making safe her den. He pulls it down and hurries up the creaking treads, terrified that she has hurt herself, that he's failed at the only important thing he's ever tried to do.

She's not hurt. She's sitting cross-legged next to the crib Héloïse couldn't bear to throw out or give away. Her fingers slip between the bars, like she's playing with a baby's ghost.

"You wanted your own children." The words he hoped she'd never say. They curl from her mouth like tangling vines.

He's supposed to say, *You are our child. We never wanted anyone but you.* But he knows her better now: knows when the approved phrases will hit their mark, and when she will deflect them with deadly force at his heart.

"We tried, yes," he says. "But it wasn't meant to be."

"Meant to be?" The phrase contorts Thora's mouth. "My parents were *meant* to look after me. I was *meant* to do well at school and go to uni and learn physics and biology and be an astronaut." Santi flinches; Thora doesn't see her blow land. "But that didn't happen. And you and Héloïse didn't get your own children, you got me." She shakes her head in fury, pulling her sleeves down over her wrists. "None of us got to choose. The only difference is you want to make it mean something. Like this was what God wanted all along. When it's just what we got stuck with."

Santi has run out of bullet points, of reasonable discussions in a calm voice. He can't confess how close her words have cut to his secret fear: that he is the worst kind of liar, taking whatever he's not too lazy to accomplish and calling it fate.

A thud against the attic window. Santi jumps in holy terror: God's fist on the glass. Thora is already at the window, carefully delineating the ghost of wings.

"Oh." A quiet exhalation. She has become another person in the time it took for a bird to die. She pushes past Santi, sliding down the ladder so fast it must hurt her hands.

He follows her down and out into the garden. "Did you find

it?" he asks, approaching her as if she is the bird: fallen, half-dead and half-alive.

Thora opens her hands. The bird is a bright, startling green: one of the feral parakeets that have colonized the city. It lies perfect as a simulacrum, wings folded, eyes closed.

"What a shame," Santi says.

"She's not dead," Thora says forcefully. She blows gently on the bird, ruffling its feathers. It twitches, eyes opening and closing.

Santi feels a surge of hope, intoxicating as wine. "Bring it inside. We need to keep it warm."

They set up a padded box in Héloïse's study, close the door to keep Félicette out. Santi shows Thora how to feed the bird water using a pipette. He watches her stroke its feathers with fingers he's rarely seen outside of sleeves or fists. He's never known her so quiet, so absorbed.

Days pass, and the bird doesn't die. Santi stops looking for Thora in her room. When he gets home, he comes straight to the study where she will inevitably be, hunched over the box, feeding the bird or watching it sleep. Sometimes she's so enthralled that he catches an instant of how she is when he is not observing her. He hoards them, those impressions of a soft, wondering girl, like jewels. It awes him, how someone as angry and self-contained as his daughter can look after this helpless thing with such tenderness. He is watching her look after herself, in the way that he and Héloïse, with their distance and their good intentions, never can.

"I've decided what her name is," she announces.

"Oh?"

She strokes the bird's feathers carefully with the tip of her little finger. "Urraquita," she says.

Little magpie. His Spanish nickname for her. He can't tell

her what it means, that it's already the name of another bird. He should have known she was smart enough to figure him out.

Thora looks at him over her knees. "Is it our fault if she dies?"

Santi takes a breath. "What do you think?"

It takes Thora a long time to answer. When she does, he pretends he doesn't hear the strain in her voice. "No. We didn't hurt her. We're just trying our best to make her better."

"Right." Santi hopes it means she's willing to forgive them, if she's willing to first forgive herself.

The bird recovers. A few days and it's hopping, then flying in short bursts around the study, making Thora giggle in a way Santi has never heard before.

"You know, parakeets are good vocal learners," he says, ducking as wings whir above his head. "You might be able to teach it to say something."

She darts him a look. "Really?" she says suspiciously.

He nods, glad to have caught her interest. "You have to really work at it. And there are no guarantees."

She's barely listening. She's focused on the bird, her busy mind already thinking of what to teach it. Santi smiles and leaves her alone to work.

He gets used to coming home and finding the study door closed. Sometimes, he hears Thora repeating something over and over, but he can't make out the words. Until one day, the door hangs open. He pauses, wondering if he should go in.

"Santi," Thora calls.

It's so unusual for her to name him, let alone request his presence, that he hesitates. "Yes?"

"Come here," she says impatiently.

When he enters the study, Thora is sitting on the sofa, the parakeet perched on her finger. Her face is open, nervous, alive. She keeps changing, too fast for him to keep up with all the versions of her. "Hey, Urra," she says softly. "Did you have something to say?"

"Help," says the parakeet. "I'm trapped inside this bird."

Thora looks up with a grin of triumph. For a moment, Santi just stares. Then he laughs, as much joy as surprise, until they are both laughing so hard they can't breathe.

"I had to say it over and over. But it worked in the end." She bounces in her seat, startling the bird into flying up to the bookshelves. "I want to teach her something else."

Santi smiles and sits back, in awe at God's work: how all his effort is nothing to a wounded bird that fell out of the sky. *Thank you*, he says wordlessly. *Thank you for this gift.*

God giveth, and God taketh away. Santi comes home the next evening to find the study empty. Heart pounding with dread, he searches the house. Through Thora's bedroom window, he sees her in the garden, sitting on the tree stump where he talked to his mother.

He goes to stand beside her. She's not crying. Somehow, that's the worst part: the profound sorrow and the absence of tears, like something inside her is broken.

"I took her outside," she mumbles. "I thought she might want some fresh air."

"Oh, no." Santi crouches down to her level. "When?"

"This morning. She still hasn't come back." Her voice is tight. "What was the point? If she was just going to fly away?"

This is the test, Santi realizes: not the nurturing, but the letting go. To take all the love and effort and detach it from yourself, no matter what vital organs get ripped out in the process. He takes Thora's hand. "There was always a risk she might. But does that mean it wasn't worth it?"

Thora snatches her hand away. "Stop it. You're doing that thing, where you ask me questions and make it seem like I'm making my own decisions, but really you're just telling me the answers. Go on. Tell me."

Santi can't help raising his voice. "You need to be proud of what you did. She wouldn't be alive if it wasn't for you."

"Then I wish I'd let her die."

He doesn't tell her she doesn't mean it. In the heart of her rage, he is sure she does. He looks out into the woods beyond the garden. He imagines the bird flying out from Thora's hand: a rush of panicked freedom, then a pause on the fence, halfway between somewhere and somewhere else. Santi has always tried to read the world for symbols. But this one—a feral thing fleeing from offered love—he refuses. His daughter is not a bird. She is Thora. And he is not letting her go so easily. "Maybe she'll come back to visit," he says.

Thora shakes her head violently. "She won't come back. Even if she did, she won't remember me. It'll be like I never existed."

"But you'll remember her." He wonders why the words feel so heavy, as if they are talking of things as vast as galaxies.

"That just makes it worse." She looks up at him, eyes wide and tearless. "I never want to see her again."

Santi is developing an intuition for Thora, like a plant's blind awareness of the sun. He needs to let her deal with this alone. He squeezes her shoulder and starts back toward the house.

His intuition is wrong. The argument isn't over. "Why do you always think you know better than me?"

Santi stops, turns. All the answers—*because I'm your parent, because I'm older*—seem as empty as lies. "I don't," he says. "Right now, it's just my job to pretend to." That's unexpected enough to silence her. He sighs. He's so tired: too tired to repress the question he's not allowed to ask. "Why are you so angry with me?"

Her face stays still. He knows her well enough now to be aware of the emotions underneath, emotions he suspects even she doesn't understand.

He steps off known ground, following his explorer's instinct that there is something out there in the wild worth finding. "Thora, I'm not the one who left you."

She stares at him, something uncanny in her eyes. "But you will."

He crouches in front of her, takes her unwilling hand. "I'll never leave you."

He shouldn't lie to her. He needs to be reliable, predictable, not making impossible promises. But in the moment he says it, he believes it. As he looks at Thora, he sees her believe it too.

"Liar," she spits. She pushes his hand away and runs into the house, slamming the door behind her.

Santi rubs his tired eyes. He looks up, where the stars he copied onto her ceiling are obscured by clouds. An old desire takes hold of him: to be up there, to see all this from an angle that could make sense of it.

It's too late; that path is closed to him now. He'll have to make do with this limited, fumbling perspective: hope that someone who sees further is guiding his steps. He sets his shoulders and follows his daughter inside.

MEANT TO BE

○ ✹ ◎

Thora is weightless.

She floats underwater, ears humming with pressure, the sea-green tips of her hair drifting over her eyes. Ahead of her stretches the hazy gray-blue expanse of the lake: an infinite world for her to explore. Echoes come through the water: the throbbing of a motorboat, the shouts of children playing close to the shore. Thora can hold her breath for a long time. She sculls with her hands, turning, and dives, aiming for the line of buoys that marks the edge of the swimming area. A few seconds and she will be close enough to swim under, make her escape to the wild freedom of the open water.

Something grabs her heel. She kicks, spasming to free herself, but the grip follows her, clamping around her ankle. A tug-of-war, a miniature battle she loses. Before she can get free, she is being pulled upside down to the surface. Water goes up her nose and she chokes, drowning.

She breaks through into the air. "You're such a dick," she gasps at her brother, who is treading water and laughing.

Santi grins, the sun off the water making him squint. "You

were going to swim under the barrier," he says, flicking water at her. "Think I didn't see you?"

Thora splashes him back. "So what?"

"What's wrong with the water on this side?"

She wrinkles her nose. "Apart from like a thousand people having peed in it?"

Santi tilts his head with an exaggeratedly relaxed expression. "A thousand and one."

"Ugh! You're disgusting." Thora kicks out, swimming away as fast as she can. As he surges into motion behind her, she switches to crawl, easily beating him back to shore. She climbs out, dripping and sinking into the sand. On this summer's day, the shore of the Fühlinger See is crowded with families escaping the city heat. Thora stamps her way up the beach, toward where the skyline of Cologne shows through the trees. She finds their towels, her copy of *The Hitchhiker's Guide to the Galaxy* lying facedown. She picks it up as Santi drops onto the towel next to her and lies back, closing his eyes. Thora tries to read, but the beach is everything underwater wasn't: loud, and safe, and full of familiar human noise. She looks over the book at her brother, as still as a corpse and about as entertaining.

"I think I'm going to get a tattoo," she says.

"Mm," he grunts.

Thora sighs. Half the time she wishes she could launch her brother into space. The other half, she wishes he wasn't so distant. It's strange to think how little would have had to change for him not to be here at all: two seconds on a wet road eight years ago, the crash that killed Santi's birth family and the version of Thora that was an only child. She remembers what she used to be like: lonely, yes, but self-sufficient, good at being on her own. Now she's dependent on this uncommunicative lump for entertainment.

"This is *boring*," she complains.

"Boredom is the sign of a tiny mind," Santi says without opening his eyes.

She flicks sand at him until he flinches. "Want to play pirates?"

He opens his eyes just long enough to roll them. "We're not twelve anymore."

It stings. She never wanted them to grow out of their old game. She doesn't really believe he has. He just knows what fourteen-year-old boys are supposed to like. Cars, and girls, and fighting: not playing at exploring the high seas with their sisters. He didn't even want to come with her today. He only agreed because he didn't want to stay home to listen to their parents argue.

Thora stares back out at the water, remembering the blue world beneath. Muted sound and ripples of light, and the feeling of a truth hidden down there if she searched long enough. "Why won't you let me swim past the barrier?"

"It's dangerous," Santi mumbles. "There are signs. You can read, can't you?"

"No," Thora retorts.

Santi opens one eye to peer at the book in her hands. She turns it surreptitiously until it's upside down. He half-smiles, but shakes his head.

Thora won't let it go. "Since when do you care about signs? There were signs all over the lighthouse in Ehrenfeld, but you still went ahead and climbed it."

Santi sits up, brushing sand off his back. "That was different."

"Why?"

"The lighthouse was actually worth exploring."

Thora snorts. "You told me there was nothing in there. It was just an empty shell."

"There still could have been. I can tell you now, there's nothing in this lake except pee and old cans."

"You don't know that if you haven't explored it." He's doing what she hates, pretending to know better. "Why do you have to be so—big-brothery about it?"

"I am your big brother."

"By like half an hour. It doesn't count." Santi thinks it means something, that they were born at almost the same moment: fate reaching back from the future, binding them together. Thora just thinks it's funny to tell people they're twins when they look nothing alike. She crosses her arms. "And you know what I mean. Acting like I'm some little kid who's going to get myself hurt. I'm not." Thora has never felt like a child. Not when she was six years old in her dad's car careening across the wet road. Not now, fourteen and angry and never allowed to express it because Santi has reasons to be angry that she could never equal. "Why don't you just admit it's because I'm a girl—"

"It's not because you're a girl. It's because I'm not letting you put yourself in danger for something stupid."

It's hard for Thora to remember, sometimes. He has lost so much in his life that the idea of losing her must feel like madness, like the God he believes in testing him beyond destruction.

"Santi, it's just a lake," she says, more gently than she knew she could. "There's no sharks. There's no tsunamis. Nothing's going to happen to me." She doesn't tell him that she *wants* something to happen to her, wants the unknown and all that comes with it, a desire so strong she can't put it into words.

"Just *leave* it," he snaps.

She opens her mouth to protest, then closes it. It's not her nature to hold back. But she'll do it for Santi. She wonders who she learned that from.

"Hey." She ducks into his view until he looks at her. "I'm not going anywhere," she says.

"My birth family didn't think they were going anywhere." He rubs his hand across his face. "No one does. Until they do."

Santi doesn't talk about his birth family. Thora sits very still, feeling like she's eavesdropping on him talking to himself.

"My father died mid-sentence." He frowns, biting his nails. "I've never stopped thinking about that. Why wouldn't God even let him finish his thought?"

Because God had nothing to do with it. Thora files that under "things that wouldn't help" and tries again. "What was he saying?"

"Nothing important. Arguing with my mother about the next turn." He shivers. "When I think of the things he could have said, if he'd been ready—"

"I guess . . ." Thora hesitates, unsure if it's her place to talk about this. "I don't know if I'd want to be ready. I feel like I'd rather just—go. In the middle of what I'm doing. Die living, you know?"

Santi glances up at her. "Are you scared of dying?"

"Yes," she says without hesitation. "Terrified. But that's because I don't think there's anything after." She shrugs. "It's different for you. You think you're going on to your parents and your—your sister."

He nods, looking away across the beach. Thora imagines the two of them dying. Here, now, a comet blazing down from the sky, sending each of them where they believe they're going. She feels a pang of strange loneliness, imagining Santi in some perfect hereafter with his real family, while she . . . She catches herself. She wouldn't exist anymore to miss him.

Santi digs in the sand, like he's trying to uncover something he can't remember burying. Thora hugs her knees, thinking about the accident, how it traded away her loneliness for Santi's pain. She has decided a hundred times over that if she could bring back his family by giving him up, she would do it. She decides it again now, closing her eyes and imagining herself alone on the beach, imagining Santi back with his real sister and his mother and father. Thora likes to dwell on things that hurt: the mental equivalent of pinching herself until her fingernails leave a pair of half-moon scars. But Santi won't let her do that anymore.

"I never told you this," he says. "But—for a while after they died, I was sure I was meant to be dead too." He laughs, mocking the child he was. "I thought God had made a mistake. Any second, he was going to realize, and then, he would come to take me." He stabs the sand in an irregular heartbeat rhythm. "The first few nights I spent in our room, I didn't sleep. I just lay there, waiting."

Thora remembers. She didn't sleep, either. She lay in her familiar bed in her familiar room, staring up at the glowing constellations on her ceiling, wondering how it was that everything had changed: the empty space on the other side suddenly filled with his dark shape, his shallow, tentative breaths.

"It wasn't hard to imagine what it'd be like. Dying, I mean. It was almost like I remembered it." A shiver comes on Thora from nowhere, a dizziness that surges and passes. Santi's voice wavers. "But I just kept thinking about all the things I'd never be. I'd never learn to fly. I'd never get to see the world, let alone the stars." He's crying now, and Thora can't look, and she's not made for this. She wants to dive into the lake, hide in the blue world where everything is silent and nothing weighs this much.

Santi rubs his hand across his face, leaving a trail of sand. "I wanted to see my family again. So much. But I didn't want to die. And I—I don't know if they'll ever forgive me for that."

He sobs, his body shaking but his mouth closed, holding everything in. Thora sits paralyzed. *Help*, she thinks, without knowing who she's asking: the ghost of Santi's real sister, maybe, who should be here to comfort him through the grief she caused. What would she do? The answer comes to Thora, not as words or even as an idea, but as possession, opening her arms and drawing Santi into them. She holds him, and he leans into her, clinging as if she can fix what is broken in him. Over his shoulder, the indifferent world goes on: a child building a sandcastle, a man sleeping with a book over his face, a long-haired man in a blue coat running along the edge of the sand. Thora has never been so angry: at Santi's family for dying, at his God for abandoning him, at the mindless universe for changing him from the person he ought to have been. She doesn't know where it comes from, her clear picture of the Santi that would have existed if they hadn't died, a version of him she never met. A version that was calmer, less angry, who laughed more: Santi as he was meant to be. And her without him: lonelier, spikier, less ready to forgive. Maybe they would still both be here on the beach, sitting apart, neither even noticing the sullen girl with the sea-green hair or the laughing boy in his knot of friends. Thora imagines them passing each other underwater, nothing but two vague shapes in the blue.

Santi pulls back from her. He's calmer now, his breathing easier, and his face is hot with shame. "Sorry," he says. "Shit, that was embarrassing."

Thora digs her fingertips into the cool sand. "I won't tell anyone," she says.

One moment they are looking at each other, Santi's eyes red and his grin sheepish, Thora half-relieved and half-triumphant, like she's passed a test she didn't know was coming. Then the man in the blue coat is falling to his knees beside them.

"Excuse me. Something's coming," he says, looking back and forth between them. "Sorry, I tried—"

Thora is not sure what happens next. She is aware of a rending, tearing noise, and a shaking that lasts an instant and seems to go on forever. Time folds, inverts: she's six years old, lights blazing off the wet road, and when the collision comes it reverberates through her whole life, from the moment of her birth to the far-off instant of her death, changing everything. She and Santi fall together, his head buried in her shoulder, her arms tight around him, as if that will save them when the world ends. *Not yet*, is the only thought that escapes her before everything stops.

She opens her eyes. Santi's grip loosens as she draws back from him. They are on the sand by the Fühlinger See, and children are playing in the shallows, and everything else is the same.

Not everything. Thora hears a sound, over the chatter of the oblivious beachgoers, the splash of the water: a chime, soft but insistent, like a clock striking an endless hour. The man in the blue coat crouches next to them, hands braced against the sand. Thora feels a brightness at the corner of her eye, but when she turns her head, it disappears. She smells smoke on the air. She coughs, trying and failing to catch her breath. Beside her, Santi is hunched over, gasping, but she doesn't look: she's hypnotized by the man in the blue coat, his worried face, his stillness.

The chime stops. The smell of smoke vanishes. Thora isn't completely sure she didn't imagine it. Still, she feels light-headed, as if she has been underwater for too long. Beside her, Santi takes a breath, his wheezing gradually calming.

The man in the blue coat sits up, looking dazed. "You're all right," he says to Santi, touching Thora on the arm. "You're all right." He says it like a line from a poem in a foreign language, memorized by heart.

"What about you?" Santi says. "Are you—"

The man's eyes roll up in his head. He collapses onto the sand. Santi leans over him. "Hey. What's wrong?"

Expressions flicker uncannily across the man's face, joy to anguish to laughter. Thora feels a roll of danger in her belly. "I think he's having a stroke."

"Fuck." Santi stares at her. "Did you bring your phone?"

She shakes her head. She didn't want to leave it while they were swimming. "Go," she says. "Find someone to call an ambulance. I'll stay with him."

Santi jumps to his feet and pelts away across the sand. Thora will remember it for a long time after: the man's blue coat spread around him like wings, the paler blue of the sky, the sand flying up from Santi's heels as he runs.

"Something happened," the man keeps saying, over and over.

"I know," Thora says, as if it will help him to know that someone is listening. "What's your name?" she asks.

The man looks up at her from his twitching, changing face, as if she has the answers, as if she can save him. "Peregrine," he says.

"Peregrine, we're getting help," she says. "Just hold on."

Part II

NOT ENOUGH SKY

○ ✺ ◎

The stars are wrong.

Santi lies on his back, the grass of the Uni Park tickling his neck, the air thrumming with a summer storm on the way. Here, in the green belt separating the city from the suburbs, the sky is dark enough to show him a scattering of lights. One set of stars, steady and constant, as if they are the only stars there have ever been.

He closes his eyes. Different stars, in different patterns, burned into his memory. When he lets himself see them all at once, the sky becomes crowded, impossible: a sea of blazing light.

Santi has always trusted in fate: that there is one way things have to go. He isn't literal enough to believe that the future is written in the stars—he's doing a PhD in astronomy, after all—but his memories of other skies still unsettle him. The idea that there are other possible configurations for the universe, that God could be running them all in parallel, cuts against everything he believes. The only way he can reconcile what he remembers is to think that it's a message, one he's not yet ready to understand. He watches the world like a detective, like a poet, waiting for the meaning to come clear.

In a square in the old town stands a ruined clock tower covered with graffiti. Over the other scrawls, someone has written in ragged black letters: NOT ENOUGH SKY. The first time Santi saw it, he stopped in his tracks. He was used to the city's verbosity, slogans in a dozen languages blooming over its walls. But those three words felt like his own thought, transmuted through someone else's mind, spoken directly back to him.

Sometimes he wonders if that's the only reason he hasn't gone mad. He is not alone. Someone else is dislocated in the same way that he is, and one day, he will meet them face-to-face.

When he opens his eyes, the stars are gone. He blinks, but it's just the storm clouds moving in. A raindrop hits his cheek, then another. By the time he gets to his feet, the rain is sluicing down like a river. Thunder rolls, chasing him across the grass to the Physikalisches Institut. He holds up his card until the doors open. Inside, he shakes the rain out of his hair. It's after midnight: the building is quiet. He still isn't surprised when he reaches the glass door of the lab and sees a lone figure inside.

"Hi, Dr. Lišková," he says as he walks in.

His supervisor looks up, blue eyes wary. She's wearing the same clothes as when he last saw her two days ago. Santi wonders if she slept here, curled up under her desk to the quiet humming of the computers. He spends most of his days with her, but his knowledge of her is entirely one-dimensional: he doesn't know where she lives, or even exactly how old she is. Her hair is streaked with white, but her face doesn't have the lines to match. Either she's gone prematurely gray, or she deliberately dyes her hair to look older. He wouldn't put it past her.

"You're soaked," she says.

"Yeah." Santi grins, running a hand through his wet hair. "It's apocalyptic out there."

"Just don't drip on any of the priceless equipment."

Part of Santi enjoys the unimpressed look she gives him. He is a little in love with her, but then he is in love with everyone: Héloïse, the pretty French girl who works in the campus coffee shop; Brigitta, the barmaid at Der Zentaur, with her Germanic stare and her careful hands.

He checks the simulation he set running when he left the lab. A mass of red error messages greets him. He swears and traces the first one back. Spotting his mistake, he laughs.

"What?"

"I gave the simulation an input it wasn't expecting, and—" He turns to Dr. Lišková. "Looks like I broke gravity."

He's surprised to see the ghost of a smile on her face. "Comes with the territory."

Humming under his breath, he starts fixing the problem. He's lost in his model universe when Dr. Lišková's voice jolts him out. "Can you stop?"

This time, when he turns, she is glaring at him.

"What?"

"Humming. It's driving me up the wall."

"Okay. Sorry," he mutters. He turns back to his computer, but his concentration is broken. It all feels futile: tinkering with a crudely simplified model of the cosmos in the vain hope it will give him the answer he's looking for. He sighs and stretches, wincing at the familiar pain in his neck.

"What is it now?" snaps Dr. Lišková.

Santi doesn't understand her sometimes: the push and pull of her, like part of her wants him to stop existing while another is always looking for a reaction. "It's nothing," he says. "Just my neck."

Her brow furrows. "Aren't you a little young for aches and pains?"

"Perk of doing a PhD, I guess," he says with a grin she doesn't return.

"I have a PhD, and my neck's fine. You must have terrible posture," she retorts, turning back to her screen.

Santi stares at her until she looks at him. "Is it worth it?" he asks.

Her eyes flick away. "If you don't know that by two years in, I can't help you."

Santi spins his chair back to his computer. "I don't know. When I was a kid dreaming of studying the stars, I thought I'd spend more time actually looking at them."

"*Actually looking* isn't science."

Santi shakes his head. "Thanks for the mentorship," he mutters under his breath. He fixes the bug and sets up the next run of the simulation, then goes to the lounge to make a pot of coffee. He drinks his first cup, kicking his feet up on the table where copies of old journals act as makeshift coasters.

He knows he shouldn't talk to Dr. Lišková the way he does. He knows she shouldn't talk to him the way she does. They simply don't work, and he's not sure if it's him or her that's the problem. It's not that he dislikes her. If they were anything other than supervisor and student, they might even get along.

As if summoned by his thoughts, she comes into the lounge for a cup of tea. The sound of the kettle rings a bell in Santi's head: time for more coffee. He picks up his mug to refill it, but it's heavier than he expected. Hot coffee sloshes over the edge, burning his hand.

He swears. Dr. Lišková watches with amusement. "Did you break gravity again?"

Santi is searching for a comeback when he remembers what he

was about to do. He stares at the full mug of coffee, at the fault line in the universe. "It was empty."

Dr. Lišková pours water into her mug. "You mean you thought it was empty."

"No. I know it was empty." Santi looks up at her. "How long have I been in here?"

Dr. Lišková checks her watch. "You've been away from the lab for thirty minutes."

Santi notes her careful rewording: confining her testimony to what she could personally observe. "Well, I was in here the whole time. Have you ever known me to take more than ten minutes to drink my coffee?"

"You do usually down it like it's juice," she admits, bringing her tea over and sitting down. "I suppose you made an exception."

Santi realizes she isn't going to take his memory as an accurate record. "It's hot," he says, showing her the inflamed skin on his hand. "It can't be the same coffee I poured when I came in here."

"So someone came in and poured you another."

He swings his legs down and sits up. "Okay, first, there are maybe two other people in the entire building right now. Second, how would I not have noticed someone standing right next to me and pouring me a coffee?"

Dr. Lišková turns to face him. Santi has never seen her so engaged in any conversation that isn't about research. "You fell asleep."

"After drinking a whole mug of coffee in ten minutes?"

She shrugs it off. "That's normal for you. I've found you in here fast asleep after drinking the entire pot."

Santi shakes his head, half-laughing. "Are you just going to keep throwing rational explanations at me?"

Her brow furrows. "I don't understand. What else should I be doing? What alternative am I arguing against?"

Santi opens his mouth and closes it. He looks down at his coffee, still there and still inexplicable.

Dr. Lišková understands. She laughs, and that's unusual enough to make Santi stare. "Oh, I get it. You think this was a miracle! All hail the holy coffee cup!" She leans toward it, making exaggerated motions of veneration.

Santi doesn't want to let her see that she's got to him. "So you think I should accept one of your explanations instead?"

Dr. Lišková's eyes widen. "Yes," she says. "Obviously, yes."

"And what if my perception and my memory tell me that those explanations are wrong?"

His forced calm is working. He can see the frustration coming off her in sparks. "Then you should conclude that your perception or your memory is wrong. You know the science, Santi. Witnesses can't even describe a car crash accurately five minutes after it happened. We're flawed, lumbering machines, crudely accidented into existence because a few cells randomly started copying themselves. I don't understand why you wouldn't accept that, instead of—of jumping to the conclusion that a big man in the sky likes you enough to stand you a coffee."

Santi glares at her, overcome by an intensity of feeling he can't explain. She glares back, as if his faith repels her as much as her cynicism does him. He sees her see him seeing her in a set of infinite mirrors and reels with a yawing sickness.

A knock on the door of the lounge snaps him out of it. "Do you mind not arguing so loudly?" says a sleepy-looking graduate student. "I'm trying to get some work done next door."

"Oh," says Santi. "Sure. Sorry."

The student closes the door behind her.

"Christ," scoffs Dr. Lišková. "We're turning into my parents."

A personal detail, offered like a flash of a fish's tail before diving back into the depths. Santi imagines a sullen seven-year-old covering her ears. The sharpness of the image makes him shiver. "I'm not jumping to any conclusions," he says, lowering his voice. "My mind is open, that's all. What about yours? Why are you so desperate not to believe?"

Dr. Lišková runs her hands through her white-streaked hair in frustration. "If God could work miracles, why would he refill your coffee cup instead of—I don't know, curing all the world's diseases? Or—or revealing the secrets of the universe?"

"Because he wanted to leave you something to do."

"Be serious."

"Fine. Maybe because something like that would be undeniable. But filling my cup—only I experienced that. I can't verify it against anything other than my own memory. And so I get to decide whether to put it down to a gap in my perception, or a miracle. And that decision—that's what makes it about faith."

"Why on Earth did you go into the sciences?" Dr. Lišková wonders aloud.

"Why did you?" he retorts. She shakes her head, sipping her tea, but he doesn't let her escape. "I'm serious! Why did you become an astronomer? There must have been a moment when you looked at the stars, and felt—something. A sense of wonder."

Dr. Lišková's face closes down. "Wonder is the denial of a need for explanation." She stands, turning abruptly to the door. "I need to get back to work."

Santi watches her leave, feeling like she has left him alone on a precipice. He stays in the lounge to finish his coffee. He expects it to taste different, but it's the same as always. He's not sure if that makes it more or less of a miracle.

When he gets back to the lab, he senses the new error message before he switches the monitor back on. He sighs. "It crashed again," he says heavily, before Dr. Lišková can ask.

"Can't expect more than one miracle a night," she says.

He has to smile. "I'll ask God not to waste it on coffee next time."

"Mm." She's gone, absorbed into her computer. As Santi pulls on his coat and leaves the lab, she doesn't look up.

He walks home to his apartment in the Belgian Quarter and crashes into bed, surrounded by sketches of the stars he remembers. By the time he wakes up, it's early evening. He showers, changes, and heads out through the sun-dappled streets of Neumarkt to meet his friends at Der Zentaur. The long, raucous table has an unexpected addition: Héloïse, Santi's crush from the campus coffee shop.

"I met someone who knows her," Jaime explains to him in Spanish, not bothering to lower his voice. "And yes, you owe me."

The summer evening passes in a stutter of refilling glasses and sinking light. Santi slingshots from conversation to conversation, switching between English and German, lapsing into Spanish with Jaime whenever they don't want the others to understand. As the tally of drinks marked on their beer mats rises, he spends more and more of his time watching Héloïse in the mirror behind the bar: the glow of her skin in the semi-dark, the way her braids swing when she laughs. He's too far down the table to talk to her directly: she's within his sight, but as unreachable as ever.

The girl sitting opposite gets up, leaving him a view of the window. At a table outside, two women are arguing. One looks tearful. The other sits drawn tight, arms crossed. It's only when she shakes her head and turns to the window that Santi recognizes Dr. Lišková.

Their eyes meet through the glass. Santi freezes, convinced she sees him, but she turns back, reaching across the table to take the other woman's hand.

Jaime bumps his shoulder. "What are you staring at?"

"My supervisor," Santi says in slow horror.

Jaime laughs and slaps the table. "Guys! That's Santi's supervisor outside!"

As one, they turn their heads to the window. Santi crouches, hiding himself. "Stop! Don't all stare at her!"

"She's younger than I thought," says Jaime.

"She's hot," says some guy Santi doesn't even know.

"Looks like she's having a fight with her girlfriend," Héloïse observes. Wonderful: *now* she's talking to him.

Santi covers his head. "Can you guys dig a tunnel to get me out of here?"

His plea is ignored. Vibrant speculation about Dr. Lišková's love life ensues. Santi bites his nails and drinks his way toward a hoped-for oblivion. Through the window, his supervisor and her girlfriend mime a passionate unraveling. After a dilated, unreckonable time, the girlfriend gets up and walks away. Surely now Dr. Lišková will leave. But she stays, an angry ghost ordering glass after glass of wine, throwing it down her throat like it's a poison she deserves. There is something obscene about seeing her like this, and yet Santi can't stop looking. The girl opposite gets fed up of him peering over her shoulder and moves to another seat.

Finally Jaime shakes him. "Hey. We're leaving."

Santi looks up, disoriented. "Sure."

"Do you want us all to huddle around you as we walk out? Like—human shield style?"

Santi considers it. "No, too obvious. I'll wait here. Just—make a lot of noise as you leave. Then while she's busy looking at you guys, I can sneak out."

Jaime laughs, but he marshals the troops. Santi watches them stagger performatively outside, whooping and reeling across the cobbles. Dr. Lišková looks up jerkily from her nth glass of wine. Santi takes a breath, puts his head down, and walks quickly after his friends.

"Santi. Santiago López. Santiago López Romero." She slurs his name but still gets it right. Given that he's seen her put away the better part of two bottles of wine, he's almost impressed. "Please stop insulting both our intelligences and turn around."

Dr. Lišková sits clinging to her empty wine glass like an anchor chain. She hasn't been crying. There's another emotion than sadness at work here. Santi thought he had seen her angry before. Now her anger is elemental, incandescent, and it is all turned inward on herself.

"How—how are you?" he asks.

It's such an absurd question that he expects her to laugh. She doesn't even smile. "Jules just left me," she says, lighting a cigarette. "So there's that."

Santi wishes for the power of flight, of teleportation, any miracle that would get him out of this conversation. "I thought it was in my control," Dr. Lišková says. "I thought I could just—choose not to let her go." As she taps the ash off the cigarette, Santi notices a tattoo on her wrist: stars, in a vaguely familiar pattern. "Maybe if I'd done something differently," she goes on. "Maybe when I asked her to move back to the Netherlands with me, I could have done it in a way that made her say yes." She takes a drag on her cigarette. "Maybe there's a universe where I did, and I'm in our beautiful flat in Amsterdam with her right now, instead of making a fucking idiot of myself in front of my student."

Santi's memory fractures. Another moment, another argument. A lock of blue hair against the night sky. He blinks the phantom away. "I don't think it works that way," he says.

"Of course you would know how it works." She tips her wine back, seems upset to discover that it's empty. She waves the glass at him. "Hey. Can your friend up there stand me another?"

Santi's fists clench. He looks away, across the square at the graffiti on the clock tower. NOT ENOUGH SKY.

"I did it," Dr. Lišková says.

For a second, he doesn't know what she means. Did what? Torpedoed her relationship? Put away enough wine to tranquilize a horse? Then he follows her gaze to the graffiti. "The message?" He stares at her. "You're saying you wrote it?"

She nods.

It can't be, but it is. Dr. Lišková, his distant, skeptical supervisor: the kindred spirit he's been waiting to find. Finally, he understands the feeling of magnetic repulsion between them, matching poles straining for distance. He laughs aloud. "It's you," he says. "You're the other person who remembers."

The directness of her drunk gaze is overwhelming. "What are you talking about?"

Out of the corner of his eye, he sees Jaime beckoning him from a side street. But he doesn't want to leave, not after what he's discovered. "The stars." He's been preparing for this moment his whole life. Now, the words come too fast, tripping over each other. "I—I remember constellations that don't exist. Whole skies that never were. Every time I look up, all I see is what isn't there." Dr. Lišková's fingers go to her wrist. He talks on into the void of her silence, waiting for an echo. "I went into astronomy to find out what it means. You went into astronomy to explain it away. But we both went looking."

She doesn't speak. The cigarette in her hand burns down, its long ashen tail like a dying star.

"It's true." Santi's voice breaks on the word. "Tell me you remember. Don't leave me alone in this."

Her lips move. Santi feels a rush of premature joy.

"You're not making any sense," she says. The cathedral bells toll as she stumbles to her feet. The wine glass wobbles and falls, rolling until it rests in a crack in the table. "I'm going home. So should you. Forget this conversation ever happened." She shakes her head. "God, I hope I will."

Santi, lost, watches her walk away.

As he crosses the square from east to west, skirting the fountain toward the tall letters of her graffiti, he looks up. For a second, he swears he sees them all: every star he remembers, overlaid in a dazzling progression toward a meaning he doesn't understand. In their silver light, the hands on the clock stand frozen at one thirty-five.

A BETTER WORLD

○ ❋ ◉

Thora stands on the fire escape of the hospital's ninth floor, watching the ash from her cigarette drift down to the street below. The old town of Cologne spreads out before her, a dark mass of crooked buildings broken by cobbled squares. The air vibrates with the sounds of carnival: the beat of a drum, the laughter of afternoon drinkers. A gaggle of people in animal suits runs down the alley, appearing and disappearing like a hallucination. To drown the noise, Thora hums to herself, a tune that's been in her head since she woke up.

"Thought I'd find you out here." Her colleague Lily comes to stand beside her.

"Mm." Thora narrows her eyes, focusing on the ruined clock tower.

Lily waves a hand across her stare. "Earth to Thora?"

"Sorry. Yeah. I'm here. I just . . . Has it always been like that?"

Lily leans the way Thora is pointing. "Has what always been like what?"

"The clock. Stopped at twenty-five to one."

"Yes," Lily says, with an inflection of the obvious.

Thora frowns. "Since when?"

"Since the past two hundred years?"

"Right." Thora rubs her tired eyes.

Lily pats her shoulder. "Do I need to send you down to neuro?"

"You're hilarious. One day I'll actually get a brain tumor and then you won't be laughing."

"Oh, I will. And you'll thank me. You'll need someone to see the funny side."

Thora turns away from the railing. "Why do we do this?" she asks Lily.

"Geriatric physiotherapy? Or were you speaking more broadly?"

"The first one."

"In your case, I'd say probably unresolved issues from your mother's early death." Lily is one of the few people who knows Thora well enough to joke with her about this. "Also, I think you enjoy throwing yourself at something impossible. As for me— honestly, God knows. I sometimes feel like he just dropped me here to give you someone to talk to."

"I don't believe in God," Thora says.

"Just as well. If you did, you'd probably want to fight him. Cause all kinds of cosmic ruckus."

Lily's trying to distract her. But Thora doesn't want to push this thought away. She wants to call Jules and talk about it, but she's away at a conference. Maybe it's just as well. They've been arguing more lately. She can sense Jules slipping away. It's a sad, tired feeling, like watching the same story play out for the hundredth time, the ending already fixed.

Thora yawns and runs her hands through her hair. She's had it short since her mother died, the same age she started dyeing it pink, but her subconscious still thinks it's long: her hands slip suddenly free, as if they were expecting it to keep going. She wonders if everyone feels it, this hunger to live every life, to exist as every possible version of herself. "There's always a moment, isn't there?" she says, flicking her cigarette end off the fire escape and watching it fall. "A moment when you choose. This path, or another one. What if I'd chosen something different?"

Lily looks at her sideways. "Then you'd be off the hook for your three o'clock."

Thora sighs. "Remind me who my three o'clock is?"

Lily looks down at the roster. "Ooh, you're in luck. Mr. López."

Thora's heart lifts. "I know you're kidding. But this is genuinely going to be the highlight of my day. Is that desperately sad?"

Lily looks at her levelly. "I know you want me to say no. But the factory didn't program me to lie."

Thora holds the fire door open, letting Lily inside. "Come on, Lil, you know what a nightmare patients can be. It's just nice to find one you get along with, once in a while."

"Sure." Lily pats her on the back. "Don't worry, I won't tell Jules about your secret lover."

Thora gives her the finger over her shoulder. In her treatment room, she pulls up Mr. López's record as the door opens. "Good afternoon, Dr. Lišková."

"Still not a doctor," she says, smiling. "But at least you got my name right. You're the only one who does."

Mr. López frowns. "I never found your name difficult to remember."

"You'd be surprised. Usually, I just give up and go by Jane Smith." As he chuckles, she asks, "And how are you feeling today?"

He smiles his craggy smile. "All the better for seeing you."

"That's enough, charmer. Show me your hands." She begins her examination. "Someone's been drawing again," she observes neutrally.

"It's the way I make sense of the world," he protests.

"It's also the way you exacerbate your carpal tunnel."

He looks up at her. "If I don't practice, I won't get better."

Thora privately wonders how much better he can get at his age. She pushes away the thought as unkind. "Have you been doing your exercises?"

"Yes. Every day." She can tell he's not lying. Another reason she likes him: Mr. López, unlike so many of her patients, is not resigned. He isn't angry, either, not like she would be in his situation. He simply does what he can, and lets the rest go. It's an attitude she respects more than she can say.

He smiles at her as she watches his face for pain. "And what about you? How are you feeling today?"

She chuckles. "You're my only patient who asks me that."

"Ah, I see. Avoiding the question."

She gives him a look. "All right. I'm feeling—odd, if you must know."

"Odd?" He frowns. "You should take a break. My hands can wait."

"No, it's nothing physical. Just—" She sits up, looking into his eyes. "Do you ever have a moment when you look at the world, and don't recognize it whatsoever?"

"Yes," he says. "But I am eighty years old. You're a little young to be talking that way."

"Maybe I'm an old soul."

He smiles. "Better than being an old body."

"You're doing very well for an old body," she remonstrates. "I'm going to prescribe you something for the pain, but otherwise, you just need to cut down on the drawing and keep up with the exercises. I know they hurt like hell, but your range of motion is great, much better than it was."

She goes back to her computer to fill out his prescription. As she types, she sees him reflected in the screen, looking around at her walls: the star chart behind his chair; the copy of the Hippocratic Oath in the original ancient Greek (her father's passive-aggressive way of saying that if she was going into medicine, she should have become a doctor); the picture of her and Jules kissing at the Christopher Street Day parade. Mr. López is from a different generation, a different culture, and she's worried he'll make a comment. But when he speaks, the question isn't what she expected. "What are you singing?"

Thora didn't realize she was humming again. "Just—a tune that's been in my head. I don't know where it's from. Why, do you know it?"

Mr. López doesn't answer. When she turns to give him his prescription, he has a strange look on his face, as if there's something he wants to say to her. Instead, his head turns back to the star chart: her public secret, daring the curious to ask. Thora follows his gaze, wondering how to explain to him that she keeps it as an anchor, to manage the vertigo she feels when she looks up at the night sky and imagines a dozen other ways it could have been. *These are the stars. This is your life. These were your choices.*

"I used to think I would go there someday," he says, tapping the chart somewhere light-years away.

Thora sees the pain in his eyes and greets it like a friend. In a few decades, she will be the age he is now: an old woman, Earthbound her whole life. "Me too," she says.

He takes the prescription from her. "It may be selfish, but I'm glad you didn't," he says. "Or you wouldn't have been here to be my doctor."

"I'm not——" she begins.

"I know." He gets to his feet, wincing. His hand goes to the back of his neck.

"Something new?" she asks.

He shakes his head. "I've had this pain all my life. This is beyond even your power to fix."

She smiles ruefully as he goes to the door. On the point of leaving, he pauses.

"Was there something else?" Thora asks.

Mr. López frowns, as if he's not sure what he's going to say until he says it. "When you said you don't recognize the world. What do you mean?"

"I mean . . ." She pauses. The appointment is over: she has a cancellation straight after, but Mr. López doesn't know that. She should really stop talking, send him home. But his eyes are fixed on her, and she doesn't know why, but she wants to share this with him. "I remember it being better."

He lets go of the door handle. "Better how?"

Thora swallows down the old hurt. "My mother—she died after a stroke when I was sixteen years old. And I feel—I can't help feeling like that wasn't supposed to happen. That there's a world where it didn't happen, and in that world, other good things came after." *Like maybe I made it to the stars.* She has to stop herself from saying it. She doesn't know why she's talking this way to a patient. But it's important to her that he understand what she means. "I used to think if I tried hard enough, if I really concentrated, I could travel there. To another world. A better one."

Mr. López is looking at her with tears in his eyes. Thora panics. "Oh. I'm sorry. Did I say something wrong?"

He rubs the wedding ring on his veined right hand. "My wife. Thirty years ago, she resisted being robbed at knifepoint, and—they killed her. I tried to stop them, but . . ." He trails off.

Héloïse. The name jumps into Thora's head. She frowns, and focuses: her patient just disclosed a personal tragedy, and she's staring into space. "Jesus," she says, forgetting that Mr. López probably believes in Jesus and doesn't appreciate her blasphemy. "I'm sorry. I guess you have your own reasons for wanting to be in another universe."

He reaches inside his jacket. Thora expects him to bring out a photograph. She already knows who it will show: a dark-skinned woman with thick braids and an uncertain smile. She waits, breathless, for him to prove her wrong. But Mr. López's hand stays in his pocket, clinging to something.

He looks past her to the window, to a city the rain turns to a blurred mosaic. "I'm—a fatalist, I suppose you could say. I don't believe it could have happened any differently. And I've found meaning in it. For it to have happened and not happened—for there to be a place where she is alive and still with me—no, with someone who is me and not me—it would make a mockery of everything I am." He dashes tears from his eyes with one shaking hand.

Thora stares at him, wondering what is happening to her. Nothing is happening to her. The name, the image, are just random firings in her brain. Nothing to do with Mr. López or his dead wife. *Prove it,* a voice whispers. *It would be easy. Say her name. Describe her and see how he reacts.* But this conversation has already gone far enough. Her curiosity, however fierce, is not worth his distress.

"I'm sorry," Thora says. "It's not my place to . . . You're my patient, I shouldn't be speculating about alternative versions of your life. I don't know what's wrong with me."

He takes in a sighing breath. "Perhaps it's a gift. To be able to see the possibility of a better world." His eyes fix her. "But I don't believe it can work like you say, that we could step into it so easily. No. We have to work to make it."

Thora lets the thought settle in her. It wakens a memory, like a vision seen in flames: sitting by her mother's bedside after her stroke, desperate to reach into the machinery and make it work again. The desire that led her off the path she thought was hers and onto a new one. The path that eventually brought her here, to a ninth-floor treatment room on a rainy afternoon in Cologne: to an old man who is looking at her with infinite patience, as if their roles have been reversed.

"You are busy, Doctor," Mr. López says. He opens the door. Thora has to fight the urge to ask him to stay. It burns her strangely that their time together is so limited. *Don't leave me alone in this*, something in her cries.

"I'm not supposed to say this," she tells him, "but you're my favorite patient."

Mr. López gives her a somber look. "If I am dying, please just tell me."

She laughs. "Nah, you've got a good ten years in you yet. Five of those with working hands, if you keep doing as I say." She takes his hand. As they shake, his gaze lingers on the tattoo on her wrist.

Thora holds the door for him. "See you next time," she says.

He blinks at her, confusion flickering across his face. "Next time," he agrees, and carefully pulls the door closed.

*   *   *

At the end of the day, Lily leans around the doorframe. "Boo. You almost finished? We're going to Chlodwigplatz to join in the craziness, if you want to come."

Carnival. A week of wild, drunken street parties, with the flimsy historical excuse of letting off steam before Lent. The idea of joining in makes Thora want to jump out of the ninth-floor window. She rubs her eyes as she switches her computer off. In the black mirror of the screen, her face looks lost. There's a thought she can't grasp, lingering in her mind like the smell of smoke in her hair. "Sorry, I can't tonight."

"Plans with Jules?"

"Jules is away. I have plans with the sofa and a tub of ice cream." She looks through her fingers at Lily. "I know it's anti-social. But—"

"But you'd rather watch *Contact* for the fiftieth time than hang out with us actual real humans. It's okay. I get it." Lily shakes her head, mock-offended. "Look after yourself," she adds as she turns away.

Paths, Thora thinks, as Lily's steps diminish down the corridor. Paths diverging again and again, infinite and terrifying. But hopeful too. Maybe she hasn't trapped herself after all. Maybe it isn't too late to seek a better world.

She locks the treatment room, wraps the scarf her father knitted around her neck, and heads down the stairs. Her phone rings. She sighs and picks up. "Hey, tati. How are you?"

"Oh, excellent, excellent." Her father sounds drunk. "How are you?"

"Not bad. Just finished at work." The automatic door lets her out into the spitting rain. "Had a bit of a weird conversation with a patient."

He makes a dismissive noise. "Not surprising. They are all senile, your patients."

No more senile than you. She hears the echo of her angry response, as if another Thora says it, but she makes a different choice. "Listen, I have to bike home now, but—I'll come and see you tomorrow. Okay?"

A pause. "Yes. Okay. See you."

The rain intensifies as she reaches her bike. She pulls up her hood and sets off, dodging a truck that nearly pushes her into a pothole. "Watch it!" she yells, in German, English, and Czech for good measure. That would have been a good ending to her little epiphany, she thinks. Killed in a bike accident.

As the rain eases off and the clouds begin to break, she cycles on through Neumarkt, skirting the Belgian Quarter and crossing the park where the mosque glitters in the evening sun. She pedals on into Ehrenfeld, passing the Turkish café, the landlocked lighthouse by the train tracks: home. As she parks her bike and unlocks the door of her building, she rubs her breast, feeling the lump Jules keeps nagging her to have checked. *Later*, she thinks, and closes the door behind her.

WE ARE HERE

○ ✹ ◎

Santi is lost.

He stands in the middle of a busy shopping street, a stone in a river of staring people. He knows what a year of rough sleeping has done to him: the haunted eyes, the tremor, the nervous tension that makes people keep their distance. But he knows that's not why they're looking. Being the center of the world is exhausting. He wishes, sometimes, that they would just stop. *Look at someone else*, he wants to say, but the problem is that everyone else is perfectly transparent: even if they all lined up in front of him, it would be as useless as trying to hide in clear water.

He's not sleeping rough these days. He has a place in the hostel now. That's where he was trying to go. But the streets of this city lead back on themselves, knot and tangle into dead ends. He reaches into his jacket for the talisman of his grandfather's knife. The key, he thinks, is to know who you are. Only then will you know where you're going.

He picks a street, follows it with his eyes half-closed. It leads him true: he comes out into the open green of the park with the sense of worlds abruptly ending and beginning, clumsily jointed. Wind chases the leaves past him, the city sliding away under his feet. As he crosses the park, flashes of sunlight break through where the mosque gleams, green space on one side and the post-industrial sprawl of Ehrenfeld on the other. The sun mingles with another light: heavenly fire, blazing invisibly bright at the corner of his eye. He takes the main road into the neighborhood's heart. The landlocked lighthouse by the train tracks taunts him with a meaning he can't grasp. A revelation is coming. Santi looks up at the sky, clouds fleeting across it like impossibly swift ships, and feels it building, inside him and out.

At the door of the hostel, he fumbles for his card, but his pocket is empty. He swears. He forgot: he lost the card this morning, in the courtyard next to the clock tower. One moment it was falling from his pocket onto the grass. The next, it had vanished. He combed the ground obsessively for an hour, but it was gone, as surely as if it had never existed. He imagines the card slipping out through a hole in the world and feels sick with vertigo. He presses the buzzer.

"Hello?" A woman's voice, compressed by the intercom.

The hairs on the back of Santi's neck stand up. "Hi. I—I lost my card."

"Okay. One second." The buzzer vibrates, and the door clicks open.

The woman behind the desk looks up as he walks in. Bleach-blond, short-cropped hair; stark blue eyes. "I guess you'll be wanting a new card," she says. Santi is about to tell her his name when she says, "Are you Santiago López?"

His skin prickles. "How do you know my name?"

"Oh, I—I've been looking through the files."

His eyes drift to her desk, where only his file lies open in front of her. His life, distilled down to a few pages: the essence of him, the blueprint for all the Santis there could ever be.

She closes it hurriedly. "Give me one second," she says, and wheels her office chair over to the card printer.

She's humming under her breath, a tune Santi knows. His eyes pass over her desk. A starscape mug filled with strong tea. A photo of her with her arms around a smiling woman.

"Here you are, Mr. López." She hands him the new card. "I'm Thora, by the way," she adds. "Thora Lišková."

He closes his eyes. "Fox."

She coughs. "Excuse me?"

"Your name." He opens his eyes, watches her face for clues. "That's what it means."

"Yes." She half-smiles. "The other staff—they told me you like to know what things mean. So you speak Czech?"

"No."

She frowns. "Your name means Wolf." She blinks, confused. "I—don't know how I know that."

Santi feels the world shift under his feet. "What are you doing here?" he says softly.

"I'm a trainee social worker. I'm new here, I just started this morning—"

"No." He cuts her off. "What are you doing here?"

"I . . ." She's familiar, everything about her is familiar: the washed-out blue of her eyes, the frankness of her gaze. She's about his age, although he knows he looks older. Life has been kinder to her, this time.

"You," he says with sudden understanding. "You're part of it."

Her expression shifts to wariness. "I'm sorry. I don't know what you mean."

"You do." The conviction burns him: she is the revelation, and she knows it. He slams his hands down on the counter. "Tell me," he shouts. "Tell me what's happening to me."

"Take it easy." She reaches under the desk for the panic button. He has seconds to get through to her. He leans across the counter, stares into her eyes. The words come to him as if he has said them before. "Don't leave me alone in this."

He sees something change in her face as the resident assistants pull him away.

Back in his room, they sit him down for a talk. They tell him he can't threaten the staff, or he won't be allowed to stay here anymore. They explain to him that one of the features of his illness is a tendency to see meaning everywhere, that his delusion about recognizing Thora is just another in a long list of symptoms.

He lets them think he understands. After they leave, he takes the knife from his jacket and slides it under the pillow: an old habit he can't sleep without. He lies on his side on the narrow bed and stares at the wall, searching for patterns in the cracks until he falls asleep.

In his dream, he's running through the hospital, endless branching corridors all leading to darkness. It's a normal dream, routine even, until he sees her, pink-haired, standing in an impossible shaft of sunlight. Even in the dream, he knows it's not right. The woman he met was blond. This is a different Thora: older, gentler, scarred by sorrow.

She looks as surprised as he is to find herself in his dream. "Mr. López," she says. Then, hesitantly, "Santi?"

The ground shakes. Santi falls. A tearing like the universe breaking in two. A rip opens up in the floor. Thora is on the other side. He reaches out, almost meeting her grasping fingers. Gravity takes them, and they fall apart, two planets pulled by the force of separate suns.

He opens his eyes to a cracked white wall. He has no idea where he is. Panicked, he searches through a kaleidoscope of remembered images: sun-yellow curtains, an open window, the cornice of a high-ceilinged apartment. Finally, it comes: he's in the hostel. He reaches for his notebook, finds what he scribbled half-conscious as he woke. A lightning-shaped hole, two figures falling.

He sits up, feeling the old pain in his neck that he puts down to his year on the streets. He turns to face the grid of images on the wall, linked with pinned-up lines of red string. The ruined clock tower in the old town; a time-lapse photo of a starry sky, constellations blurred into streaks; the imprint of a bird on a window, ghostly feathers on glass. Together, they form a map that he hopes will one day lead him to meaning.

He looks down and starts to draw: image after image of Thora, old and young, her hair all the colors of the rainbow. The ruled lines of the notebook cut each picture, interference on a transmission coming from impossibly far away.

He tucks the notebook into his jacket and follows the rising sun outside. His shoulders tense as he passes through reception, but the person behind the desk isn't Thora. He stops to pet the skinny black cat that haunts the hostel door. She meows at him plaintively, as if she's trying to remind him of something important.

He begs a slice of burek from the Turkish café across the street. He eats half and keeps half for later, dropping the crumbs for the parakeets. The birds are talking in the trees, muttered fragments of conversations he's heard before. This world is overlaid with itself, parts reused to patch up what is worn out. He wonders if he is made of fragments too: if somewhere he can't see, his skin flashes feathers. If he jumped from the top of the clock tower, would a fragment of feather be enough for him to fly?

He walks on, into the city's tangled heart. Sooner than it should, the cathedral looms, a vision of darkness against the sky. Santi still remembers how his throat went dry the first time he stepped inside: how the space between him and the vaulted ceiling gave him the illusion of movement, as if the whole thing were about to lift off and carry him to the stars. He should have taken it as a warning, not a promise. He should have left the city then, while he could still afford to. Now, he's stuck in the labyrinth, wandering in circles until he finds a thread to lead him out.

He walks on across the Hohenzollernbrücke, averting his eyes from the padlocks. Inside the Odysseum, he holds up his hostel card until the clerk waves him through the turnstile. A tremor of meaning follows him into the room of false stars. The museum is quiet. One other person stands next to him on the gantry, staring up at the velvet dark studded with random lights. He knows before he looks that it is Thora.

There is a message here, a code for him to decipher. As usual, he can't concentrate hard enough to understand. Thora stands next to him without looking at him, following the unwritten rule of public spaces. Santi savors the asymmetric knowledge it gives him. Alone, together, they look up at the map of a cosmos that never existed. Her hand moves as if to catch hold of the glowing lights.

"Why are you with me?" she says quietly.

Santi's heart jumps. Then he sees the phone cradled in her other hand, hears a woman's voice on the other end. He listens, eyes fixed on the stars.

"I mean, what did I do?" Thora asks. "When was the moment you decided—this is it, it's working, I'll stay?"

Santi hears the distant echo of an answer. Whatever it is doesn't satisfy Thora. She turns, paces away from him. "There must have been a moment. There must have been something I did that made it different." A pause. "Not different. I mean . . ." She puts a hand to her head. "Sorry. I just—I had a really weird day yesterday. Yeah. I'll tell you about it when I get home. Okay. Love you." She hangs up. She breathes into her hands, then lifts her head to the velvet sky.

Santi can't hold back any longer. "You're a stargazer too."

She turns. When she recognizes him, he sees fear in her eyes. "Mr. López. I—didn't know it was you."

He realizes: she thinks he followed her here. Something in him responds by wanting to reassure her. "I come here a lot," he explains, although what kind of explanation is that?

"Do you now," she murmurs.

He can tell she doesn't believe him. It brings a different emotion, belonging to a different person: anger, at how dismissive she can be. He hears his voice adjust, a stranger speaking through him. "What are you doing here?" Because he has to know, has to unravel this before it unravels him.

"They gave me the day off, after—yesterday. This place calms me down, when I feel—" Mid-sentence, her attention snaps back, as if she's just caught sight of herself. Every second of this interaction is another stain on the carefully controlled relationship her job requires them to have. If she were anyone else, Santi would expect her to walk away. But he has already learned that his expectations are no map for her territory. "I shouldn't have done that," she says. "Guessed your name, told you what it means. They—they told me that's one of your triggers. Thinking people know more about you than they should."

Her words let another ghost in to possess him. This one is wry, certain, her equal. "But you do, don't you?"

She takes a breath. "I don't want to lie to you," she says. "I do find you—familiar." She meets his eyes with frank annoyance. "But that doesn't mean you're right. All it means is that this kind of delusion can happen to anyone."

It's so unexpected, so off-script, that he laughs. "Why did you tell me that? You're supposed to just tell me it's all in my head."

She looks at him seriously. "I want you to trust me."

He doesn't know what to say. But what comes out, surprising him as much as her, is the truth. In all the different versions of him she brings out, there is one constant. "I do."

She nods, looking away. Visibly, under her breath, she says, *Fuck it.* "Can I get you a coffee?"

She buys him a black coffee without asking how he takes it. They head out the back way, past a closed-off room marked "Under Construction" into a playground filled with fiberglass models of the planets. The breeze off the river is cold. Thora pulls a mustard-yellow scarf out of her bag and wraps it around her neck before climbing up to sit with her feet on the rings of Saturn. She offers Santi her hand. He clambers up to sit next to her, on the same planet as another person at last. Two meters and four hundred million miles away, two small children battle to throw each other off Jupiter. Santi feels a strange sense of loss. Beyond the riverfront plaza, the Hohenzollernbrücke stretches over the water, tying them back to the city.

"Have you ever looked at the locks?" he asks.

Thora raises an eyebrow. "I'm sorry?"

He points. "On the bridge. All those padlocks. Two tons of them."

Thora takes out a pack of cigarettes, offers him one. He takes it for later. She lights hers, blows the smoke away from him. "I've seen them, yes. Joey plus Bobby forever, et cetera."

"But have you ever *looked* at them?" He sits forward. "I mean, really looked at them. Walked all the way across the bridge, following the fence, paying attention."

"No, I haven't." Again, that smile, sending him spiraling through responses: fondness, pride, resentment. "To be honest," she goes on, "I've always found the whole thing a bit stupid."

"They repeat." He blurts it out before he reminds himself to slow down. "If—if you walk across and keep your eyes on the locks, after a while, they start to repeat. The shapes, the colors. Even the names."

Her mouth opens a second before she speaks. "There are only so many brands of padlock. And with people coming here from all over to do the same thing, some names are bound to repeat. That's just statistics."

He shakes his head violently. "It's not like that. It's not random. I've seen the same names, over and over again, in the same order." He rolls the cigarette between his palms. "It's a pattern, a message for me. I just need to learn how to decode it."

She laughs, throwing her head back. The gesture is so familiar it staggers him. Who is she? Why does her presence make him feel partial, fragile, on the verge of crying? "You think it's a message for you," she says.

"Yes."

She looks down at him. "How many people live in Cologne?"

Their roles shift again: she the patronizing professor, he the resentful student. "I don't know. A million?"

"A million people. How many of them walk across that bridge every day?"

A different reaction, a different self. Brother to sister, weary and superior. "A thousand. Fifty thousand. Does it matter?"

"Why do you think the message is for you, and not for any of the other thousand or fifty thousand people who might happen to walk by?"

Santi puts away the cigarette and sits on his hands. He hates feeling like a marionette, his gestures controlled by memories that can't possibly all be his. He focuses on what makes him real. "Because no one but me sees what's wrong with the world."

She frowns. "What's wrong with the world, Mr. López?"

That the stars keep changing. That the city repeats itself, over and over. That I'm the only one who's really here. The answers stop at his lips, destabilized by the fact that his illusion of a constant self dissolves every time she speaks. Was he as unreal as the world, all along? Is he just another dream, being dreamt by a hundred changing Thoras?

She speaks quietly, as if she's afraid someone will overhear. "Why do you come here to look at the stars?"

He turns toward the glass wall of the Odysseum, sees their reflections watching them. "Because the stars in there don't change."

She looks at him with growing disquiet. "You remember different stars?"

"Yes." He swallows. "Sometimes, when I look up, it's like I see them all superimposed. Like the light of them all together could blind me."

"And then you blink, and look again," she says softly. "And they're just the stars as they are. And all you know is that things didn't used to be this way."

Santi stares at her. He doesn't know if she is speaking for herself, or if he is witnessing an act of empathic imagination. Right now, it doesn't matter. No one has ever talked to him about this as if they understood.

"That's why I went into social work," she says. He focuses on her expression, thoughtful and self-conscious: another letter of an alphabet he's remembering how to read. "I felt so dislocated, so lost. I thought even if I couldn't fix myself, maybe I could fix other people who felt like they didn't fit. Make the world better for them." Her eyes flick up to meet his. "But I never met anyone who felt exactly the way I did."

"Until you met me."

"Until I met you."

He looks at Thora like a treasure he thought he'd lost in a fire. He knows this woman, better than he knows his own fractured self. It's someone else's knowledge, but for a moment he lets himself drown in it, the certainty he so rarely feels in this life. His fingers itch to draw her: a girl resting her feet on the rings of Saturn, head in her hands. Wordless, he pulls his notebook from his jacket and hands it to her.

She leafs through, hesitant at first. "You'd better not show this to anyone in the hostel," she says dryly. "They'd kick you out sooner than you can say *stalker*."

"I'm not—"

"I know," she interrupts him. "But they won't." She keeps turning the pages. "Where did you get all this from?"

He looks at her. "I dreamt of you. But not as you are."

A grin spreads across her face. "Just the idea," she murmurs. "That I could be all these different people." She turns the page. In this picture, she's younger, haloed by stars, blue hair flying in the night wind. "What am I doing here?" She rotates the book, squinting. "Is that the clock tower in the old town?"

Santi nods, fingers digging into the surface of the planet. "You were sitting at the top," he says. "Watching me fall."

Thora looks up at him. "In your dream. Were there different versions of you as well?"

"I don't remember." *I don't want to remember.* But he's starting to understand: every one of her ghosts drags one of his own out with it, until he's drowning in reflections, none of them exactly right. He has worked so hard to hold himself together, to fight the catastrophic falling-apart that drove him away from Héloïse and onto the streets. Now he feels it happening again, his center dissolving, his edges bleeding out to nothingness.

He climbs down from Saturn. He needs to get his feet on the earth. "I—I have to go."

Thora looks down at him, uncomprehending. "Okay. Can I walk with you?"

He recognizes another constant: she never really understands him. It's stabilizing enough to make him nod, offer his hand to help her down. Maybe there is a clue here, a direction for his map of meaning, if he can hold himself together long enough to find it.

They walk across the bridge into the city that seems to Santi to repeat again and again, the same angle of walls meeting, the same pattern of cobbles, haunted by itself. It's how he feels, walking by Thora's side. With every step, he lurches between selves: an angry young man in an argument with an older woman, a father trying to make a connection with a sullen daughter.

"It's lucky I work in the hostel," Thora says brightly, as they turn down the river path toward the old town. "It'll make it easier for us to keep talking about this."

Santi thinks of the hostel, his hard-won sanctuary, turned into a laboratory where he will be dissected day by day. The staff there may not understand him, but they have helped him. In another world, Thora could have been one of them. But in this one, she knows him too well. *No one can be everything to someone*, he thinks, and wonders why the thought makes him buzz like a bell struck sideways.

As they reach the old town, a gap between the buildings shows them the clock tower. Santi is sure it shouldn't be visible from here: as if the gravity of the two of them together is warping the world. Thora takes the alleyway to the square, and Santi follows. They stand side by side at the foot of the tower. The clock is frozen at five minutes past midnight. Santi is still sure he can hear it ticking.

"I guess doomsday already happened," says Thora.

Santi can't shake the feeling that doomsday is yet to come. "Maybe we're waiting for the next one."

Thora frowns. "But the clock's stopped."

Santi shakes his head. "I don't think it has."

Thora throws him a puzzled look. Before he can try to explain, someone grabs their shoulders and turns them around.

"Excuse me." A long-haired man in a blue coat looks between the two of them in shifting delight and confusion. "I—I need to tell—" He cuts himself off, starts again. "You're—you're here."

Thora looks at Santi. He reads her unspoken question. *Do you know this man?* He shakes his head, uncertain.

"I'm sorry, we don't . . ." Thora frowns. "What did you say?"

The man looks at Santi. "You're here. *Here.*" His face crumples in distress. "I—I need to tell you—you—"

Thora tries to meet his eyes. "Listen. Do you need something to eat? A place to stay?"

The man looks at Santi in despair, as if he doesn't understand what Thora is saying. "You're here," he says again, hopelessly. "Here."

Santi shakes his head. "I'm sorry," he says, although he doesn't know what he's apologizing for.

The man wrings his hands and turns away, wandering off across the square.

Thora watches him go, biting her nails. "I'll call the hostel later. Ask them to keep an eye out for him."

Santi's eyes follow the man's vague progress, his blue coat flapping in the wind. There is too much meaning in the world, more than it can hold.

"He's right, anyway," Thora says.

Santi looks at her, puzzled.

"We *are* here," she says. "Both of us. Whatever that means." She presses her hand to the wall of the tower, scrawled with messages in the city's hundred voices. "I guess that's what all these people were trying to say." She pulls a marker from her jacket. WE ARE HERE, she writes in an empty space.

Santi understands, and he doesn't, the meaning sliding away from him like wind-blown leaves. He hates words, he decides. He wishes the ruin was covered in pictures instead. Murals, spreading all across the city like portals to other worlds.

As Thora lowers the pen, he glimpses something on her wrist. His hand moves out to catch her. She steps back, wary again. He holds up his hands. Wordlessly, he pulls back his sleeve, showing the stars inked under his own skin.

Thora makes a soft, disbelieving sound. She grabs his arm, rubs at the tattoo as if she expects it to come off.

"What is it?" Santi asks.

"A constellation," she says. "One that doesn't exist anymore."

He stares down at the pattern of stars: the first thing he drew in his book after he arrived in the city. It felt so important that he went straight to the Belgian Quarter to have it inscribed on his skin. But it doesn't even belong to him: it belongs to Thora, to the bewildering tornado of existences she brings with her.

He steps back, pulls his sleeve down. He wanted to understand. But if the price of understanding is his own unraveling, he doesn't think he can survive it.

"What's wrong?" Thora asks.

Santi laughs. He points to her words, written on the wall of the tower. "*We are here*," he says. "But—who are we? Where is here?"

Thora steps hesitantly toward him. "We can find out," she says. "Together."

Santi shakes his head and continues backing away. He returns to the thought that led him out of the labyrinth: the thought that felt as solid as his grandfather's knife under his hand. "We can't know where we are if we don't know who we are. And I—I can't know who I am when every moment I spend with you breaks me into a hundred pieces." He walks away from her.

"Santi," Thora calls after him, the same way she said it in his dream: his name so tender in her mouth, like a cat carrying her kitten by the scruff of the neck.

"I never told you to call me that," he says without turning around.

He hears her footsteps following him. "I still have your book!"

"Keep it," he yells over his shoulder. "I don't want it anymore." He quickens his pace, running past the fountain where the water bubbles over coins as bright as constellations. For an instant, he sees each droplet freeze in midair.

He won't go back to the hostel. On the streets, he will still have himself, even if everything else dissolves around him. As he runs, he feels the clock tower lean impossibly after him. For the first time he can remember, he can't hear it ticking.

TILL NEXT TIME

○ ✷ ◎

"López!"

Her partner looks up from gazing at the cobbles, gleaming damp in the foggy night. "Yeah. Sorry. I thought I saw . . ." He trails off.

Thora crosses her arms. "If the end of that sentence isn't *the suspect*, I'm not interested."

López grins darkly. "Fine. I won't tell you."

Of course, now she's desperate to know. As usual, López has trapped her with her own words. "Tell me when there isn't a knife-wielding maniac on the loose." She shakes her head. "I can't believe you're basically my age. I swear it's like working with a toddler. Can you just focus for five minutes?"

López follows her into the Heumarkt, past the temporary ice rink that curves around the statue of Friedrich Wilhelm III. "I am focused," he argues over the crowd that parts at the sight of their uniforms. "On the big picture."

"The big picture is that innocent people are going to die if we don't pay attention."

López raises an eyebrow. "Isn't that a little dramatic?"

Thora laughs. "I wonder who I learned that from." She mimics him. "I am focused. On the big picture. The deepest mysteries of existence. Your petty mind is too simple to understand."

López shakes his head sadly. "I can't believe you are wasting time mocking me. Lišková, innocent people are going to die if we don't pay attention."

It's New Year's Eve, twenty minutes to midnight. An hour ago, a drunken man stabbed two people in a beer hall and fled. Now, she and López are part of the team tasked with hunting him down. Their official search area is Heumarkt and the square to the north, but they might as well be trying to search a moving labyrinth: the stalls of the Christmas market and the crowds of revelers form infinite paths, opening and closing behind them as they force their way through. Thora scans the square, looking for someone who matches the killer's description. She keeps thinking she catches him, then turning and seeing someone else, as if his face has been copied again and again onto the shifting crowd. Her blood fizzes with anticipation. This is the part of the job she loves most: the joy of seeking, the promise of discovery, the undercurrent of danger that makes her feel alive. Beside her, López reaches inside his jacket, a nervous motion she recognizes.

"Bringing a knife to a knife fight?" she asks.

He shakes his head. "Don't dismiss my choice of weapon just because you don't have the skills to use it." He pulls the knife out without unfolding it, points the handle at her. "This can bring a man down in minutes if you do it right. Under the left arm, straight into the heart." He demonstrates on her.

Thora bats his hand away. "May I remind you we shouldn't be aiming to kill anyone?"

López smiles. "You know I'd never use it. It's symbolic."

"Everything's symbolic with you," Thora grumbles, as a queue for glühwein bars their path. They cut through into a knot of swaying people, lost in laughter until Thora yells "Polizei!" and they scatter, giggles turning to drunken screams. Thora grimaces. "Why did this guy have to pick New Year's Eve of all days?"

"Why, did you have something better to do?" López asks.

"Of course not. Making the city safer is my life." She gives him a sideways look. "If I was joining the party, I'd have picked better company." She's not worried that he'll take it to heart. She never has to watch what she says with López; she speaks to him almost as she would speak to herself.

True to form, he smiles. "You don't think we'd be friends if we weren't colleagues?"

"You mean if I wasn't your boss?" She catches his wry look. "Why, do you?"

He avoids the question. "You're the one who loves speculating about parallel universes. I'm content with the one we have."

Not speculating. Fragments of other lives, other selves, so vivid they sometimes overtake Thora's current existence entirely. "You don't think any universe could be better than this one?"

López scratches his stubble. "How about the one where we catch this guy before he hurts anyone else?"

"Sounds good to me." Thora leads them farther into the square. "So, what were your New Year plans?" She keeps scanning the crowd as she talks, her attention more on the job than on what she's saying. "I guess if you weren't on duty you'd be doing something devastatingly romantic for Héloïse."

"Héloïse and I broke up."

Thora snaps back to him, surprised. "That's a shame. She was lovely. Too lovely for you, obviously." She's trying to provoke him, but he doesn't bite. "Seriously. Why didn't it work out?"

López climbs up on the rung of a barstool to get a better view. "Because I knew her too well."

"What's that supposed to mean?"

"I mean—it felt—unfair," he says hesitantly, as if he's having trouble articulating what he means. "Like I was always a step ahead of her."

Thora follows him through the hot breeze from a roast chestnut stall. "Honestly, that sounds ideal. You could make her fall deeply in love with you by anticipating her every need."

López looks back at her. "Wouldn't that violate her agency?"

Thora doesn't miss the ironic echo of her lectures on the subject of women's autonomy. Typical López, turning her own arguments against her. "It's not violating her agency if it's what she wants."

He laughs. "I would love to hear you explain that to Héloïse."

"So what happened?" Thora asks. "You brought her a cup of tea unprompted and she flipped out?"

"No. I tried to explain how I was feeling, and . . ." He shrugs. "She told me she didn't know what to say. Right after that, she left."

Thora stops, tracking a man's progress through the crowd, but it's a false alarm: he turns and he's someone else, too young, smiling. She looks back to López. It's tempting to mock him again, but instead she chooses a brief moment of sincerity. "I'm sorry."

He gives her a tired smile. "Still lasted longer than I expected. It surprises me that anyone puts up with us for long."

Thora snorts. "Speak for yourself. I'm a fucking catch, and one day, some lucky person is going to realize it."

"That's not what I mean." They're approaching the edge of the square, moving more freely as the crowd thins out. "We both know we're not ordinary people."

Thora smiles wryly. "What could you possibly mean by that?"

"We know things we shouldn't." López keeps pace with her. "About other people. About each other."

Thora makes a face. "I don't think we *know* anything. I think we're both just wired to see possibilities. Other ways things could have been, if the world was different. If we'd made different choices."

López shakes his head. "I don't think they're glimpses of what might have been. I think they're clues, pointing us to a larger truth."

"Ah," says Thora in exaggerated understanding. "Of course. The big picture."

López stops in his tracks, his face earnest. "I believe we were meant to work together," he says. "To be here, in this place, at this time. The things it seems like we remember—I don't think they're memories at all. I think they're part of a message. Directing us toward each other, since before we ever met."

"A message from who? From God?" Thora shakes her head. "Sorry, don't believe in him."

López frowns. "But you must want to explain it."

The truth is, she does. But she doesn't want to get dragged into a theological discussion with her notoriously argumentative partner when they have a job to do. "In the words of my father the philosopher," Thora says, "the world is a bloody weird place. You and me are far from the weirdest things about it." She focuses on where they've stopped: between two alleyways, both leading through to the next square.

"Which way?" López asks.

Thora looks from one to the other, fighting a strange unease. She wishes she could split herself in two. Send one Thora down each path: catch up with the one who succeeded, erase the one who failed. "You pick."

"You're in charge, remember?" López says with a sly smile. "No pressure. Only innocent people's lives."

"Isn't that a little dramatic?"

López laughs.

"Left," Thora decides, and starts walking, stomach already lurching with the conviction that she's chosen wrong.

"Left it is," says López with a disappointed sigh. She ignores him and moves on down the alleyway, one hand on her weapon. Then she sees.

She stops dead, presses back against the wall. "Wolfie," she says softly.

López catches her up. "What?"

She points ahead. López tenses. The silhouette of a man, head in his hands. Thora can't see his face, but he meets the description she was given: he's the right height, with a shaved head and an FC Köln football shirt.

"Left it was," López breathes into her ear.

The smell of smoke in his hair makes her want a cigarette. She laughs silently. "It was a fifty-fifty chance."

"Guess we're just lucky this is the universe where you got it right," López teases her. He starts forward, then pauses, hand on his radio. "Maybe we should call for backup."

Thora shakes her head. "He's one drunk guy with a knife. We don't need backup."

López smiles at her, teeth bright in the semidarkness. "Why do you act like you're immortal?"

Like so many things he says in jest, it cuts close to the truth. Thora doesn't want to admit that it has something to do with him, with the fact of his presence. While she's with him, part of her believes she can come to no true harm. "You're the one who thinks all this was meant to be," she retorts. "Is God going to let us get stabbed by some random maniac?"

López looks troubled. Without meaning to, she has sent him off into one of his contemplative spirals.

Thora sighs. "We don't have time for this. If he moves, we're going to lose him in the crowd. You double back and take the other alley—"

López interrupts, completing her thought. "Head him off from the front." He's already on his way.

Thora feels an odd anxiety watching his silhouette diminish, the shadow that defines him blending into the greater darkness of the alley. *Shit*. She presses hard on her temples. Now is not the time for one of what Lily calls her cosmic migraines. It comes on her now, pushing her backward through the wall into a darkness filled with rushing noise. The world is unstable, flickering in and out of existence every time she blinks; they are collectively re-membering it wrong, over and over. She holds her breath, hoping to stem it, but it only gets worse: towers crumbling and knitting back together like bad crochet, a burning hole in the center of it all like a hellmouth. *This isn't real*, she tells herself, closing her eyes. *It's happening in your mind. Step forward. Open your eyes.*

She steps forward. She opens her eyes. She's back in the ordinary darkness of the city, the wall solid again behind her. In the meantime, her target has moved. He stands at the mouth of the alley, leaning out into the square. He's going to make a break for it, too soon, before López can get around to head him off.

"No no no," Thora says under her breath. As if he hears her, the man lurches forward into the square, shoving his way through the crowd.

Thora swears. She sprints down the alley, following the man

into the surging mass of people. "Lišková!" she hears López yell. She's aware of him somewhere to her right, drowned in the impossible brightness that burns at the corner of her eye, but she doesn't waste time looking for him: she is busy tracking the commotion ahead of her, a ripple pointing across the square toward the ruined clock tower. As she ducks and weaves and pushes her way forward, a thought comes to her as clear as a revelation. Causality in this city has a downward slope; the tower stands in a valley where possibilities narrow to zero. She looks up to see the clock already at midnight, a premature renewal. In this square, it will be New Year's forever. The man she is chasing breaks through the edge of the crowd, sprints for the gap in the wall of the tower. He checks over his shoulder before he disappears inside.

Thora pounds to a stop at the foot of the tower. López fetches up beside her, chest heaving. "Where did he go?"

Thora points to the jagged hole in the stones.

López is silent. Thora is used to her partner disappearing, even as he stands next to her: as if he's communicating on a deeper level with the world, fitting together a puzzle made of cobbles and fragments of sky. But this is different. The expression on his face dislocates her: another moment, another López, a duality she can't explain.

"Hey," she says, touching his arm. "You okay?"

He jumps. "Yeah. Is he—did he . . ."

Thora crouches by the entrance of the tower, peering inside. She straightens up and comes back to López. "He's climbed the stairs inside. About twenty meters up. I can see him there, pressed against the wall."

López stares at the tower, rubbing the back of his neck. As Thora radios their location, he starts to walk toward it, slow at first and then determined.

Thora lowers the radio. "What are you doing?"

López sounds half-asleep. "Climbing up to get him."

Thora stares at him. She sees it so clearly: López climbing, loose-limbed and unafraid, the possibility of falling never entering his mind. Rage takes hold of her, a possessive, violent refusal. "No."

He doesn't seem to hear her. Thora strides past him, physically puts herself between him and the yawning gap. "Hey. I'm the senior officer, remember?" *Remember.* Her voice echoes off the cobbles, comes back to her the same but altered. "You're not going up there."

López's gaze drifts, focuses on her. "Why?"

Her mouth moves. The reason won't form itself into words; it's nothing but an inarticulate scream. "I just—I'm not going to let you kill yourself falling." *Again.* She bites back the impossible word. Her head pounds, another migraine drowning her in images. A yellow scarf on a nail, blowing in the night wind. An old man smiling, leaving her treatment room for the last time. A hospital bed, Santi tied up in tubes and wires—she is losing him by pieces and their daughter has to watch, and she's too young, why couldn't the cancer have waited until Estela was grown, until she could understand—

López steps close to her. His voice is demanding, desperate. "Tell me why."

Thora's throat is dry. She can't say it. But she can: this is López. She can say anything. "Because you died here."

He smiles, almost in relief. "I know." He turns to look up at the tower. The harsh lights in the square turn his face to an orange-and-black skull. "I remember falling. I remember not believing it, not understanding how the universe could have allowed my hand to slip." He looks at her. "It felt like I had a long time to think about it. And by the time I hit the ground, I knew. It was right. I was meant to die, there and then, and there was nothing I could have or should have done about it."

"It was my fault," Thora says, cutting him off. "Not God. Not the universe. It was my fault it happened then, and I'm not going to let it happen now."

López laughs. "Thora," he says gently, as if she's a child who still doesn't understand.

He's never called her by her first name before. Not in this life. Thora meets his eyes. She doesn't see her colleague, the partner she fell in with so easily that Lily joked they must have known each other in a past life. She sees her teacher, her student, her brother, her husband, her father: a vortex of realities spinning and collapsing together.

"Santi?" she says, as the universe explodes.

A boom, deep and reverberating. Then another. Thora looks up. The sky is full of stars, bursting and falling, burning out in trails of smoke. The New Year's fireworks, exploding above the river. Between the blasts, the cathedral bells toll an interrupted midnight.

They have two seconds to look at each other. Two seconds to share the revelation that is turning them inside out: a blossoming, a bonfire, an ecstasy of remembering. Then everything happens at once. Thora sees the man emerge from the gap in the tower. Santi sees her face and turns. Before Thora can move, the man is already slashing at Santi's throat.

Thora launches herself at the man without even pulling out her weapon. It's madness, but she is not afraid. She is Thora Lišková, and she is immortal, and she will not let God or fate or the universe take Santi away from her, not this time.

She hits the man with all her strength. He stumbles but keeps his feet, turning to lunge at her. In her delirium, she can't tell if the knife misses or passes clean through her. She dodges, grabbing his wrist and wrenching it until the knife falls. Thora yells, knees him in the stomach, and brings him down. He huffs out his surprise as she cuffs him cleanly.

The backup team swarms in. Someone lifts the man to his feet, escorts him away. Thora stands unmoored, empty with victory. Then she sees Santi on his knees, fingers at his throat slick with blood.

"No." She falls to her knees beside him, hands searching uselessly for the artery. "López. Santi. Wolfie, come on." Sirens wail, not close enough. Thora feels like she's observing it all from afar, a tiny figure in a distant universe. "No, no, no, *fuck* you, *no!*" She holds on to him, tight and desperate. "Don't leave me alone in this."

Santi's mouth opens, his eyes fixed on hers. "Remember," he says, before he goes limp in her arms.

LOOK BEHIND YOU

○ ✳ ◉

Santi wakes on an unmoving train.

He lurches forward, wincing at the pain in his neck. Where is he? He peers through the window into a high, vaulted space. Cologne Hauptbahnhof: his destination.

He sits back, pressing his eyes until he sees stars. Didn't he just come from here? It feels as if he got on the train backward, rode it the wrong way through time to end up where he started.

The conductor strides through the carriage. "Bitte aussteigen! Der Zug endet hier!"

Everything ends here. Santi gets to his feet like a man in a dream. He stumbles down the steps from the platform to the busy concourse. He planned to get a taxi to his hotel, have a shower and rest, ready to start the job that is the reason he moved here. Instead, he lingers, scanning the faces in the crowd. He knows no one in this city. Why does it feel like someone should be here to greet him?

He walks in the opposite direction from the taxi rank, out into the cathedral square. The day is mild; rain has just started to fall. He doesn't know why it seems to him that the air should be cold, the ground slippery with frost. The smell of damp cobblestones, the pungent waft of currywurst, follow him up the steps to the cathedral. Santi stands in the spitting rain and feels the city rush through him, a river of meaning he can grasp if he only gives himself up to the current. "I'm listening," he says under his breath.

He was looking forward to visiting the cathedral. Now, the Gothic walls seem transparent to his eye, no mysteries left within. He continues into the old town. As he walks, he sings to himself, a melody that was in his head when he awoke. The rain stops. The clouds let through pale shafts of sun, fingers pointing to everything at once. Santi walks the squares and alleys of the old town like a blind man walking a maze he was born in. The buildings are a façade, paper-thin, veiling something greater. He stops under the ruined tower, looks up to see the clock still stopped at midnight. *Still.* He doesn't know where that knowledge comes from, or why it seems wrong, as wrong as the season. As wrong as being alone here, when someone should be standing by his side. His eyes drift down to a message written in bold black paint. LOOK BEHIND YOU.

Santi turns. Across the square, under the sign of a centaur raising his bow to the stars, a teenage girl waves at him from an outside table. She's younger than he remembers. The thought comes before he can make sense of it. How can he remember her older than she is? Her hair is a bright, shocking red, the color of arterial blood.

His hand goes to his throat. Dying in Thora's arms, as the fireworks burst across the sky like exploding stars. The last time they were here. The first time they remembered.

He stumbles toward her in the kaleidoscopic sunshine. She stands, knocking her chair onto the cobbles. Laughing, they collide. Santi pulls back, gazes at her in half-terrified amazement. "How—"

"I have no fucking idea!" she yells. The other customers stare, but Santi barely notices; he's focused on Thora, impossible Thora, sad wonder in her eyes like she's seeing a ghost. She rubs his arm. "Shit, it's so good to see you."

You watched me die. Santi remembers her face staring down at him, the last thing his old self saw. His words come haltingly. "How much longer did you—after I . . ."

"Made it to fifty-five. Breast cancer. Again." Thora rights her chair and drops back into it, glaring at him. "You left me alone."

"I didn't intend to." Her expression doesn't soften. Santi almost laughs as he sits down opposite her. "Thora, you can't blame me for getting stabbed."

"Can't I?" she says under her breath, as if he's set her a challenge. How can she be simultaneously so ageless and so teenage? "Glad you finally turned up, anyway," she continues, waving to get Brigitta's attention. "I've been waiting for someone to order me a wine."

Santi, still half-absorbed in the life that brought him here, tries to focus. "How old are you?"

"Fifteen." She looks him up and down. "What are you, fifty?"

"Forty-five." He blinks at her in confusion. "Why am I older again?"

"*That's* your question?" She throws her head back in a laugh. "Shit, we have a lot to talk about. Where have you been?"

Brigitta comes to take their order. Santi asks for a glass of red wine and a Kölsch. "Spain," he says. "Then France. I was . . .' He closes his eyes, trying to reconcile the version of him that awoke on the train and the myriad others that are waking now at the sound of Thora's voice. "I—wasn't happy with what I was doing. Consultancy. It felt—hollow. I wanted to do something real. Make the world better." He shakes his head in dismay. "I moved here to take a job with a nonprofit helping refugee kids. I was so sure I'd finally found what I was meant to be doing." The certainty already seems quaint, the lost dream of a dead man.

"So far, so Santi." Thora accepts her wine from Brigitta and takes a gulp. "Couldn't you have had your epiphany a little sooner? I've been here for years."

He shakes his head. "I only remembered when I got here."

"Convenient. Meanwhile, of course, I've known since I was ten." She swirls the wine around her glass. "That led to some interesting conversations with my parents. My mum basically improvised an entire treatise about Western ideas of the immortal soul in relation to Eastern ideas of reincarnation."

Santi frowns. "I thought the idea of reincarnation was that you don't come back as the same person."

Thora stares at him. "We don't." She lowers her voice, looking around at the other tables. "Santi, we were *married*. Don't take this the wrong way, but even if we were the same age, the person I am now would never." She sits back, regards him critically. "And I don't think you would either. Not as you are."

He shrugs. "Details."

She looks at him in disbelief. Then she laughs.

"What?"

"I feel like I've had this argument with you before."

"We've probably had them all before."

"We've never argued about whether we've had this argument before," Thora points out.

Santi smiles. "I guess not."

"One thing never changes. I always win," says Thora with satisfaction.

Santi presses his hands to his temples, trying to marshal his thoughts. "So your parents don't remember."

Thora shakes her head. "I don't think anyone else does. Just you and me."

Santi thinks of his constants. His mother. His father. Aurelia. Jaime. Héloïse: his wife, his girlfriend, his ex. He remembers the strange loneliness of being with her last time, the gnawing familiarity of every moment that was new to her. "Why only us?" he asks Thora. "What does it mean?"

Thora looks at him like she's been waiting to have this conversation for decades. With a lurch of warping time, he realizes she has. "Okay, so here's my theory," she announces. "We're dying."

Santi frowns. "We're dying?"

Thora nods vigorously. "We—I don't know, had a car crash or fell off a bridge or something, and now we're lying in hospital and our brains are just—going over and over different versions of our lives." She mimes brain activity with her fingers.

Santi gently catches her hands and sets them down. "If it's all in our heads, why is it in both our heads at the same time?"

Thora shrugs. "Maybe it's only in one of our heads. Maybe you're a figment of my imagination. Maybe I'm a figment of yours. Does it matter?" For the first time, Santi sees a lightness in her, a borderline hysteria he didn't initially catch. He was so focused on her being the same Thora that the differences passed him by. What has it done to her, dealing with this alone for so long?

"Clearly it matters," he says. "I don't think I could imagine you. And I know I'm not imaginary."

Thora rolls her eyes. "Of course I'd imagine you saying that." To his unimpressed look, she says, "All right then, genius. What's your theory?"

He doesn't think he has one until she asks. But it seems so obvious, fresh from the renewed memory of his most recent death, that it comes to him at once. "Maybe we're already dead."

Thora makes a face. "And heaven is a provincial German city?"

"Not heaven."

"Hell?"

He shakes his head. He can't yet form it into words: the way he has felt in so many of his lives, the drive to fulfill a purpose he doesn't yet understand. "We come back," he says. "The same, but different. Each time with new challenges, new ways we can be better or worse." He knocks the table, emphasizing his words. "Again and again, we've been given another chance."

Thora's eyes widen. For a moment, Santi thinks she is with him. He feels a bone-deep relief, a loneliness he has never understood finally easing. They are in this together. "You're right," she says. "We always get another chance. Infinite chances, to take every single path."

Santi feels a lurch in his stomach, the beginning of an endless fall. "No. That's not what I'm saying." He leans forward. "I'm saying there's one right path, and we have to find it."

Thora's nose wrinkles. "Right according to who? And why?"

"That's what we have to find out." He nods, filling in her agreement for her. "Maybe that's part of the test. To find out what all this means."

"What it means?" Thora laughs. "It *means* we're fucking immortal. It means we never have to get stuck with a wrong choice again."

After so many lives, he still forgets how alien her mind is to his own. "I don't think that's—" he starts, but she cuts him off, her face alight with revelation.

"I didn't understand until you put it that way. But do you realize, this is what I've wanted my entire life? My entire *lives*. A way to go back. To see how it would be if I did things differently." She shakes her head in wonder. "I've always been so scared of choosing wrong. Now, I don't have just one choice. I can live every life I want to. Explore every version of who I can be."

He speaks carefully. "You can't control everything that happens to you."

"Maybe not. But I remember all the ways things go wrong. Now I can learn from that. Make them go right." She leans across the table, her eyes fever-bright. "I've already started. Even before I remembered. My mum and dad—you remember, my relationship with them used to be terrible. But I know how to deal with them now. I've learned, over lifetimes and lifetimes." She laughs. "If I can learn that, I can learn anything."

Santi can't articulate the horror he's feeling, endless as their existence, stretching back and back to a beginning he can't remember. Thora touches his hand. "Hey. What's wrong? You can do the same. Figure out your perfect life—your perfect lives— and make them happen."

He shakes his head mechanically. "You can't have more than one perfect life."

Thora snorts. "Speak for yourself. I've always wanted to do everything. Be everything. Why should I have to settle for one version? Why can't I live them all?"

"I can't live like that. In—in pieces." He takes his head in his hands, as if that will contain the selves that are spilling out, leaving nothing behind. "It all needs to make sense together. The stars, the clock—we have to explain it . . ." He looks up, pleading with her. "There has to be a cause. There has to be a meaning, somewhere at the heart of all this."

Thora looks at him, level and serious. Then her focus shifts, caught by something she's seen over his shoulder. Her breath catches. "Jules."

Santi follows her gaze to the girl hurrying across the square. He remembers her crying on the other side of a rain-spattered window, Thora's arms around her in photograph after photograph, as if she could hold on to her through every life.

"Each time we've been together, I've fucked it up somehow." Thora gets to her feet. "But now I remember. I won't make the same mistakes again. I can finally make it work."

"Thora—"

She runs, chasing after Jules, after the first of her perfect lives.

Santi watches her go, her empty wine glass left on the table, his untouched lager sparkling in the low autumn sun. In all his lifetimes, he has never felt so alone.

Part III

THE VANISHING NOW

○ ☀ ◎

Thora dozes in Jules's arms, the light of a summer afternoon fil-
tering through the dusty windows of the Ehrenfeld flat. In the
next room, the baby sleeps, leaving them in this precious oasis
of quiet.

Thora stills her rushing mind, fixes herself in how this feels: to
have this life and to know how good it is. To be happy and know
she is happy. Maybe it's only possible because she remembers all
the other ways it has been: Jules yelling at her from the doorway,
Jules crying drunk at a table outside Der Zentaur, Jules calling
her selfish, incapable of being happy where she is. And now, she
is here: her head pillowed on Jules's breast, Jules's hand tangled in
her hair. She wants to freeze herself in this moment. She already
has eternity: can't she have an eternity of this?

She knows the answer. One day, this life will be over, and she
will move on to the next. She could make it happen again, she
muses. Sweep Jules off her feet with words honed over lifetimes.
Thora has become an expert in her, a connoisseur of her moods,
a cultivator of her joys.

As Jules murmurs and shifts in her sleep, Thora feels a flicker
of doubt. This isn't the first time she's tried. Sometimes she can't

find Jules, no matter how long she searches. Sometimes Thora is the wrong version of herself, too impatient or angry or cynical to make it work. Some lives, she barely stays upright under the weight of all the things she can't control. She tilts her head to look up at her wife's sleeping face. Even if she tries to do everything the same, nothing will ever be quite like this again.

The buzzer rings, stark as an alarm.

"I'll get it." Thora kisses Jules on the forehead, slides out of her embrace to pad to the intercom. "Who is it?" She never would have checked before. Now, with a brand-new human in their care, every action ricochets out to shape Oskar's whole future.

"I'm here to steal your baby." Santi's voice: the ultimate proof of the end and beginning that wait for her when this life is over.

Thora breathes in, readjusts her perspective. What matters is who he is in this life: her friend, come to meet her child for the first time. "Come on up," she says cheerfully, and presses the key to let him in.

He arrives at the door with a bag of shopping.

"Hey, Wolfie." She accepts the bag one-handed, embracing him with the other as he leans in to kiss her cheek. "You're an angel," she says, going through the bag: ready meals, snacks, a cornucopia of hands-free food.

"My mother is the angel. She's the one who told me what you would actually need right now. Thanks to her, you don't have ingredients for a risotto."

"Thank fuck for Maria." She takes his hand. "Come on. His Majesty is receiving visitors."

They go softly through to the old spare room she still has trouble thinking of as a nursery. Jules, yawning, sits by the cot, one of her fingers grasped in Oskar's tiny fist.

"Look at his beautiful brown eyes," Jules whispers to Santi as he comes in.

Thora elbows him. "We know whose fault those are."

Santi shrugs. "I told you, you should have gone the anonymous donor route. Asked for the best Viking DNA they had on file."

"You're perfect, you know that," says Jules, and kisses him on the cheek as she stands up. "Anyone for tea?"

They both nod without looking away from the baby. "He looks like Estela," Santi muses.

"Shh." Thora looks to the door, but Jules is still in the kitchen.

"It's true." He's doing what he always does: pushing her to admit this is not her only life. It's a game they play, an old argument flipped upside down through the prism of their knowledge.

Thora reaches into the cot, lets Oskar grab her finger. "Estela's nose never looked like that," she argues quietly. There's a reason Santi usually wins their game: the riddle of their lives is a mystery she can't resist coming back to.

Santi laughs under his breath. "You just don't want to think about the last time we did this."

"There was a last time?" says Jules, coming back in with tea. "You never told me about that."

Thora shoots Santi a warning look. He smiles, taking the mug from Jules. "Of course we didn't tell you. Our secret love child is our business."

"Well, at least tell me when their birthday is," says Jules, sitting down next to Thora. "I'd like to send a card."

Thora laughs, half-nerves and half-relief. She draws her wife in for a kiss.

Jules leans across and pokes Santi solemnly in the shoulder. "Hey. You. All that stuff in the kitchen. You shouldn't have."

Santi waves her off. "Least I can do for my favorite nephew."

Jules looks worried. "You can't afford all that."

"They pay me enough."

"No, they don't! They pay you minimum wage," Jules retorts. "Speaking of which. My boss is looking for an assistant. Money's crap, but it'd be more than you get right now. And there'd be potential. Progression." Jules leans forward until Santi has to look at her. "The chance to use your prodigious brain, instead of numbing it on a production line."

He laughs. "Thank you. But—I already have my work. It just isn't how I make my living."

Jules raises an eyebrow. "Well. That's certainly mysterious."

"It's not easy," Santi says. "Finding the right path." His eyes meet Thora's until she looks away.

After he leaves, Jules sits down at the kitchen table, the little furrow between her brows that Thora adores. She bends to kiss it. "What's up?"

"Santi." Jules sighs. "He looks too skinny again. And did you see his sweater? Full of holes."

Thora blinks. "I didn't notice." She sees Santi as she expects to see him, a portrait drawn more by her overlaid memories than by this reality. "Santi's fine," she says. "He's made his choices. If he wanted help, he'd ask."

"Would he?"

"He already did, remember? Otherwise we wouldn't be stuck looking after his terrible cat."

"She's not terrible." As if to prove Jules wrong, the cat chooses that moment to hop up on the table, almost knocking over her tea. "Jesus, Félicette!"

Thora strokes the cat, looking into her green eyes. "I'm sorry your owner went mad. But don't worry. We'll take care of you." Félicette rubs against her knuckles with a soft, reproachful meow.

"I just worry about him," Jules says, chin propped on her hand. "That job's destroying him, and he spends every spare moment either volunteering or scribbling in that book of his. What's he writing in there?"

Thora looks at her wife. At moments like this, she's consumed with the desire to tell her. *I've waited for you for lifetimes.* But that would mean telling her about the other times they were together, about the versions of herself that weren't right. She doesn't want Jules to know any one but this.

"Who knows," she says. "A theory of everything."

She doesn't see Santi for a month. She's used to him disappearing for weeks, reappearing with a head full of questions and a book full of notes and drawings. She's not exactly sure what he does without her. Mostly, she's too absorbed with Jules and Oskar to wonder. Only sometimes does she get a feeling like an itch inside her, a prodding from the part of her that always needs to explore. *Next time*, she tells herself. She's in no hurry. Her life is no longer bounded by her birth and her death: perhaps no longer bounded at all.

She's up feeding Oskar at two in the morning when the buzzer rings. She lifts the receiver. "Santi, it's two in the morning."

"I know. Can I come up?"

"What's wrong?" she asks when she opens the door. "Did you get kicked out?"

"How did you die?"

Thora blinks. "I'm sorry?"

"The life where I was your teacher. I died a year after you left, of a heart attack. How did you die?"

"Keep your voice down!" Thora grabs his arm and pulls him

into the kitchen. Santi takes out his tobacco pouch and starts rolling a cigarette. "You'd better not be planning to smoke that in here."

He gives her a look. "Of course not. Stop stalling and tell me."

Thora arranges herself with Oskar in a chair. "I died in an accident when I was eight," she says. "First term in the new school. Served my parents right for moving me, I guess. Remember when that cable car fell in the river?"

Santi nods.

"I was in it."

He looks up, his attention caught. "You drowned?"

"Yes. That's one death I'm not keen to try again." She can't deny that it's a relief to talk about this. She watches Santi finish the cigarette and pull his memory book from his tattered coat. "Jules was asking what you're always writing in there. You'd better not ever let her see it." He ignores her. He's busy writing what she just told him into a square in a neat grid. "Your handwriting's different," Thora says, tracing the italics that lean forward as if they can't get their message out fast enough. "Guess it's not surprising. Your personality's different."

"Graphology is a pseudoscience," he mutters.

Thora smiles. "So you're still committed to the idea of being one Santi? Constant through eternity?"

He doesn't reply. She holds her free hand out for the book. Surprised, he slides it across to her. She pages through endlessly repeating versions of the two of them: police partners, fireworks bursting in haloes above their heads; teenagers chasing their wavering shadows down the beach. He's getting better. She remembers when his drawings were tentative, unsure. Now, they are almost masterful. She supposes he's had plenty of time to practice.

"I keep thinking if I just draw them all out, I can find the pattern," Santi says. "Find out which one was real."

"Which one was real?" She stares at him. "Santi, they're all real or none of them are real. Don't go raking through broken glass looking for diamonds."

He holds her gaze, eyes tired. "I don't understand. You're really content not to ask why?"

Thora bites her lip. She wants to tell him about the nights she wakes and hallucinates the stars, racing across the ceiling of her and Jules's bedroom in all the constellations she remembers. But Oskar is warm in her arms, and Jules is sleeping meters away, hers at last. "If I ask why," she whispers, "I'll lose this."

Santi shakes his head. "I think it's more than that. I think you're afraid."

Thora snorts. "Oh, really? What am I afraid of?"

"That I'm right. That this is a test. That it requires something from us, something we may not want to give."

"I think *you're* afraid," Thora shoots back. "You can't face the possibility that this doesn't mean anything. That it's just some kind of cosmic mistake." She lowers her voice, shifts Oskar's weight in her arms. "You've been trying to pass this test, walk the right path, for lifetimes already. Where has it gotten you?"

They glare at each other until Félicette jumps up between them. Santi pets her absently. "You think she remembers?"

Thora strokes the cat's soft black fur. "Maybe Félicette's the key to it all."

When he leaves, Thora presses a spare key into his hand. "No buzzer next time."

He kisses her cheek and disappears.

* * *

Two months later, Thora is emailing pictures of Oskar to her parents when she hears a key in the door. "You're back early," she calls, expecting Jules.

"What about when you were my PhD supervisor?"

"Nice to see you too," Thora remarks as Santi comes into the living room. "I assume it's the death question again?"

He nods and sits down on the sofa, opening his memory book.

Thora casts her mind back to the brittle loneliness of that life. "In my bed, of old age. Or so I assume. Of course, there's a chance an assassin broke in and murdered me in my sleep." She watches Santi scribble in his book. "What about you?"

"Stroke," he says without pausing. "I was only thirty-five."

"You really have all the luck, don't you?" She drops down next to him. "What are you planning to do with all this?"

"I'm close to something." He scratches his stubble, looks up at her, wild-eyed. "What if, each time we die, it's because we're meant to?"

It takes her a moment to understand. She chokes. "I'm sorry. Are we back to the fate thing again? I thought our whole situation made the concept of fate redundant."

"I told you. You have to stop thinking of each life as self-contained. It's the big picture. It's the whole." He sweeps his hands wide, as if words aren't enough to get his point across. "When we were partners, chasing the man with the knife. You remembered I died climbing the tower, and you stopped me to try and save me. But I died anyway." He hits the arm of the sofa to emphasize his words. "Because I was meant to."

"I don't . . ." Thora closes her eyes in frustration. "How would you even disprove a theory like that?"

He looks at her blankly, as if that's the wrong question. For a flashing moment, Thora sees him as Jules sees him: worryingly thin, dressed in old, dirty clothes, dark circles under his eyes. She sighs. "Santi, look at yourself. You're barely functioning. You're sleeping less than me and I have a three-month-old baby." She puts a hand on his arm. "You need to take care of yourself."

"Like you're doing?"

Thora stares. "What's that supposed to mean?"

Santi pauses, as if this is a conversation he doesn't want to start. "We've been given this knowledge for a reason," he says finally. "What are you using it for? To manipulate Jules into wanting to be with you. Using memories she doesn't share to make yourself seem like a better person."

"Excuse me?" Thora draws back.

"I mean—" Santi starts, as Jules's key sounds in the lock.

They both freeze.

"Fix your face," hisses Thora as she gets up. "She's going to think we're having an affair."

Jules comes in. "Hi, my love," she says, as Thora takes her in her arms and kisses her. Jules laughs. "What was that for?"

"Just for my favorite wife," Thora says, trying to make her voice sound normal.

Jules gives her an indulgent look. "Out of all the wives you've had before?"

"Yes," Thora says without hesitation.

"All right." Jules scans her face, brow furrowed. Why does she have to be so observant? "Your favorite wife is going to take a quick shower. Hey, Santi," she says, waving over Thora's shoulder.

"Hey," he says, heartbreak in his eyes.

Thora lets Jules go. As the bathroom door closes, she sits back down on the sofa. "I'm sorry. You were busy telling me how I'm exploiting my wife?"

Santi rubs his eyes. "Forget it."

"No. You said it, you don't get to take it back." Thora pinches her forehead. "I just want to make sure I understand. Living in a squat and—and scribbling in a book is the right path, but me raising a family with Jules isn't?" She stares at him, almost laughing in fury. "The way you live is *selfish*, Santi. You think you're the hero, the noble martyr sacrificing his comfort so he'll be found worthy. But you know what? It makes you a shitty friend. Jules and I worry about you constantly. Your poor mum—"

His face closes down. "At least I'm trying to do more than just maximize my own happiness."

"You're not even listening." Thora throws up her hands. "You always know best, don't you? Honestly, you're my dad *one time*—"

"And you still act like my supervisor." Santi glares at her with the anger he rarely shows, carved into his natural peace like a tracery of scars. She remembers him as her brother, the night she found him in the garage kicking an old washing machine to pieces.

He exhales. "What about next time? What will you do?"

"I told you. I want to do everything. Be everything. Maybe I'll join the circus. Maybe I'll get rich and buy a mansion in Rodenkirchen. Maybe I'll finally become an astronaut." She watches his face. "What, you disapprove of that too?"

He shakes his head. "It won't mean anything if we don't understand."

Thora laughs. Santi bears her laughter patiently, as he always does. She hates that she remembers that. "Why are you the one who gets to decide what means something and what doesn't?"

Santi stands up. "There's no point talking to you when you're like this."

"Like what?" Thora feels cold with anger. "You can't do this. Burst in and tell me my life is meaningless."

Santi paces across the room. "Let me tell you what you can't do."

"Keep your fucking voice down," she warns him.

But he's beyond listening. He turns to her, eyes flashing. "You can't draw a line around me. Say, I want this much of you and no more. We're beyond that, Thora. We've been too much to each other." She needs to stop him, to shut him up, but he is elemental, uninterruptable as a hurricane. "You don't get to use me as an accessory for your perfect life. Hushing me when it suits you, listening when you're bored."

She hates the way he gets in her head, says the things she barely admits to herself. "I don't get bored."

"Liar," he spits. "You're like me. You want to *know*. You want to *understand*. You want to seek, and find, and—and touch what you can't explain. Not—bury yourself and hide away from it." He's shouting into her face, but she refuses to flinch. "Why are you pretending to be someone else?"

Thora stares at him. She can't say it. *Because that's who Jules needs me to be.* She doesn't know where it comes from, this conviction that seeking elsewhere and being with Jules are mutually incompatible: that she can only have one if she gives up the other.

"What's happening?"

Thora turns, heart in her mouth. She doesn't know how long Jules has been standing there, towel-wrapped and dripping.

"Fuck." Thora panics. She heads for the door. "I have to go."

"Where?" Jules reaches for her. "Can we talk about this?"

Thora shakes her off, pulling on her boots. "I'm reliably informed that there's no point talking to me when I'm like this."

Jules stands shivering, water beading on her shoulders. Her expression, pinched and wary, is too familiar. This is how she looks when it all goes wrong. "Thora, please—"

Thora hovers on the threshold. She had one plan for this life: Jules above everything. But she can't stay here, teetering on the edge of the chasm Santi has ripped through their lives. She crashes down the steps, drowning in echoes: a hundred stairwells overlaying each other, and she's running down them all at once. She bursts out onto the street where the lighthouse points like an accusing finger at the sky. It all looks wrong to her now: the city she has been trying so hard to see as real, disintegrating into fragments before her eyes.

"Thora!"

She looks over her shoulder to see Santi running after her. She ducks down a side street, emerges by the mosque on the edge of the park, its high glass windows mirroring back a hundred fractured selves. She keeps running as if she could leave them all behind.

Santi finds her in the church where they once got married. She knows it's him as soon as the door creaks open. She doesn't turn. She keeps staring ahead at the altar, at the hanging, expressionless Christ. In her peripheral vision, Santi pauses in the aisle to cross himself.

"I thought this was literally the last place you would look for me," she says.

He slides into the pew next to her. "That's why I came here first."

Thora sighs. "Is Jules okay?"

He shakes his head.

Thora doesn't have to ask more. She bites her nails, tastes the bitter coating she painted on them in an effort to break the habit. "I finally learned her. I finally know how I have to be, how to make her stay. I didn't fuck it up this time. This one is on you." She takes a drowning breath. "Did you tell her?"

"No," he says softly.

Thora stares at the flickering candles. She narrows her eyes until the flames splinter, merging with the brightness at the corner of her eye. She remembers walking up this aisle in a blood-red dress, Santi waiting for her at the altar. The gap between that self and this one is wide enough for her to fall into and disappear.

"When you were my daughter," Santi begins.

Thora braces herself for some sage advice. "Yes?"

"Do you remember how we died?"

"Of course I remember." Thora hugs herself, the pew hard against her back. "We were in the car. It skidded on a patch of ice, and—" She shudders, feeling again the obscene, unimaginable pain. "You died first. I was alone in the car for half an hour." The bitterness of that self floods back, possessing her like a vengeful ghost. "You promised you'd never leave me. But you did."

He gives her a rueful look. "I came back."

She scoffs. "As my annoying twin brother."

"Older brother."

She rolls her eyes. "By half an hour—"

They stare at each other. Wordless, she holds out her hand for his book. He turns to the right page and gives it to her. Her eyes flicker from point to point in the grid. "It fits," she says. "Always. You die first, you're older next time. I die first, I'm older. We die at the same time, we come back the same age." She meets Santi's eyes, consumed by the thrill of discovery.

"I knew it," Santi says. "I knew it meant something."

Thora's joy leaves her as quickly as it came. She slumps in the pew, handing the book back. "So what? We're still going to die. Does it really matter if you're older or I'm older next time?" She goes to bite her nails, shoves her hand under her leg to stop herself. "As long as I'm the same age as Jules, I don't care."

"I thought you always were."

"Not exactly. She's a year younger than me." Thora smiles. "She always says it must be some kind of admin error, because she's clearly the mature one."

Santi pauses before he speaks. "What I was trying to say earlier. I didn't mean—" He starts again. "It's not for me to tell you how to live."

Thora snorts. "You could have fooled me."

"But one thing I think is true. Your relationship with Jules is built on knowledge that you have and she doesn't. That's not fair. And I think you know it."

Thora looks away. There's an emptiness opening up inside her, a loneliness she can't bear. "I just want to be with her," she says miserably.

"Then be with her," Santi says. "But you have to be honest. With her, as well as with yourself."

He stands. Thora looks at his offered hand as if it's a choice. But it isn't, not really. She has been living her life with Jules inside a glass box. Now, she has to break them out of it, see if they can make something of the shards.

"I do want to know why," she says. "You think I've stopped asking, but that's not what it is. Just—catch me again when I have less to lose."

Santi gives her a serious look. "I will."

She takes his hand and lets him pull her to her feet. "Maybe we're both just crazy," she remarks as they walk down the aisle under the dark stained glass. "Locked away in a little room somewhere, dreaming of other lives."

They walk out into the summer night, through the old town back toward Ehrenfeld. Thora tilts her head up as they cross the park. The brilliance of the stars looks false, lights on a too-close ceiling. "I remember how scared I was," she says to Santi. "The first time I realized they'd changed."

He follows her gaze upward. "What scares me isn't that they changed," he says. "What scares me is that they stopped changing."

"What?" Thora squints, trying to match the scattered lights to the myriad star maps in her memory. "Since when?"

"They've been the same for lifetimes now."

She looks at him, trying to figure out if he's playing a trick on her. But she knows the Santi of this life. He wouldn't joke, not about this.

"I guess I stopped looking," she says.

His silence is enough of an answer.

Thora sighs. "Tell me, then. What does it mean?"

Santi shrugs. "Everything."

She snorts. "That's such a typical thing for you to say. And having known a lot of you, I can speak with authority." She blinks, and the stars disappear. Then they're back, steady and waiting. "Why do you think we never made it up there?"

Santi looks from the stars to her with a fond smile. "There's no never," he says. "Not for us."

Thora shudders at it: a horror and a comfort, that this isn't their last chance. She laughs, a strange hilarity overtaking her.

"What?"

"You know what I need right now?" She looks at him, his haunted eyes that never really look back, always fixed on forever. "A friend. Like you're supposed to be, in this life. Not—whatever the hell we are in the big picture. Can you just—be that for me? Just this once?"

His eyes linger for a moment on the sky. Then he offers her his arm. "Come on," he says. "I'll take you home."

Jules is waiting for her when she gets back.

Thora stands by the door. Maybe this is when she fucks it up, when Jules walks out and never comes home. She could lean into it, like closing her eyes into a fall. Or she could fight to rise, stubborn against gravity all the way to the stars.

"I'm so sorry," she says. "I shouldn't have left. I should have stayed and talked to you."

Jules doesn't speak. Thora gets the unsettling feeling that her wife can see right through her, all the layers and versions, to the emptiness inside.

"Was Santi right?" Jules asks. "When he said you were pretending? Because—if you do feel trapped, if you want something else, I . . ." She shakes her head, dashing tears from her eyes.

Thora touches Jules's chin, lifts it so she looks at her. "This is all I want." She says it with complete conviction. For this version of her at this moment, it's true.

Jules gathers her into her arms, sighing. "You're still with me?" she asks.

Thora kisses her deeply. "Always."

They make love, for the first time since Oskar was born. Afterward, lying in Jules's arms, Thora feels like crying, but she doesn't. She never does. Life after life, there is just this burning in the back of her throat, this dryness in her eyes, like some crucial part of her is missing.

Jules winds Thora's hair—bright orange up to the roots where she hasn't had time to dye it—around her finger. "What's wrong, love?"

Thora looks at her: the face she's known for so many lives, the eyes that know only this version of her. Santi's right: it's not fair. How can Jules forgive her for all the ways she's done her wrong, when for her, those lives never happened?

"There's something I have to tell you," Thora says.

Jules turns sideways on the pillow. "What is it?"

Thora closes her eyes. "I don't remember the beginning," she says. "I don't know when it started, or if there even was a start. But here is how it's been, for me."

She tells Jules everything. It's a strange relief to share this with someone who isn't Santi. She can tell it like a story, without being interrupted, without his perspective intruding on her own. Through it all, she keeps her eyes closed, not daring to look at Jules's face.

When she's finished, she waits for Jules to speak. Instead, she hears her shift in the bed. When she opens her eyes, Jules is sitting up, facing away from her.

"Jules." The first stab of panic. "Talk to me."

Jules doesn't move. Thora sits up, takes her shoulders to turn her around. Jules stares at her. She's not angry. It's worse than that: her face is blank, confused. Gently, she detaches Thora's hands. "I don't know what to say." She stands, starts getting dressed.

Thora's heart freezes. She remembers another night, pushing her way through the New Year's crowd. Santi told her about him and Héloïse. *I tried to explain how I was feeling. She told me she didn't know what to say. Right after that, she left.*

"Jules." Thora follows her wife out of the bedroom, into the nursery. Jules bundles Oskar into his carrier. "You're not—" Thora tries to say. "You can't—"

Jules looks at her, heartbroken. "I can't leave him with you. You're not yourself."

Thora can't help it. She starts laughing, painful gasps that rack her like labor pains. "Who am I, then?" She follows Jules into the bathroom, back to the hallway, to the door of the flat. "Please. Jules. Tell me who I am."

Jules shakes her head and closes the door behind her.

Thora gasps. She's drowning again, icy water dragging her under. She swears, gets dressed, and runs down the stairs, fumbling for her phone to call Santi.

He answers immediately. She's not sure he sleeps anymore. "Jules," she says, as she makes it down the last flight. "She's leaving. It's your fault. You have to come and fix this. You have to—"

"Thora, slow down." She hates how calm he sounds. "Where are you?"

"At the flat. You have to, she's—" Thora hangs up when she sees Jules already in the car, Oskar buckled into his seat in the back. The engine starts. Thora stops, frozen. Then she makes a choice. She runs for her bike. It's absurd; she'll never catch up. But the other choice, to stand and watch the best life she has known recede into the distance like it never was, is no choice at all.

*   *   *

Five minutes later, lying in the gutter, Thora shakes with pain and rage.

"You told me to do this," she says, wheezing with agonized laughter. "You told me if I wanted to be with Jules, I had to tell her the truth. And then she left. You knew she'd leave, like Héloïse did. You knew I'd chase her. You probably knew a fucking truck would fucking run me over. You know it all, don't you?"

Santi is there, of course, beyond the twisted wreck of her bicycle, beyond the paramedics who buzz like orange flies at the edge of her narrowing vision. "Hold on," he says.

"You were wrong," she gasps at him. "This isn't *right*. I'm not *meant* to die now. I'm meant to live, and love Jules, and raise Oskar, and drink tea and waste time and—oh, God, this *hurts*. Where's Jules?"

"She's coming, Thora, she's got Oskar, just hold on."

"Hold on," she echoes. "That's what I was trying to do." The world is ebbing, flickering in and out like a guttering candle. "I don't even get to say goodbye to them. How unfair is that?"

His voice shakes. "You'll see them next time."

"No, I won't. She won't be the same Jules—I won't be the same Thora—Oskar won't even exist—" It hurts to breathe, but she doesn't want to let him have the last word. "You'd think I'd be used to dying by now. But it never stops being terrifying."

He takes her hand, squeezes it hard. He's crying, of course. He'll always cry for her, and she'll never cry for him. "I'll look after them," he says.

She laughs, even though it hurts more than she could have believed. "Fuck you," she says, with all the sincerity she can muster. She understands now, the revelation coming to her in waves of pain: the choices she has made because of him, the ways her life has warped around him. "It's you," she spits. "You're the problem. You're what gets in the way."

"Thora," he says, hurt spilling out of him. "We'll talk about this. I'll find you, next time."

The sirens wail like wild birds. Thora narrows herself to a point, pushes her lips to form the last thing she will say to him. "I never want to see you again."

NEVER MEANS NEVER

○ ✹ ◎

Santi sees his reflection in the glass, hooded and wary, before he smashes it. Pulling his sleeve over his hand, he reaches through the jagged hole and opens the window, brushing the shards off the sill so he can climb through. He drops and crouches, waiting for the echo of broken glass to give way to silence. When he's sure he's alone, he straightens up in the nighttime hush of the university's alumni relations office. Somewhere in this dusty room, crammed with old computers and filing cabinets, he will find Thora.

He's been hunting her since he arrived in Cologne six months ago. Not by train, this time: in the passenger seat of a stranger's car, in the middle of a long, straggling hitchhike across Europe, fleeing the mess he'd left behind him in Spain. He never meant it to be the end, just another stop on his journey. But when he saw the skyline of the city, he wept without knowing why.

His driver looked across in perplexed sympathy. "You been traveling a long time, man?"

"I guess." But as the city coalesced around him, Santi couldn't shake the feeling that he had never really been anywhere else.

His driver dropped him at the Hauptbahnhof. He walked out

into the cathedral square, memories coming to him in snatches, a melody heard through broken headphones. Sitting on these steps, sketching the twin spires into his notebook. Hurrying out of the station on a frosty morning, gulping the last of his coffee as he headed for the police headquarters. He still didn't understand until a man in a blue coat came up to him and touched his arm. "You're here."

Santi stared at him, his haunted face, his long hair knotting in the breeze. He couldn't shake the idea that the man was transparent: that if he looked hard enough, he could see through him to what he stood for.

"You're here," the man said again.

Santi looked up at the cathedral. "I am here," he echoed. The words slid through his mind, solidified into an image, stark capitals on a wall. The letters shifted. Not I. *We.*

Thora, the last time he saw her. Gasping with pain, her hand tight on his, clinging to the life she was desperate not to leave.

The man in the blue coat was walking away. "Wait," Santi called after him. "Where's Thora?"

The man looked at Santi as if the question didn't make sense. "Here," he said.

Santi worked it out as he ran through the old town, stumbling over lives and deaths to find the one that mattered. Last time, he outlived Thora by forty-five years. He was thirty-five now, so she must be eighty. *God, let her still be alive.* He quickened his pace, the last words she had said to him burned into his mind. *I never want to see you again.*

He didn't seriously think she had meant it until he arrived at Der Zentaur and she wasn't there. He stood scanning and re-scanning every table, looking for an old woman with Thora's eyes.

"Can I help you?"

Brigitta, familiar as a ghost. Santi reached for her in relief. She backed away, holding up her hands.

"Sorry," he said, clenching his fists. "I'm looking for someone. She—she's a regular here. An older woman, tall, English accent. Her hair—she might have dyed it."

Brigitta shook her head. "I don't recognize that description."

When Santi left the bar and looked across the square, he laughed. Written on the clock tower in bold black letters was Thora's message: NEVER MEANS NEVER.

It should have convinced him she meant it. But a message telling him to stay away was still a message: words she chose to write, knowing he would read them. He couldn't help taking it as a challenge.

A challenge that led him to this dark office, papers blowing across the floor in the breeze through the broken window. Something moves in the corridor. Santi presses himself against the wall, heart thundering. He remembers, in other lives, being calm, confident, a person with solid edges. Now, he is unraveling like a piece of his mother's crochet, loose threads catching on every sound. He takes in shallow breaths, trying to get himself under control: not his own, but the control of something he is not sure anymore whether to call God.

He tried to do this the right way first. After half a year fruitlessly haunting the Odysseum, the arts cinema, the LGBT center, the Turkish café in Ehrenfeld, the tattoo shops in the Belgian Quarter—every place that spoke to him of Thora, everywhere she could have left some trace—he went in desperation to the university.

"I'm trying to get in touch with someone," he said. "She might have gone here sixty years ago."

The receptionist looked at him over his glasses. "Do you have a name?"

"Thora Lišková." Saying her name aloud was like uttering a prayer. As he spelled it out, he remembered her hand carving the letters one by one into the tower, so many lives ago.

The receptionist frowned. "Sorry, nothing's coming up."

Of course. If she was hiding from him, the first thing she would have done was change her name. "Can I—can I see some pictures? I'd know her if I saw her, I would—"

The receptionist looked him up and down: his old clothes, his foreign accent, his shaking hands. "I'm sorry. Are you an alumnus of the university?" Santi shook his head. *Not this time.* "Then I'm afraid I can't help you. We have to protect the privacy of our alumni. I'm sure you understand."

And so he left, and came back at night through the window he had already noted as a possible point of entry. The habits of a criminal lifetime are hard to break. Now he sits down at the computer, bringing up the login screen. In another life, he worked here: a summer job when he was an engineering student. He longs for the focus, the quickness of that self. Why can't he will himself to change, even when he remembers being otherwise? Those first few weeks after he arrived, it was almost a relief to remember. He had been so lost, this life: ten years out of prison, haunted by all the ways he had failed. To know he hadn't always been this way felt like a gift. Now, it feels more like a curse, his memory crowded with better versions of himself he can never be.

He thinks back to the decisions that led him here. A youthful theft to impress a girl, falling in with the wrong crowd, risking bigger and bigger scores until the one that landed him in prison. Decisions made blindly, without the conviction that has been taking root in him for lifetimes, that the way he and Thora live their lives matters. He can't help resenting the unfairness of it. How can he seek the right path, when the life he lived before his memories returned has molded him into a shape he can't alter?

Santi. Focus. He imagines Thora's voice, her steadying hand on his shoulder. The login screen glows, awaiting his input. The password used to be *heimweh*. It still works. Shaking his head, he brings up the records of alumni who were students sixty years ago. He pages through, eyes flicking to the glass of the office door, checking for light and movement. He almost skips over her before he goes back. There she is: a low-res photo in the top right corner of the screen.

"Jane Smith," he reads. He can't help himself: he laughs aloud. The name she joked about using to introduce herself. The name he guessed, in the life where he married her. She could have chosen anything else. It confirms his first thought on seeing her message. Part of her wants to be found.

He looks through her record. He remembers when he could scan this kind of information effortlessly, but now his mind judders, skipping from place to place. Courses she took in undergrad, none of them familiar: literature, economics, theater. An address, recently updated, with a phone number and a note saying, *Regular donor—stay in touch!*

His hands tremble as he takes out his memory book. He writes down the phone number and the address: in Rodenkirchen, a rich southern neighborhood beside the river. Santi has never known a Thora who lived there. He hears her voice again, low and sarcastic. *Maybe I'll get rich and buy a mansion in Rodenkirchen.* Another clue she left for him. He stares down at her address in the midst of his drawings and has to stop himself from laughing at the miracle: the inexplicable solidified, imagination made flesh.

A light shines through the office door. He swears. By the time he has shoved his memory book into his jacket, the security guard is already unlocking the door. It's too late to go for the window. Santi prays wordlessly for a miracle. He runs straight at the guard, hoping to knock him off his feet. Instead, the guard dodges. Before Santi can change direction, he's running into the wall: no, *through* the wall, passing cleanly from existence to non-existence and back.

He finds himself outside, grass under his feet, trees and night sky above his head. He gasps in wonder and terror as he looks up: the same stars again, bright and constant, letting in the light.

He calls the number the next morning, from his damp apartment in Kalk on the other side of the river. The gray curtains, the stained carpet, all blur to unreality as he listens to the electronic pulse.

"Hello?" A brisk voice, not hers.

He clears his throat. "I—I'm looking for Jane Smith."

"This is her daughter," says the voice. "I'm afraid my mother's very ill. I'm sorry, who's calling?"

A daughter. He imagines a grown-up Estela he never got to see. The heart-shock makes him forget his own name. "I—Santiago López," he says. "Would you tell her I called? Just—say Santi. She'll know."

A pause. "All right," she says, clipped, and she's gone.

He doesn't expect her to call back. He's halfway out of the

door, on his way to the address in Rodenkirchen, when his phone rings less than a minute later.

"She doesn't want to see you." Thora's daughter sounds upset. "She says she thought she'd made that clear."

Santi hesitates. How can he explain that he doesn't care about a dying woman's wishes, that he will see Thora even if he has to break every window in the city to find her? But the daughter isn't finished. With a ghost-familiar dryness, she continues, "She also told me to tell you she's in the central hospital, and that visiting hours are until six."

Santi laughs into her silence. "Which ward?"

"Oncology," she says, and hangs up.

Cancer. He wishes God could have more imagination. At least she made it to eighty this time. He still remembers visiting his young physiotherapist in the same ward, the crack it made in his old, tired heart.

He catches a bus to the hospital. As it crawls across the river, he twitches in his seat, wishing he'd walked. He gets off a stop early and runs, the spring wind tugging at his jacket. At reception, he gives his name and takes a seat. After an eternity in a plastic chair, a harried-looking woman approaches him. "Mr. López?"

He stands. "Yes?"

"I'm Andromeda. Jane's daughter. Will you come with me, please?"

Andromeda looks nothing like Estela, nothing like any of the Thoras he remembers. He follows, wondering for the first time if this is all a mistake: if he is about to impose on a dying woman who happens to look like his imaginary friend. *She told you to come*, he reminds himself, as he enters a corridor full of staring family.

The daughter turns. She's upset, but hiding it well; now he sees Thora in her. "She asked to speak to you alone. We want to respect her wishes, but she doesn't have much time left. We'd all appreciate it if you kept it short."

He considers telling her that Thora, like him, has nothing but time. "I'll do my best," he says, and goes in, closing the door behind him.

Thora lies in bed, gnarled hands gripping the coverlet. Her hair is the ice-cream blue of old women, permed into unnatural curls. He's never seen her so old. She must have had a good life, this time around. A safe life. He thinks of his scrabbling childhood that ended in two years of jail and feels a sick resentment. He won't live to see her age in this lifetime.

"You're late." The old woman's voice is barely more than breath. Still, it's Thora's. She is real, and she's right in front of him, just in time for him to lose her again.

He sits down in the chair by her bedside. "Looks like you're the one who's about to be late."

He's relieved he can still make her smile. He runs a hand through his hair, and the way she watches him do it, with half-annoyed recognition, breaks his heart.

"I'm sorry," he says. "I would have come sooner. But you did a good job hiding. I was starting to think you were right about being a figment of my imagination."

She snorts, unimpressed. "Really. You think you could imagine me?"

"You're right." He meets her eyes—Thora's same blue eyes, looking at him out of the ruin of an old woman's face. "I couldn't have imagined you thinking Andromeda was a reasonable name for a child."

Thora grits her teeth. "I'd hit you if I had the strength to lift my arm."

He laughs. As she shifts her hand on the covers, he sees that the place where the tattoo should be is blank. He's too ashamed to roll up his sleeve and show her the copy done from memory on his own wrist, at the last tattoo shop he searched in the Belgian Quarter.

"How long have you been in Cologne?" he asks.

"Sixty-two years."

Santi quakes with wasted time. For thirty-five of those years, he's been alive. For fifteen, he's been a free adult. He could have come here, found her before it was too late. "I only remembered when I got here. Again. Was it the same for you?"

She nods, eyes closed.

He leans forward. "What is it about this place? Why do we always end up here? Why do we never remember until we arrive?"

"Maybe if we left, we would forget." She coughs, the deep, terrifying cough of the terminally ill. "You should try it," she says when she catches her breath. "Too late for me."

The last thing Santi wants to do is forget. And he doesn't want to let her forget, either. "I looked after them," he says. "Jules and Oskar, after you died. Like I promised."

Thora's clouded gaze doesn't waver. "Am I supposed to be grateful?"

"Yes." He is shaking with rage; for a blessed moment, he is not the scattered Santi of this life, but the driven one of last time. "I had a mission. I was trying to find the right path. But I gave it up, to be there for them. Because of what they meant to you."

"You always have to be such a martyr." She fumbles with the blanket, veined hands shaking. "I would have been there to look after them myself, if it wasn't for you."

Old guilt weighs him down. She was happy with Jules; he shouldn't have interfered. But he was so consumed with the greater truth that he couldn't fathom why she would want to hide from it. *The way you live is* selfish, *Santi*. Her words, coming back to him in his own voice. A thought strikes him, startling as sunlight. What if they are not being tested, but punished? What if the way he is now is a judgment on his failure last time?

He closes his eyes, rubbing his aching neck. He's so tired. Lord knows when this will end, when he will have seen enough, done enough, been enough.

"Speaking of which," Thora says, "I think you've kept me from my family long enough."

He follows her gaze through the glass, where her loved ones watch with understandable suspicion. A man half her age they've never seen before, showing up at her deathbed. He gives them a wave. They look back at him, stony-faced. He stands. "I'll leave you to say your goodbyes."

"You should. I don't know if I'll see them again. You, on the other hand, I can't escape."

She says it like a joke, but by now he knows Thora well enough to hear real anger there too. He wants to ask her why she hid from him, why she left him alone. But her rage is a wall between them, hard and smooth as glass.

He takes her hand gently, the papery skin sliding over the fragile bones. Thora, mountain-tall in his imagination, reduced to this. She leans back against the pillow, closing her eyes. "Till next time," she says.

At the door, he turns for one last look, angry and heartbroken in equal measure. She doesn't open her eyes. He leaves, hurrying past her family before they can ask any questions.

* * *

She dies the following week. Andromeda lets him know with a text message and a grudging invitation to the funeral. He doesn't go. The memory of seeing her put in the ground, Jules weeping at his side, is too fresh. Instead, he goes to the address he found in her file. From across the road, he stares disbelieving at a big, boxy house framed by climbing roses. It bears no relation to any of the Thoras he has known: as if she knew the only way to hide from him was to distance herself entirely from what she was. His own words on the tower come back to him, as if young, blue-haired Thora whispers them mockingly in his ear. *We'd be the same people whatever happened to us.* She has turned her entire life into a point in their never-ending argument.

Someone is watching. A neighbor at the window, phone in her hand. Santi sees himself from her perspective: a young man in a hoodie and dirty jeans, staring intently at a dead woman's empty house. He shoves his hands in his pockets and keeps walking.

That night, he comes back and breaks in. As he climbs through the back window into what looks like a library, he thanks his criminal childhood for teaching him the skills he needs. The sense of a pattern, a plan, gives him serenity as he pulls the window closed. He moves away before clicking on his flashlight.

The house is big. More unnerving, it's immaculate, everything in its place. He wonders again what happened to Thora this time, what turned her into the kind of person who collects horseshoes—fifty of them, nailed in regimental order above the range cooker—and, apparently, plays the piano. He imagines his fiery, impatient Thora sitting down to practice her scales and has to stifle laughter.

He pans his flashlight up the stairs, illuminating photographs:

a life flayed and hung on the wall. In most of the pictures, Thora is alone. In some, she stands next to a tall man with broad shoulders who Santi assumes is her husband. It's odd seeing her with a man rather than a woman, until he remembers that he once stood in that place. It seems so strange to his current self, so outside anything that he would want or need from her. It feels more like a dream: the kind you wake from with a wry smile, shrugging at the tricks of the subconscious.

The husband accompanies Thora through the years, grayer and more stooped until he drops out of frame. Santi lingers on the last picture: Thora in her seventies, still tall and strong, hair hanging iron-gray to her shoulders. It took illness to reduce her to what he saw in the hospital.

Nothing so far to hint at her life being any more than ordinary. He remembers her words to him in their last life. *Catch me again when I have less to lose.* But she had a lot to lose this time too: a husband, a daughter, a house bigger than this version of Santi has ever been inside, let alone dreamt of owning. He turns away from her picture and continues exploring upstairs.

Fragments of the Thoras he has known lie strewn through this stranger's house like shrapnel from an explosion. A diploma from a physics course she took as a mature student, framed above the piano; her collection of vintage sci-fi, shoved like a guilty secret behind a trailing plant. Parts of her constant self she couldn't repress. He feels it like a victory every time he uncovers another. *See, Thora? You're still who you are. You could be born on an alien planet and still be yourself. You can't hide from that, not in the biggest house in Cologne.* The idea recasts what he's doing, turns it into a macabre game of hide-and-seek. Thora's body is in the ground, but by searching through what she left behind, perhaps he can recover her ghost.

The thought finds him at a locked door on the second floor. He's lost count of how many rooms he's explored: this is the first one that wasn't left open. Behind this door is what she values. He jiggles the lock, considers using his knife: but no. He senses that this room is meant for him. Thora would have left the key somewhere he would know to find it.

He steps back, clicking off the flashlight. When they lived together, in their apartment in the Belgian Quarter, they kept the spare key outside the front door, under a boot scraper shaped like a cat.

Santi peers through the warped glass of the front door, checking for passing lights before he cautiously opens it. There, on the step: the same boot scraper, or its near-identical twin. "Hi, Félicette," he breathes, missing the cat he never had in this world. He lifts it gingerly and finds the key underneath.

The secret room opens. Feeling like Bluebeard's wife, Santi pushes the door inward, meeting resistance. He gropes his way past bulky shapes to the window and pulls down the blind before clicking on the flashlight.

A smile spreads across his face. This is Thora's house, all right. The chintzy order of the public rooms gives way to a chaos he remembers. His flashlight flits over childhood toys, some he recognizes; books that didn't make it onto the overflowing shelves; a perplexing collection of china shards, as if one day Thora destroyed all her crockery in a fit of rage. A skull sits propped on a dressmaker's dummy, a memento mori to which he gives a respectful nod. Around the dummy's neck, tied in a careful knot, is a familiar mustard-yellow scarf.

A desk in a blocked-off fireplace draws his eye. Propped against it is a corkboard covered in scraps of paper and string. Santi remembers a hostel room, the map of his madness pinned on the wall. A map Thora never saw. Still, she has unconsciously copied it here, in the life where she tried to distance herself from him the most. Santi thinks of the neatly arranged rooms of her sprawling house, of this room lurking inside, a container for his ghost. He can't help the smile that breaks across his face. A part of her couldn't resist trying to solve their mystery, no matter what she had to lose.

The collection spills off the edge of the corkboard, colonizing the wall. He follows threads like he's following Thora's thoughts, ending in knots of memory. She's not an artist, like him. Instead of drawings, he finds snippets of different-again handwriting, like fungus growing over her respectable old-lady wallpaper. He wants to gulp her thoughts like water, but this version of him has never been a strong reader, and Thora's latest Gothic scrawl doesn't help. *We are who we are*, he makes out. *We'd be completely different people.* Jules, underlined. *Cologne*, she writes inside a circle, as if she intended to start a mind-map, but nothing connects. Then: *Why do we both want the same thing, and why do we never get it?* Finally, stuck to the wall like an afterthought: *I'm trapped inside this bird.* Santi picks up her pen and sketches a quick cartoon of a parakeet, a speech bubble containing the words.

The trail ends at the bookshelves. Santi casts his eyes over the volumes, recognizing some of his own recommendations. On the shelf below is a collection of books on memory, past lives, reincarnation. He picks up one of the more New Age volumes and opens it to the title page. *Bullshit*, Thora has written, underlining it three times.

There's something else: he feels it, tingling at the tips of his fingers. He goes back to the wall where a star map is pinned, half-obscured by scribbled notes. He slides his hand up behind it and draws out an envelope addressed to him in large, self-conscious letters. He unfolds the letter inside with shaking hands.

It wasn't written by the woman he talked to in the hospital. The paper is old, for one thing, folded and unfolded until the creases start to become tears. But even if it had been pristine, he would have known from reading it that it was the work of someone much younger.

Dear Santi,

I once asked my father if it was possible to remember someone you'd never met. He, of course, turned it into a philosophical treatise about the nature of memory: how remembering is an act of reconstruction, increasingly distant from the experience that formed it. But that wasn't what I meant. I meant you. You, my brother, my friend, my partner in so many ways, all your selves scattered across my memory like the fragments of light cast by a prism.

I thought I'd know better who I was without you. But in trying to hide from you, to kill any part of me that you might recognize, I've only ended up hiding from myself. It's too late for me to make a different choice. This is my life now. Until the next one.

I wanted to live every life, to be every possible version of myself. But losing Jules and Oskar taught me that you were right. We can't live in pieces. Now, I wish I could forget. Part of me thinks that if I can make it through one life without meeting you, then the cycle will end, and I'll be free. Maybe we both will.

But part of me still imagines it. Maybe one day you'll walk up to me, with that impossibly remembered smile, and say it's all part of the plan. I can't say I'll be pleased to see you. It would mean you knew how to find me, even when I couldn't find myself. It would mean there really is no escaping you. But it would be a relief to stop missing someone I've never met.

Day by day this world feels more shallow to me, more full of holes. Perhaps one day, I'll fall through one of them. Perhaps I'll see you there.

þ

Santi traces the thorn of her signature and realizes he's crying.

He reads the letter again, imagining the words spoken by the woman he saw in the photographs. He gets the feeling he would have liked this version of Thora. The ease of her life has given her space to blossom, pushing back the tendency to bitterness that grows so readily in her. Maybe she was right, in a way she didn't recognize: maybe she is a better version of herself without him.

Absorbed, he doesn't notice the flashing blue light through the edges of the blind until the police are already banging on the door.

He swears. He wasn't careful enough: the neighbor must have seen him. He shoves Thora's letter into his pocket and pelts down the stairs. He hears the door splinter, heavy footsteps behind him. For the second time, he closes his eyes and prays for a miracle. This time, God doesn't answer. One of the officers grabs him and slams him to the floor. In the dazzle of the flashlight, Santi sees the echo of another light—a flame, speechlessly bright—before it swings away.

The trial is brief: neither Santi nor his lawyer put much effort into his defense. The mostly local jury are not inclined to be lenient to a dark young man with a foreign accent caught breaking into the house of a dead old lady. The sentence comes down: three years in prison. His mother cries and promises to move to Cologne to be near him; his sister Aurelia is angry. He tries to comfort them, but it makes no sense to him to grieve for something inevitable. From the instant he remembered Thora, no other path existed.

He writes to her from prison. He knows the letter has nowhere to go but her grave, but he imagines it piercing the veil, going on somehow to the place they will meet next.

Dear Thora,
The last time I met you for the first time, you were in a hospital bed. You were older than I've ever seen you. But I knew you, just the same.
This life hasn't been good to me. I miss the one where we were happy. You know the one.
(How likely is it that we're thinking of different worlds?)
There's a song, stuck in my head. There's a tattoo on my wrist. I bite my nails, and I want a cigarette, and I don't know how much of me is me anymore and how much of me is you. I used to be so sure of who I was. Is that something you stole from me? Or are we both drifting now, both as lost as each other?
Maybe you're right, to want to forget. Maybe it was easier when we didn't remember, when we thought each life was our only chance. But when I look back now, I can't remember not remembering. It all feels like one thing: a path leading us step-by-step to where we need to be.
I know why you've resisted thinking about the meaning of all this. I know you like explanations, and you're afraid there might not be an explanation for what's happening to us.

I think we are the explanation. I don't know if that makes sense to you. I've never been that good with words.
  I wish I could tell you

He trails off. There is too much he wants to say to Thora, not enough space in the words to hold it. He folds up the letter and keeps it under his mattress, always intending to finish it.

Between the daily déjà vu of prison, between visits from his mother that leave him sadder and calls from Aurelia that remind him there is life outside these walls, he turns his mind to the mystery of him and Thora. The police confiscated her letter; Santi assumes they gave it to Andromeda. He imagines her in the chaos of her mother's secret room, staring up at the map of her madness. He wishes he could go back there, read Thora's notes, have something to work from. Instead, he is trying to solve a puzzle with half the pieces missing and one hand tied behind his back: the handicap this life has given him, of a brittle mind that can't focus on details. Still, he tries, writing out the notes he remembers and sticking them on the wall, mimicking Thora's chaotic display. In the center, he places a drawing he did from memory of one of the photographs: Thora in her youth, but no youth of hers he's ever seen. She's astride a horse, her face round and healthy, her eyes creasing up with laughter. On the days his head hurts from trying to work out who they are, what their purpose is, he looks into her eyes as though she could somehow look back. "I need you," he says softly. "I need you to help figure this out."

"She your girl?" Jaime asks, coming in sweaty from exercise in the yard. It's a comfort, having his old friend as his cellmate, even if as far as Jaime is concerned they just met.

"No," Santi says. "She's the old lady I stole from to end up in here."

Jaime laughs. "You're crazy, López," he says, swinging himself onto his bunk.

Maybe we're both just crazy. Thora, last time, under the unchanged stars. *Locked in a little room somewhere, dreaming of other lives.*

Santi raises an eyebrow. "That's one possibility."

He flicks through his memory book, filled with drawings of himself in every lifetime: better selves, smarter selves, who would have had a chance of finding the right path. He thought that made the test unfair, but he was wrong. He pauses on a picture of his old science classroom, Thora upright and self-conscious in the second row. He hears his own voice: *If God's test were easy, it would be meaningless.* He will try to pass it with the tools he has been given, the self he is this time. If he doesn't succeed, perhaps the next version of him will. Each time they reawaken is another chance to get it right.

He closes the book and looks up into Thora's eyes. She is already taking that next chance. While he languishes here, she's growing up, the time since her death shaping her into the person he will know next. By the time he gets there, she will be formed, and he will be a novice, doomed to learn everything over again. One comfort: there's no chance of him living to eighty in this life. The lost years transform into a gift, a promise of finding her sooner.

He doesn't have to wait. He could follow her, catch her up. He thinks about it sometimes: looping a sheet around a beam, letting gravity take the blame. But he never goes further than thinking. Even though he knows he will come back, sure as he knows the sun will rise, he still believes that killing himself to follow her would be the deepest kind of sin. He is being tested, and it is imperative he not fail.

*   *   *

When he gets out of prison, he moves with his mother into a flat on the outskirts of the city. He picks up odd jobs, painting houses, digging gardens. In his spare time, he works as a volunteer cleaning up litter from the streets of the old town. Working outside soothes him, grounds him in what he is determined to think of as the real. He tries to pursue the puzzle Thora left for him, but his mind glances off it like a fly off a window, repelled by a truth too big for him to see.

The letter he started writing to her, he leaves unfinished. One day, he will know what he wants to say. Then he will write it down, and on his deathbed he will read it over and over until he has it by heart: until the words, in his next life, are the first thing he remembers.

NOTHING TO LOSE

○ ✴ ◎

Thora is running away.

She pulls her hood up, leans into the bus window until her breath fogs the glass. She's been a seventeen-year-old girl enough times to know that traveling alone as one attracts attention. Outside, the fringes of the city slide past, gray and empty as a dream.

She gets off at the end of the line, in an industrial zone with a schematic, unreal look she doesn't trust. She walks north, keeping the setting sun on her left. The city cannot go on forever. There must be an end to it, as there was a beginning, the invisible line in the air that her plane crossed when she arrived with her parents two months ago.

It didn't take her long to remember. The first time she walked through the old town, she felt it as a dread dogging her steps, a shadow cast the wrong way against the sun. When the cathedral bells boomed hollow through her bones, she stopped where she was, under the ruins of the clock tower. "No," she said softly. "Not again."

Santi wanted to understand why they only remember when they arrive here. To Thora, it's no mystery. The city is so overlaid with their shared lives that there is no living here without remembering.

She looked up to the hands of the clock still stuck at midnight. She heard the echo of her own words to him last time. *Maybe if we left, we would forget.*

She tried the train first. She didn't even think about where she wanted to go. She just got on the first one she saw and waited for it to leave. Looking out of the window, she wondered how it would be. Would she forget all at once, awaken in a glorious elsewhere with no idea how she had got there? Or would it be more gradual, a kind of healing dementia, stealing her other lives fragment by fragment until even the memory of Santi was gone? A pang tugged at her, but she resisted. Remembering had done nothing but make them miserable. Better to start afresh, even if that meant never meeting at all.

The train hummed to life. Her head snapped up. Her escape, beginning at last.

The hum cut off, the lights flickering out. A disembodied voice announced a fault. The other passengers grumbled and disembarked. Thora sat transfixed, furious, almost laughing.

She tried again and again. Sometimes, the trains got as far as crossing the river before breaking down. One stopped on the Hohenzollernbrücke with the bang of an exploding fuse. Thora sat staring at the shackles of the padlocks on the fence, forty thousand relationships left to rust. When the train pulled into reverse, she felt time unwinding, unraveling her back to where she started.

It was after she got off that train that she decided to trust nothing but herself. She won't break down. She will walk until the road runs out, and then she will keep walking.

She climbs through a hedge and strikes across a scrubby meadow. She's beyond the city limits now, in an endless dream of fields and fences. She holds down a coil of barbed wire to clamber across. When she lets go, it slices her thumb. She sucks the blood away and walks on.

North, always north. The setting sun throws her shadow sideways across the fields. Darkness falls, revealing the stars, but she doesn't look up. When she glances behind her, the city never looks any farther away, no matter how many hedges she crawls through, how many fences she climbs. Thora imagines the great mass of Cologne tearing loose from its foundations, edging along in her wake on flat concrete feet. She walks faster, breaking into a half-run. She's pushing down the next fence when she sees a dark stain on the wire. Her blood.

She stops, laughing in despair. The same field. She's been crossing the same field, over and over.

"This is fucking absurd," she shouts. "Why am I trapped here? What did I do?"

No one responds. But even unanswered, her instinctive question feels like a revelation. This is a punishment, designed specifically for her. What could be worse than a world with no elsewhere?

She lies down, flat on her back on the cold ground. Out here, far from the city lights, the stars look like silver paint sprayed on the inside of a solid dome. She could stay here, wait to die of thirst or exposure. She hasn't experienced either of those before. She suspects they would probably hurt.

Or, she can keep trying.

She gets to her feet and calls her mum.

In the passenger seat of her mother's car, Thora looks through the window, through the world, recognizing it for the simulacrum it has always been. She remembers the holes she saw in other lifetimes, without understanding what they meant: her childhood window that looked onto the impossible, the mirror behind the bar in Der Zentaur that showed her a view from the sky. Perhaps, somewhere at the city's edge, one of those holes waits to let her out.

"Thora. Are you listening?" her mother asks, in the falling question inflection she carried over from Icelandic.

Thora blinks. "Yes."

"Then answer me. Where were you going?"

"Nowhere," Thora says, looking out at the city streaming past. "Absolutely nowhere."

Her mother's fingers tense on the wheel until they turn white. Thora has learned how to dissolve the bitter pill of her anger, just as she has learned to defuse her father's scorn. But right now, she doesn't want to. Why should it always be on her, to change to fit their constancy? Why should she be the only one cursed to remember?

"You are such a teenager sometimes," her mother says under her breath.

Thora stares at her. She wants to tell her mother she is no such thing: she is ageless, immortal. But her mother doesn't know that. She just hears the same sullen daughter she's known lifetime after lifetime. Thora's weary mother-self comes back in a wave of reluctant empathy, remembering Estela at the same age. Is this how her life will be now? Feeling every age at once, unable to honestly inhabit a moment without drowning in reflections?

"Sorry," she says. "I won't do it again."

But of course, she does: carefully, gradually, so as not to risk her parents finding out. She spends her weekends mapping the limits of the city, pushing at the fringes where reality blurs. She stumbles into endless woods, crosses and recrosses the same road, wades through water that deepens into shallows, stranding her back where she began. She hunts obsessively for a hole that will lead her out of the lie. But her jailers have built her cage too well. If there are gaps between the bars, none are wide enough for her to escape.

She is nineteen, crossing a scrubby field, when she sees the setting sun cast her shadow due east. The circle closes. She has tested every inch of the city's boundary and found no way out.

Something in her snaps. She throws her head back and screams, pulling at the barbed wire until her hands are bleeding. "Let me *out*. Fuck you, fuck you, let me out!"

The wind blows her voice away. There is no one to hear her.

Not yet.

In her memory, Santi sits awkwardly by her hospital bed. He looked in his mid-thirties. She counts forward to his possible deaths—days, months, or decades after hers—and backward to her birth. He could already be here. Or, she could have as many as thirty years left to wait.

She wraps her bleeding hands in her father's scarf and catches a bus back to the university. In her dorm room, she dresses her wounds, looking past her reflection into the mirrored darkness of the prison where she awaits her cellmate's arrival. When she's finished, she rides her bike to the old town. She wonders, as she props it against the railings of the courtyard by the clock tower, if the Santi she met in the hospital still lives, just the other side of where her fingers can touch. She thinks of him as she saw him last: scruffy, tired, the signs of a hard life etched on his face. She adds nineteen years, imagines him standing now beside her, looking up to where the hands of the clock clasp as if in prayer.

She takes the spray can from her backpack. NOTHING TO

LOSE, she writes, big enough to be seen across the square, across the distance between worlds. When he sees it, he'll know what it means. That she's finally ready for them to find a way out of this together.

When enough time has passed after painting her message that she's sure he's not already in the city, she relearns enough Spanish to call the hospitals in the town he is usually born in. She's sure she becomes a local joke, the foreign girl with the bad accent who keeps asking for the child who doesn't exist. Spain isn't the only possibility: in some lives, his parents move to Cologne before he is born. Every week, she flicks through the local paper to the birth announcements, scours them like a hurricane survivor haunting a missing-persons board. After a few years, she stops expecting to find him there. It becomes a game to her, a quirk to her friends, used to her leafing through the *Stadt-Anzeiger* and reading out the most ridiculous names as they drink coffee at her big kitchen table.

She's a doctor now, training to be a surgeon. It was her plan before she remembered, and a resentful part of her didn't want to give it up. She leafs through the paper as Lily laments over the same guy she's been obsessed with for lifetimes, feeling five hundred years old.

Lily leans over her shoulder. "Dennis," she says. "Imagine that. Baby Dennis."

Thora gives her a look. "Where did you think all the adult Dennises came from?"

"Made in a factory," Lily says, but Thora barely hears her, because there he is, in a small announcement at the top of the page: Santiago López Romero.

Her ears fill with thunder. He's here. He's alive.

"Thora?" Lily waves a hand in front of her face. She follows Thora's gaze. "Ooh, Spanish. Hot name." She frowns. "Is it weird to say that about a baby?"

"Yes," Thora says and turns the page, already thinking about how she can meet him.

She tries the hospital first, but Santi and his mother have already gone home. She redirects her attention to finding out where that home is. In the worlds where they live in Cologne, Santi's mother usually works in a shop in the city center. On her lunch breaks, Thora begins an irregular circuit of likely candidates. She's two months into her search when she walks into a mini-market near the church where she and Santi once got married and sees his mother standing behind the counter.

Thora stares, stricken by something like fear. She ducks into the magazine section, pretending to browse. Maria Romero: her mother-in-law, her best friend's mum, the other end of an overheard phone conversation coming through as static and noise. Thora's knowledge of her is partial, one-sided, but it will have to be enough. She picks up a magazine about crochet and brings it to the till. "I'm a beginner," she announces.

Maria makes a noncommittal noise.

Thora fumbles for change. "Not sure how much I can learn from a magazine, but . . ."

Maria takes Thora's money and smiles. "Good luck," she says in friendly dismissal.

Thora leaves, temporarily defeated. She scans back through her memories of Maria: slow to trust, especially in a foreign place. There is no way to get through this but patience.

She buys the magazine every week. Sometimes, she just gives Maria a friendly smile. Sometimes, she drops in a remark about a project she's excited to try, or laments a technique she hasn't been able to master. Six weeks later, Maria says, "We have a circle that meets at my house on Mondays. You should come."

Thora feels like she has solved a fiendishly hard puzzle. She moderates her grin to what she hopes is normal. "That would be amazing. Thank you."

Maria scribbles an address on a torn scrap of paper. "See you Monday."

Thora leaves the shop with a spring in her step. "That was easy," she congratulates herself, until she realizes she has two days to teach herself to crochet.

She spends a grumpy, tangled weekend in her flat. She hated crochet back when Santi tried to teach her as her long-suffering father, and the hatred has endured across lifetimes. Still, by Monday, she has enough of the basics to pass herself off as an enthusiastic amateur. She keeps her head down as she approaches the third in a series of identical tower blocks. At Maria's door, she knocks and hangs back, crochet basket in hand, tempted by the urge to run. Santi is a baby. What is she expecting, to pick up where they left off?

Maria opens the door. "Thora, isn't it? Welcome." A small figure clings to her leg. "This is my daughter Aurelia."

"Nice to meet you." Thora looks down at the dark-eyed toddler. Aurelia, killed aged nine in a car crash. Aurelia, who moved to Cologne to help raise Estela after Santi died.

Aurelia gives her a mistrustful look and runs away.

Maria laughs. "Ignore her, she's in a bad mood. Come in." She ushers Thora through a hall carpeted with children's toys into a kitchen where four other women already sit chatting over coffee.

Thora didn't expect to meet Santi right away. But she didn't expect to spend an hour actually attempting to crochet. As she fumbles with her needles, she tunes out Maria and the others, listening intently for a baby's cry. She hears nothing. Of course Santi would be quiet, even at three months old. She imagines him serenely contemplating the universe from his crib, and her anger with him builds until she stabs herself in the finger.

The others leave one by one. Thora can tell Maria wants her to go. "Would you like another coffee?" she asks pointedly.

Thora has had three. Her hands are already shaking. "No, thank you." She looks up, feeling nauseous. "I was wondering, do—do you have any other children?"

Maria gives her an odd look. "Why do you ask?"

"I thought I heard a baby." She follows it up with an unconvincing grin. "I just love babies."

She's barely even fooling herself. She waits to be thrown out. Unexpectedly, Maria laughs. "I'm sorry. You just really didn't seem like the type." She stands up. "Yes, I have a new baby. Come through and meet him."

They enter a dark room. As they move toward the cot by the curtained window, the absurd suspense makes Thora want to laugh. Maria picks up a swaddled shape, impossibly small. "This is Santi," she says. "Would you like to hold him?"

Thora fights the urge to run away screaming. She holds out her arms.

She has held babies before: Estela, and Oskar, and Andromeda. But this is different. Thora knows a moment of pure panic, as she feels the warm weight and knows she is the only thing between him and falling.

The doorbell rings. Maria turns. "I'm sorry, I have to get that—do you mind—"

"Oh—no, it's fine," Thora says, while her mind screams, *No, don't leave!*

Maria hurries off, leaving Thora with the baby.

He looks up at her with wide brown eyes. For a moment it's Santi as she has known him, trapped in this helpless form like a fly in amber. Then it's just a baby, cooing and wriggling in her arms. She tightens her grip to stop him escaping. "Now, now," she says quietly. "I only just found you. You're not getting away from me that easily." She starts humming, the song she doesn't know if she learned from him or he from her. By the time Maria comes back, Santi is smiling.

"He likes you!" Maria exclaims. "How strange. Usually he's very fussy about who holds him."

Thora looks into his face, lets him hold on to her finger with his tiny, strong hand. "I'm honored."

It's easy to fall into being Maria's friend. Thora goes from attending the crochet circle to dropping by for coffee to offering to watch the kids once a week. In this world, Santi's father died of a heart attack, and Maria is drowning. Thora tells herself she is a good person for reaching out to save her, even as she knows it is the most purely selfish thing she has ever done. She is almost sure Santi will forgive her once he's old enough. Right now, though, he can't even say his own name. She watches him crawl across the floor in pursuit of a ball he can barely grasp and feels helpless, like she is what he is trying to hold on to.

She remembers from other lives how it feels to know someone as a child, then meet them again full-grown: the shock of seeing a person emerge from such chaotic potential. Now, for the first time, she sees it from the other side. She has known so many Santis: her father, frazzled but trying his best; her intense, philosophical student; her absent-minded police partner. Now there is just this ball of curious sensation that she has to periodically prevent from destroying itself. Inside are the seeds of all the Santis that could exist. Or not quite all: the trajectory of this life, his parents moving to Cologne, his father's death, have already set him on a path away from some of the people he might have been. Uneasily, she adds herself to the list. What might it do to him, spending so much time with someone who has such a clear notion of who he should be? How might her responses, to something as simple as him pressing a pointed star into her palm, push him off one path and onto another? A dozen times, she decides to remove herself from his life, come back when he's older. But Maria has come to rely on her, and even Aurelia is thawing, coming to sit with her, braiding her hair while she tells her about her stuffed animals and their adventures. And even if Santi isn't Santi yet, even if he can barely say her name, she is not strong enough to willfully detach her fingers from the only ledge between her and an endless fall.

And it seems the feeling is mutual. Each time she leaves for the hospital, he clings to her, wailing his distress.

Maria rescues her. "Thora has to go make people better, mi hijo," she says, clawing him off Thora's leg. "I'm sorry."

"Fora," Santi says insistently. The terror in his eyes isn't natural. It's the same as when he sat by her hospital bed, as when he held her broken body in the gutter.

"I'll come back," she tells him, a bitter promise he doesn't yet understand. "I always come back."

She teaches him how to write her name. He's five now, a restless, inquisitive boy: getting him to sit still and focus is a challenge.

But he will do it for Thora. She shows him the thorn, then gets him to copy it. He concentrates, tongue sticking out of the corner of his mouth.

"You won't have to use this one in any other words," she explains. "It's a special letter, just for my name."

"I know," he says irritably. "I remember."

She freezes. Maria is across the room, brushing Aurelia's hair.

"You remember?" Thora says.

"Yes." He goes over the lines of the thorn like he's carving it. "You showed me. When we were up on top of the tower."

Thora looks up at Maria, but she's laughing. "Santi, you do love to make up stories."

His brows knit together. "It's not a story," he insists.

"You're right," Thora says. She looks Santi in the eye. "It was real. It happened."

From then on, he watches her with a new kind of attention. Thora relives the loneliness of remembering, no one less than a world away who could understand. Whatever effect she might be having on Santi, at least he gets to grow up with the one person who can tell him he's not crazy.

She tries to learn from the gaps in how he once raised her. Where he was stern, she is gentle; where he tried to give her space to find her own answers, she tells him frankly what she thinks and lets him decide whether or not he agrees. Even as his memories fill out, she longs to hurry him, fill him with truths he's not ready for. He's only eight, talking about going to Australia one day, when she snaps.

"No, you won't," she says. "We can't go anywhere. This is it, for you and me."

He looks up at her, lip trembling. "Why?"

She knows she should soothe him, tell him she was only joking. But she's furious, and for an instant all her fury is directed at him. *Grow up*, she wants to scream. *Grow up and help me find a way out.*

"That's a really good question, Santi," she says instead. "You know what I think? I think it's because we're being punished."

His brow furrows. "What did we do?"

"Who knows?" Thora says brightly. "But it must have been something really, really bad."

Santi's eyes go wide and frightened. "I'm not bad. You're lying." He flees to his room and doesn't talk to her for the rest of the day.

When Maria comes home, she's puzzled. "What did you say to him?"

That his dreams are dust and ashes. Thora shrugs helplessly. "He's sensitive. You know what he's like."

He's quieter after that. Thora feels guilty, but she can't feel sorry. Better he knows the reality of their situation before he grows up. And grow up he does. She thought her impatience would make it endless, but in what seems like a year he is twelve, then fifteen, then going to university. And he is Santi, familiar and all new, youth burnishing him while she feels herself dulling into middle age.

When his mother dies during his first year at uni, he goes to pieces. It's not Aurelia he runs to: it's Thora. At three in the morning, he shows up on her doorstep drunk and sobbing. She lets him in and holds him until his crying is done.

"You'll see her again," she says. He's half on the sofa, half on the floor, face pressed into her shirt while she rubs his back. It should confuse her, how she feels like his mother and his sister and his lover all at once. But the worlds have scraped away her capacity for confusion. "She'll be back next time, just the same."

"It still hurts to lose her," he mumbles wetly into her shoulder.

Thora can't repress her impatient thought: now Maria is gone, now he is grown, there is nothing to stop them from looking for a way out. "Wouldn't be much of a punishment if it didn't hurt," she murmurs.

Santi pulls back from her. He frowns, rubbing the tattoo he got on his eighteenth birthday: the stars that haven't been in the sky or on her wrist for lifetimes now. "Can we go somewhere? We need to talk."

Thora blinks. "About what?"

"Everything." He looks down with a bitter smile. "It's not like there's anything to stop us now."

Thora shivers at the echo of her thought. "Of course."

She lives in Agnesviertel this time, a futile attempt to make the city seem new. The streets are still deadly familiar, winding around them like a closing noose. Santi leads the way, south toward the cathedral and the old town. "I guess it's good that we don't have to speak in code anymore."

"Code." Thora laughs. "Like when you yelled at me, 'You're not my sister this time'?"

"That's not fair," Santi says. "I was six."

Thora senses she's upset him in a way she doesn't understand. Shouldn't she get him by now? Shouldn't she be able to see inside him, find the problem, and fix it?

He meets her eyes in challenge. "So you still think we're being punished?"

"Still?" Thora is puzzled until it comes to her: his crying eight-year-old face, a guilt that hung over her for days. "Oh. I didn't think you'd remember that."

He gives her a dark look. "Of course I remember. I was eight years old, and you told me I was trapped forever because of something bad I'd done. That sticks with you."

Thora looks away. "Sorry I traumatized you with the truth."

He turns on her, all teenage anger, a Santi she doesn't recognize. "How do you know it's the truth?"

Thora spreads her arms wide. "What else could this be? Take two people who want to go everywhere and see everything, and trap them in one city for the rest of their infinite lives. Seems pretty perfect to me."

"So what are we being punished for?" he asks her. "What did we do?"

"I told you, I don't know! Maybe we murdered someone," she says, half-joking.

Santi shakes his head. "We're not killers."

"Speak for yourself." She takes out a cigarette—correlation or fate, that she always smokes in the worlds where she's a medical professional?—and lights it. "I feel more murderous every day I spend in this place."

"If you think it's a punishment," Santi argues, "you must think there's someone doing the punishing. It means you think this is deliberate. Designed."

Thora snorts. "Well, yes. Discovering reality literally has a wall around it did change my perspective somewhat." Before Santi can go on, she adds, "I don't think it's God, if that's what you're wondering. No, this level of malicious fuckery is all too human."

"Whoever it is," he says as they pass under the medieval gate of the Eigelstein-Torburg, "if they're punishing us, there has to be a chance of redemption. They must have designed a way out."

"I told you, I've tried leaving the city a hundred ways—"

"I don't mean a physical way out."

Thora smiles. Maybe he's not so different from the usual Santi after all. "Oh, I remember," she says. "The right path."

They enter the tunnel that leads under the train tracks. Santi's voice echoes back to her strangely. "I don't think about it that way anymore. If all of our actions matter, that creates too many paths for just one of them to be right."

"I'm glad we agree." Thora follows his shadow through the dark. "What are you thinking instead?"

"That there's something specific we have to do to atone."

"Atone?" Thora catches up with him as they emerge from the tunnel. "How can we atone when we don't even know what we're being punished for?"

Santi lifts his chin. "We'll know it when we see it."

"How? How will we know?" She pursues him as he turns toward the cathedral. "Take last time. Obviously we failed, according to your reasoning, because we're still here. But what would have done the trick? If I'd sold my house and moved into a bungalow? If you'd given back to all the people you stole from? Then what, there'd be a bright light and a chorus of angels and we'd finally be free?"

Santi looks at her, uncertain and close to tears. She forgets how vulnerable he is in this world, how much he needs her approval. Her fault. "I don't know," he says. "But whatever it is, it won't be easy. You can't atone without making a sacrifice. Giving up something you really don't want to lose. Freely, of your own choice."

The wind blows cold across the cathedral square. Thora pulls her jacket closed and keeps walking. She's furious with him, and it takes her a moment to articulate why. She rounds on him, walking backward into the wind. "So you believe we have a choice now? What happened to God's hand? Everything happening because it has to happen?"

"That was when I thought there was one universe."

Thora laughs, throwing her head back like a mad witch.

Santi scowls. "What's funny?"

"What's funny is we've swapped places." She grins at him maniacally. "Go on. Ask me what I think."

He pouts like the sulky teenager he is. "What do you think?"

The wind whips Thora's hair into her eyes as they come up the steps to the cathedral. "We have no meaningful choices at all," she says. "Our actions don't matter, because whatever we do has the same result. We die, we come back, we die again. Forever."

Santi's face contorts with frustration. "Why?"

She shrugs violently. "Because someone decided that's what we deserve. You want to think we're going to learn from this, that it's all going to add up to something in the end. But it isn't. It's just going to go on, and on, and on—"

"Thora!" Santi yells. His hand reaches out. Thora grabs it without thinking, lets him pull her forward: remembers his tiny fingers, clinging to her like she was the only thing in the world.

A high-pitched singing, impossibly loud. *A chorus of angels*, Thora thinks, as something shatters behind her. She turns to see the paving littered with shards of black stone. "What the fuck?"

"A tile from the cathedral." Santi tugs her back down the steps. "The wind must have blown it loose. It was—it would have hit you." She lets him lead her to the shelter of the train tracks. "Are you okay?" He looks strange, drawn, as if he's seen something he can't bear.

"I'm fine. What about you?" Thora searches his face. "I don't want to know what you're thinking, do I?"

He's looking up at the cathedral. "You almost died. And I saved you. Just like you did for me, at the clock tower. Before—" He shudders. His hand goes to his throat.

"Fuck." Thora stares at him. "What are you saying? That I'm fated to die now, and the world's just going to keep trying until it kills me?"

"Maybe—" Santi bites off the word, looks away. "Maybe that's part of the plan."

Thora doesn't have the breath to laugh. She looks past him, up at the cathedral that sent her death singing down to her. "So what, next time I'll have to wait even longer?" Her voice shakes. "Fuck that. I can't go through this again." She pushes his arm off her and keeps walking, like she kept walking across the field that never ended.

Santi catches up with her. "There's nothing we can do."

She considers retorting: *Actually, there is. It's called a murder-suicide. What do you say?* But she knows Santi would never agree to it. Some things are always sacred to him. However much it hurts her to know she'll die before him, she can't be the one to tear that away. "Why?" she says instead. "Because it's destined? I don't care. I'll thwart destiny."

A smile breaks through his troubled expression. "If anyone could, I'd bet on you."

Thora snorts. "And from anyone but you, I'd take that as a compliment." They come out through the narrow streets of the old town into the clock tower square. Her heart is steady now, her mind almost resolved. In the shadow of the tower, her fingers trace the words of her message. NOTHING TO LOSE. She takes a breath and ducks through the jagged hole in the wall.

"What are you doing?"

She turns. Santi stands in the light, like she's seeing him

through a portal to elsewhere. She wonders how she must look to him: a shape in the darkness, already half-gone. "Taking the only way out I can."

She knows his face so well. The part of her that helped raise him cries out in protest. She doesn't want anything to hurt him. "What do you mean?" he asks.

"I'm not waiting around for the universe to kill me." She looks up at the dark space above her. "If I'm going, it'll be on my own terms." It's a peaceful feeling. Like being in a nose-diving plane, her hands coming to rest on the controls.

She starts to climb. After a moment she hears Santi's footsteps behind her. She turns, meeting his eyes in the dark.

"I don't want you to be alone," he says.

She should tell him to leave. He's still a little drunk: he could slip and fall, and she would have another of his deaths on her conscience. She goes along with it anyway, because every terrible idea resonates to the frequency of her misery.

The tower is taller than she remembers. She stops while they're still inside, on a ridge of the crumbled steps where there's just enough room for them to sit. She gasps, getting her wind back; Santi, of course, is hardly out of breath. It hammers in what lies in store: the sickening repetition of another childhood, another rush of memories, another half a lifetime alone in the déjà vu city. She scrapes her hand against the brick until it grazes. Lifetimes ago, climbing down, she looked through a gap and saw herself endlessly refracted.

"What are you thinking?" Santi asks.

She looks at his open, concerned face. Fuck it: if she doesn't say this to him now, she never will. "I never told you what it was like. To wait." She looks down at her boots hanging over the drop. "Twenty-five years, Santi. Longer than your whole life so far. That's how long I was alone. Just—waiting for you to show up. And then you did, and"—her voice breaks on her laughter— "you were a *baby*. Can you imagine? You're right there, but you're not you, you're this formless thing that can't even talk, and I see glimpses of you in there, but it's not enough, and everything I do to try and help you become yourself again might—it might—" She stops, swallows, finally speaks the fear that has gripped her since she first held him. "I worry I did too much. I worry I tried to turn you into someone, and I worry that it's worked."

His gaze is not troubled enough. "Whatever you did, you can't have made me into a different person. I'm still me."

"Which is exactly what I'd expect you to say." Thora can't articulate to him the terror of it: the only person she can't see through becoming a mirror of herself, a creature of her own construction. She breathes out, trying to exorcise the long tension of this life, the feeling of everything being on her shoulders. "What I said before—I meant it. I can't do this again. I can't be so far ahead. I can't wait for you to grow up." Far below them, fallen leaves rustle invisibly in the dark.

"Before," Santi says, his voice shaking. "When I said there wasn't anything we could do about it. I was wrong, wasn't I?"

Thora looks at him. His eyes flick unmistakably down.

A chill runs through her. She stares at Santi: not Santi, but something uncanny, a monster pieced together from her projections. *What did I do to you?* "Don't be ridiculous. You—you're at the beginning of your life—"

He shakes his head. "I want to do the right thing. I want—I want to help you."

For an instant, Thora sees all the way into him: his deep uncertainty, his willingness to let her nudge him into a death he's known before. Another Santi falling. Another Santi standing at the foot of the tower, mourning his own death, accepting it as God's will. He is, in this life, so much what she has made of him. If she told him to climb down, he would. But she's not strong enough to do this alone. "Okay," she says, her voice breaking.

Wind whistles through the gaps in the tower. A song in the unreal city's voice. *Do it.* A thought worthy of another Santi, obsessively counting the locks on the bridge. Thora doesn't truly hear it, but she knows one thing: if they climb down, this moment will never come again.

Her blood hammers in her ears. She has died so many times, but never like this. There is nothing familiar about hanging above this drop, knowing the crunch and shatter at the end, knowing it will be her own doing. Everything inside her screams, her body a palace of alarms telling her to back down. But she has never been one to do what she is told.

She turns to Santi, kisses his forehead. Their hands come together. "Find me, as soon as you remember," she says. "I'll leave a message for you."

He presses his forehead to hers. She can feel him trembling. "I'll wait for you."

"I'll wait for you." Her hand tightens on his.

Together, they jump. As they fall, Thora knows a moment of sickening regret. *No. I take it back.* But it's too late. Santi's hand loosens from hers, lets go. She hears him cry out before they hit the ground.

At the moment of impact, she sees something else. Brightness beyond belief, hurting her eyes; then, in the dimming darkness, the shadow of a face looking back at her.

FOLLOW THE LIGHT

○ ✻ ◉

Santi is waiting under the lighthouse in Ehrenfeld when Thora walks through the wall.

She looks the way she always looks to him, like reality precipitating from a dream. It's a heart-shock to see her. She's his age: of course, this time they must have been born at the exact same second.

She grins at him. "You figured out my message."

Santi nods. He can't trust himself to speak. He almost couldn't bear to go to the clock tower; it felt like stepping on unholy ground. He only stayed long enough to read the words she had written there. FOLLOW THE LIGHT. It hit him like a cruel joke. What else has he been trying to do, all these many lives? And what has Thora done but drag him again and again into darkness?

She knocks his arm in friendly rebuke. "What took you so long?"

"I only just arrived."

Thora frowns. She's settled on a hair color, the rainbow he remembers dulled to the blue of an evening sky. He wonders if it's a Thora costume, her way of making believe she's the same person every time. When did she start thinking that way? When did he start thinking of himself as multiple, a series of watercolor portraits on glass? Like Thora said last time, they have been slowly changing sides. "I don't get it," she says. "We died together. We're clearly the same age. Why did we still arrive here at different times?"

We died together. How easily she says it: as if they crashed in the same car, or fell victim to the same slow disease. He remembers taking her hand. He remembers falling in the dark, terror and rushing air and too-late regret. But he doesn't recognize the person who made that memory. The act is a horror: a fault line in who he is that he doesn't think he will ever come to terms with.

He remembers the moment of impact, the face that looked back at him when he died. Long-haired, shadowed, with eyes that saw him at his lowest and knew him for what he was.

He was sure—is still sure—that what is needed from them is atonement: a meaningful, deliberate sacrifice. There, inside the darkness of the tower, he believed that what he had to sacrifice was himself. He marvels at how completely Thora twisted his thinking. Joining her in self-annihilation was the easy way out. The true path to redemption will be harder: so hard that when he sees it, his soul will cry out against it. He is determined that this time, he will not fail.

Thora tilts her head. "Are you okay?"

Santi blinks. "You just walked through the wall," he points out.

"Yeah. I've been busy." Thora holds out her hand. He hesitates. Impatient, she grabs him and pulls him through solid stone.

It's a strange feeling—a humming in his ears, a split-second gap in his existence—but not unfamiliar. Santi emerges into the dark interior of the lighthouse with the same wonder as when he passed through the wall in the university to find himself under the stars. "A miracle," he says under his breath.

"A mistake." Thora lets go of his hand. "We're not supposed to be able to get in here."

"Not at ground level, anyway." Santi climbed into the lighthouse as a teenager lifetimes ago, through a broken window in the lantern room. The interior is how he remembers it: a gray sketch, the lack of detail almost uncanny. Now, the monotony is broken by a mattress on the floor and a bucket filled with chip packets and bread. "You're living in here?"

Thora nods enthusiastically. "I figured a landlocked lighthouse accessible only by mystic portal was the closest I could get to elsewhere."

Something about the bucket strikes Santi as odd. He empties it out. He's not imagining it. Three of the same oddly shaped bread bun, four of the same pack of paprika chips. The same exact apple with the same bruise on one side, repeated over and over. He looks up at her. "Where did you get all this?"

She grins. "Come with me and I'll show you."

In the crowded aisles of the Alter Markt, Santi watches Thora reach out and take a bun from a bread stall.

"Thora," he starts.

"Before you call the police, just wait." She points steadily at the corner of the stall. When Santi looks again, another identical bun has appeared in the place of the one she took.

He blinks. He remembers a cup of coffee, unexpectedly heavy in his hand. "That happens every time?"

"Loaves and fishes," Thora says, grinning.

Santi shakes his head in wonder. "How did you find this?"

Thora bites into her prize. "I've been here five years," she says around a mouthful. "Plenty of time to learn all this place's tricks." She takes another bun and shoves it in her pocket. "Once you get the hang of it, they're pretty easy to spot. You just have to look at things the right way." She grabs his arm, her face lighting up. "Which reminds me. There's one you have to see."

He pulls back. "I can't stay. Héloïse will be wondering where I am."

"Héloïse?" Thora stares. "I thought you were finished with Héloïse. You said being with her didn't feel fair."

Santi rubs his eyes, still reeling from the twenty-five years that have passed and not passed since he and Thora last saw each other. He remembers moving to Paris, meeting Héloïse, their wedding in the Art Nouveau church in Montmartre under the impossible brightness of stained glass. Images, tied up with emotion, connected by the illusion of a self that experienced them. If his and Thora's lives in the city are the melody, then perhaps the pauses also have meaning, like the rests in music. He shrugs. "We were already married when I arrived."

It's not an answer, and Thora knows it. But if she senses there is more he's not telling her, she doesn't seem to care. "Fine. But before you go and hang out with your fake wife, let me show you this one thing." She tugs his hand, leading him through an alleyway back toward the clock tower. Santi drags his feet, but Thora is relentless. She leads him around the side, into the grassy courtyard where they once met as first-year students.

"There," she says, pointing at nothing.

Santi tilts his head. "What am I looking at?"

"Observe." Thora hefts the remainder of the bun and throws it straight ahead. As Santi watches, it disappears in midair. He steps forward, fascinated. "It's like—an invisible door," Thora says. "It un-exists things."

Santi's eyes drop to the grass. A memory comes: searching for an hour with nail-bitten and dirty hands, not comprehending how something could disappear so entirely. "My hostel card," he murmurs.

"What?"

"Nothing."

"I tried walking into it, of course," Thora says airily. "But it doesn't work on me. I assume it won't work on you either." She gestures. "Give it a try."

Santi pauses. Maybe this is another trap Thora is leading him into, a second suicide. But he believes in treating the world as real. There is nothing here for him to be afraid of. He walks forward, through the invisible door.

Nothing happens.

"I call it the annihilation portal," Thora says cheerfully. "There's something therapeutic about it. One time, I got all my least favorite books from the library and just sat throwing them in one by one." She settles cross-legged on the grass, picking up pine cones and tossing them to non-existence by Santi's feet. It sickens him: the repetitive, angry motion, the nothingness left behind.

"Thora, what are you doing?" he asks.

She blinks up at him. "What do you mean?"

"You said you've been here five years. Has this been your life? Stealing impossible food and—and throwing things into the void?"

Thora stares at him in disbelief. "I thought you loved miracles."

Santi rubs his face, exhaling. "I don't think we're supposed to exist this way."

"Come on. What's the alternative? Getting a job?" She scoffs. "Besides, it's not like I'm stealing *from* anyone. Unless the ether has property rights."

Santi shakes his head. "It's not right. It feels like—like cheating."

"Maybe if this were a game we had agreed to play. But I don't recall signing up." She drops her last pine cone and stands, confronting him. "Last time, I told you we had no meaningful choices at all. But I realized—that's not true. We have one. To refuse to play by the rules."

Something is building in Santi, a rage made from lifetimes of trailing in Thora's wake, picking up the damage she leaves behind. "This isn't a game," he says. "Not to me." He points past her at the tower, shaking with regret. "I ended my own life. I left Aurelia to live with knowing what I had done. Can you imagine how that hurt her?" He presses his fingers to his temples. "How could I do that? How could you let me?"

Thora crosses her arms. "It was your decision."

"How could I make my own decisions when you had made me who I was?" He doesn't know how to explain it to her: how meeting her so young made her the center of his world, something between a second mother and a saint.

Thora rolls her eyes. "You were the one who said you'd be yourself no matter what happened to you!"

"I was wrong."

The admission silences her. Under different circumstances, that would make him laugh. Finally, he has found a way to stop their endless argument.

Thora shakes herself. "Santi, it doesn't matter what you did.

Because you didn't actually do it. None of this is real." She gestures at the invisible outline of the annihilation portal. "What more proof do you need?"

"I'm real." He steps toward her. "You're real."

She shakes her head, a strange smile on her face. "Real people don't die and come back. Real people don't regenerate into a hundred versions of themselves until all that's left of them is anger and fear." She paces away from him. "Maybe we were real once, a long time ago."

Santi watches the hard line of her shoulders. She has retreated into the holes in the world, leaving him alone again. But he can't do this alone. His actions mean nothing without her: if they are both being punished, then they both need to atone.

"I'll prove it to you," he says. "I'll show you something you can't dismiss as unreal."

Thora turns her head. A smile creeps up her cheek: she can never resist a challenge. "Go on then."

"I need some time. Meet me at Der Zentaur, a week from now."

Thora crosses the courtyard back to him. She scans his face curiously, but he gives nothing away.

"Fine," she says. Her eyes flick up to the tower. "I won't ask what time."

He nods. "Let's make it midday, not midnight."

Thora smiles. She kisses his cheek and vaults the fence, loping away until she disappears behind the tower.

When he gets home, Héloïse is pruning her bonsai tree. She sits in the window in the last of the winter light, swearing softly in French as she wrangles the branches into a more pleasing arrangement. She doesn't know it has been a lifetimes-long project.

Like his drawing, Santi thinks; but without the chance to remember, to grow, Héloïse still never quite gets it right.

For a moment, he just watches her, this woman he knows so asymmetrically: each version of their relationship new to her, while he sees only the echoes of what came before. There is truth here, he realizes, in the place where all their histories intersect.

"You're late," she says without looking up.

Santi stoops to stroke Félicette as she rubs against his ankles. "I ran into an old friend."

Héloïse abandons the tree with a dismissive gesture and comes over to kiss him. Her brown eyes scan him as she pulls back. "Hmm. Evasive." A smile plays around her mouth. "Is this your way of telling me you're running off with a hot German?"

He could say yes. He could walk out now, with no explanation. Or, he could do what he did the last time he was with her, the same thing Thora did to Jules: tell her his truth until it breaks her. As he watches her face, he doesn't sense that any of it would come as a surprise. He recognizes the constant note in their relationship: she is always, somehow, waiting for him to leave.

Perhaps, for once, he can surprise her. "Not this time," he says, and draws her into his arms.

A week later, at Der Zentaur, he is arguing with Thora. It's cold for sitting outside, but she wanted to smoke. Santi feels the ghost of a previous self's craving as she taps away the ash.

"I don't understand why you don't understand." She leans across the table. "I'm saying you were right, about you and me. We're not made to live in the world like other people. We'll always, always want what's beyond. We'll always want out."

"I agree," he says. "But what you're doing—living in the gaps, refusing to engage with it as reality—that's not getting out. That's going further in."

Thora sips her wine. "How is acting like this is real going to get us out?"

Santi pauses. He considers telling her that he is still looking for atonement, for the freely given sacrifice that will lead him to redemption. But he's afraid she will pull him away from his purpose, like she has done so many times before.

"I'm still waiting for my proof, by the way," Thora adds, drumming her fingers on the table. "I hope it's not supposed to be the wine. I've had my doubts about that since before we started to remember."

Santi checks his watch. "Should be here any minute now." He looks up and sees the woman crossing the square toward them.

Thora follows his gaze. "No." She gets up so violently that her glass falls from the table, wine spilling red over the cobbles. "No, I'm not doing this." She walks away.

Santi goes after her, grabs her, and turns her around. Jules stops.

"Hi," she says, waving awkwardly. "I'm Jules. You must be Thora."

Thora's body is angled away, her eyes downcast, as if she doesn't trust herself to look.

"Tell her she's not real," Santi says in Thora's ear. "You can't. Can you?"

Thora takes a breath, like she's about to plunge into icy water. She looks at Jules for a heartbeat before closing her eyes. When she opens them, she's looking at Santi in fury. "You told me once this wasn't hell," she says. "You were wrong. What's worse than a face you love that doesn't remember?"

Jules frowns, a soft confusion in her eyes. "I'm sorry. Have we met before?"

Santi feels like a monster. He swallows what he wants to say to Thora. *I'm sorry for following you from life to life like a starving dog. I'm sorry for haunting you with your wife's ghost.* He has to make her understand. "That's the point," he tells her. "This wouldn't hurt if it wasn't real."

Thora shakes off his hold. "I'll show you hurt." The glance she gives him before she walks away is murderous.

Jules comes up to Santi, watching Thora leave. "Is she okay? I thought you said she wanted to meet new people."

Santi looks at Jules, puzzled and friendly, always ready to give a stranger the benefit of the doubt. He thinks about how he got her here: tracking her down through her work, befriending her under false pretenses, using old memories to manipulate her into wanting to help him. Is he any better than Thora? "I'm sorry," he says. "She's having a bad day." *A bad series of lifetimes.*

"That's okay. Another time." Jules squeezes his shoulder, as if part of her remembers the years she's known him. "Tell her she's cute," she says with a wink as she walks away.

Santi goes back to the abandoned table and sits down, staring at the wine-edged prints of Thora's boots. Their bloodstained path across the cobbles is comforting and horrifying: something he's come to think of as the essence of her. *I'll show you hurt.* He knows her well enough to understand it as a promise.

He doesn't hear from her for weeks. He hears *of* her, in the conversations that drift past him as he walks the city, looking for his chance to atone. Stories of a woman who can vanish into walls: a thief, a trickster, uncatchable as a ghost. He dreads running into her, and wishes for it, often at the same time. He can't tell which causes the jump in his heart when he returns to his apartment one morning with coffee and pastries for Héloïse and finds a note on the kitchen table.

Meet me at the tower, it says in Thora's wide, looping hand.

He's surprised by the fact that he recognizes her handwriting. Parts of her are becoming more constant: this, the blue hair, the way she dresses. Flashes of the real reflected in this flawed mirror, like the look on her face when she saw Jules across the square. A phrase from the Bible surfaces in his mind. *En un mal espejo, confusamente. Through a glass darkly.* He wants to believe that each lifetime, they come closer to seeing each other face-to-face. But now he feels her fleeing from him, back turned as she fades into the dark.

The apartment is quiet. Too quiet. Héloïse should be up by now, singing to Félicette as she measures out her breakfast. "Cariña?" he calls.

No answer. He drops the coffee and pastries on the table and goes through to the bedroom. The bed is hastily made, the wardrobe hanging open. Héloïse's shoes are missing from their place by the front door.

He grabs his keys and leaves the apartment, a shiver of foreboding riding his shoulders. As he nears the old town, the streets ahead of him echo with crashing noise. It sounds like the city is at war. He's afraid it's Thora, that she has done something terrible, when he remembers: it's carnival. Crowds collect around him, raucous and already half-drunk. Santi pushes through until he reaches the tower. FOLLOW THE LIGHT, Thora's words shout, but she's not there. He circles the wall, searching. Drums pound, a bassline to the crowd's shrill screams. On old reflex, he reaches into his jacket for the handle of his grandfather's knife.

Dizziness hits him, so intense he sees stars. Then he sees Thora, standing in the grassy courtyard.

She's dressed for carnival, in a devil mask and horns. She is holding something it takes him a moment to recognize as a cat carrier. Through the bars, he sees Félicette meowing piteously. She hates confined spaces, he thinks. Then he sees where Thora is standing.

"Roll up, roll up!" Thora calls, seeing him coming. "For the greatest magic trick the world has ever seen!"

Next to her, looking half-puzzled and half-amused, is Héloïse. As Santi watches her, standing meters from a doom she can't even see, lifetimes of love turn to a rush of cold fear inside him.

He vaults the fence and strides across the grass to Héloïse, taking her arm. "What are you doing here?"

"She said she was your friend. Thora, right? She's doing a magic show, but she was scared no one would come." She laughs, a warm Héloïse chuckle that penetrates to his bones. "Carnival. Anything can happen."

Thora gives her a courtly bow. "You are absolutely right, my lady. Prepare to be amazed." She opens the carrier and lifts Félicette out.

"Stop." Santi hears the desperation in his own voice. "Thora, please."

She gives him a wicked grin. "Don't worry. Cats always land on their feet." Félicette wriggles in her arms, yowling. Thora tightens her grip. "Come on. We're going on an adventure." She carries Félicette toward the portal. The cat screams, spits, struggles to get free, but Thora holds fast until, at the threshold, she lets her go. Félicette bounds out of her arms and vanishes.

Héloïse jumps. She stares at Thora, then laughs and claps, looking sideways at Santi. "Mirrors?" she says in an undertone.

Santi can only stare at the empty grass, the void where something beloved once was. He doesn't understand why it feels like such a violation: worse, somehow, than if Thora had drowned Félicette before his eyes.

"Why are you upset?" Thora looks at him, head cocked in fake confusion. "She wasn't real. This proves it."

"Thora." He steps forward, takes her arm. "I know this is about Jules. I know it hurt you, seeing her again. But you have to see how that proves you shouldn't be doing this."

Héloïse touches his shoulder. He reads her frown. *Why are you being so weird?* "Santi, calm down. It's a magic trick." She turns a smile on Thora. "A very good one."

Thora blows Héloïse a kiss. "I'm glad someone appreciates my art." She offers her hand. "And now, madame, it's your turn! Are you ready to brave the annihilation portal?"

Héloïse laughs. "I thought you'd never ask." With a conspiratorial glance at Santi, she takes Thora's hand.

Thora leads her forward. "Don't worry," she says. "If you're real, you've got nothing to worry about."

Santi watches Thora lead his laughing wife across the grass. He wants to reach out, to pull her back, but that would mean admitting in his heart that Thora might really do this. He doesn't believe she will. She's just trying to scare him. Any moment now, she will stop and turn back.

Héloïse looks over her shoulder with a warm smile. "Santi, what if—"

She's gone. Mid-sentence, like his father in their crashing car so many lives ago. Thora startles. She looks down at her empty hand. "Shit," she says quietly.

That—the acknowledgment that this was half a game to her, an experiment she didn't know the outcome of—is what breaks him. He roars and runs for her. When he grabs her by the shoulders, he sees it in her eyes through the mask: part of her is appalled by what she's done. But in her voice he hears only defensive triumph. "See? I proved it," she says. "They're not real. They never were."

Santi shakes all over with an anger that staggers him. This is what Thora does, time and time again: take his hope and belief and desire for meaning, and drown them all in nothingness. For so many lives, he has tried to persuade her that their actions matter, in the belief that this was a test they had to pass together. But perhaps the real test was to recognize her for what she is: his enemy. The reason he is still trapped here.

Finally, he understands. His gut cramps with the knowledge of what he must do. All too easy, to sacrifice himself. This is the truly hard thing: to willingly give up Thora, to finally redeem her sins and his own. "I'm sorry," he tells her, as he reaches for his grandfather's knife.

Thora sees the blade a full second before she understands. The expression on her face will follow him for lifetimes. "Santi, no. Wait—"

He strikes fast and true, aiming for her heart.

She makes a terrible sound. Santi pulls out the blade, and her blood comes with it, warm on his hand. She's staring at him, mouth open, disbelief frozen on her face. He pulls her close as she shudders, the life pulsing out of her.

"Sorry?" she wheezes. He can hear the blood in her voice. "You're sorry? Fuck you!"

"Shh," he says, holding her. "Don't talk. It'll be over soon."

"Damn right it will." Every breath must be like twisting the blade inside her, but this is Thora: she has to have the last word.

For a vivid moment, he hallucinates his sullen daughter looking up at the false stars. "You think I'm not taking you with me?" Her hand gropes for his knife. Willingly, he lets her take it. Perhaps that is a sin too, but truly, he doesn't want to outlive her. He holds her close, and when she strikes, he welcomes the dark.

WHO WE ARE

○ ✳ ◎

Thora sits on the edge of a hole in the sky, swigging from a bottle of red wine. Behind her, on the other side of the mirror, the hum of conversation in Der Zentaur continues oblivious as she swings her legs over the twenty meter drop to the cobbled square. One quick leap and she would be on her way down. The thought of falling doesn't scare her anymore. But it wouldn't be an escape. She would only wake, and remember, and follow Santi again and again into the dark.

She doesn't know if he's in the city yet. For the first time, she hasn't left him a message. Pain flares behind her ribs, as if her heart is still recovering from his knife. She takes a gulp of her wine, staring down at where the fountain gleams in miniature like a carefully painted simulacrum. What hurts, even more than the phantom pain in her chest, is the memory of his face after Héloïse vanished and Thora knew she had done something irrevocable. She screws her eyes shut, wishing she could erase the memory, but it sits there, indelible.

Thora used to think of herself as infinite. Now she knows what she truly is: a spiral narrowing to a point that contains all the worst things about her. She looks at herself now, sitting on a patch of nothing, getting drunk alone on the same old stolen wine, and feels a rush of disgust. On impulse, she upends the bottle to send the wine down as impossible rain on the square below. The red liquid bubbles out of the neck and stops, sticking in midair.

Thora blinks. "Wow," she says aloud, to the whipping wind and the impossible sky. "Looks like I broke gravity."

The words resonate in her memory, bringing an echo back. Santi, hunched at his computer in the astronomy lab, saying the same thing about his simulation.

Thora sits bolt upright, almost losing her balance. Santi's refilling coffee cup. The miracle food she has lived on for the past two lifetimes. The hole where she sits right now, a door between two places that shouldn't be connected. Bugs, all of them, in a simulation more complex than she would have imagined possible. And hovering just below her, another bug, but with a difference. She made this one happen.

The Santi who was her student tips back in his chair, humming that same infuriating tune. *I gave the simulation an input it wasn't expecting.* Thora peers at the frozen trail of red hanging between her and the cobbled ground. "I guess they didn't expect anyone to pour wine through a hole in the sky."

She laughs, caught in a rush of discovery she hasn't felt for lifetimes. If she can break gravity in a single patch of air, there must be a way to break everything. Tear the city apart from the inside. All she needs to do is give the simulation inputs it wasn't set up to handle, until she triggers a bug catastrophic enough to make it crash.

Elated, she climbs back through the mirror into Der Zentaur. Brigitta glares at her. "What are you doing behind my bar?"

Thora waves her arm through the mirror. "What's a hole in reality doing behind your bar?"

Brigitta blinks, confused. Thora remembers the same look on Jules's face and feels a tug like the pull of an old scar.

She sighs. "I know. You don't know what to say." She pats the barmaid on the shoulder and walks out, already planning her next move.

Thora pries another padlock off the Hohenzollernbrücke and hurls it down into the river. She waits for the faraway splash, then turns back to check her progress. Three-quarters of the fence stretches empty behind her; the rest still gleams with mismatched and sentimental eyesores. Soon, it will be clear, and the simulated river will have two tons of unexpected metal to contend with. "See how you handle that, universe," she mutters. She crouches again, maneuvering her wrenches into the shackle of the next lock. She's so absorbed that she doesn't immediately notice when someone walks past her humming a familiar tune.

Her head turns. The man is walking away, but she'd know his gait anywhere. She watches Santi head for the opposite bank. The last thing she wants is to face him. But she burns with the need to know where he's going, if he's trying to find his own way out.

She packs her wrenches away in her rucksack and follows. Staying at a safe distance, she tracks him to the Odysseum, camouflaging herself in the crowd as he heads inside. He does a leisurely circuit of the planetarium and the hall of astronauts before turning into the quiet corridor with the room marked "Under Construction." Thora watches as he sits down on a bench opposite the image from the Kepler telescope and starts sketching. Every so often, he looks up, as though he's waiting for someone. For her, Thora assumes as she ducks out of view; but why not wait at Der Zentaur, where she would know to find him?

He stays for half an hour. When he gets up to leave, she follows, tailing him back across the bridge to the cathedral square; through the old town to the clock tower; onto a train to Fühlingen, where he sits on the beach by the artificial lake where they once swam as brother and sister. In every place, the same pattern: sketch, pause, scan the crowd for a face he doesn't find. When he leaves the beach, Thora watches him cross the main road and pass through a rusted wrought-iron gate into an abandoned three-story mansion.

Her scalp prickles with curiosity. She settles down in the bushes of the overgrown garden to wait.

Finally, as the sun sinks behind the house, he emerges. Thora waits for him to pass through the gate before she sneaks up the drive, under the arched cloister, and through the house's open doorway.

She's not sure what she expected. But as the evening light falls through the empty windows, she finds she isn't surprised. Santi has turned the house into his memory book. Murals cover the crumbling brick walls: world after world of the two of them, the city, the cathedral, the clock tower. And the stars, over and over, filling the gaps between.

She follows the trail of paintings up the stairs. Some lives show up again and again: the pair of them in their police uniforms, fireworks bursting around their heads; the life where they were adopted twins, Thora underwater, Santi reaching to grab her heel; two students at the top of the tower, looking up at the bewildering stars. One wall shows their parents, Thora's sharply observed, Santi's more impressionistic, as if it is easier for him to capture what he is less close to. On the opposite wall, their other constants: Lily and Jaime and Aurelia, Héloïse and Jules. Thora slides past them with a kind of vertigo, not daring to meet their eyes. She stops under the portrait of a long-haired man in a blue coat wearing a worried expression.

"I know you," she says under her breath. "How do I know you?" She hunts back through her memories. A hand on her and Santi's shoulders as they stood under the clock tower. A flash of blue against the sand, when he collapsed beside them on the beach. In a rush, it all connects. The beach. The clock tower. The Odysseum. Santi has been looking for this man, in every place they have seen him.

"Thora."

She whirls. Santi stands in the doorway.

Thora stiffens against the wall. "Don't come any closer."

"I'm not going to hurt you." He holds up his hands. "I saw you on the bridge. I know you've been following me."

She stares at him. "Why didn't you say something?"

His grimace is almost a smile. "I was too angry."

"*You're* angry?" Thora almost chokes. "You stabbed me in the heart!"

"You un-existed my wife!"

From the wall behind her, Thora feels Héloïse's eyes boring into her back. The woman who was once her mother. The woman she led by the hand to her annihilation. Sickness rises up in her throat. "I shouldn't have done it," she says, looking away. "But— it's always so easy for you to destabilize me. Like you did last time. Just show me Jules, and I'm a wreck. But you—you're always so fucking serene, so in control. I just wanted you to *react*, for once." She takes in a deep breath. "I did what I did because I knew it would make you angry. But I never thought it'd make you angry enough to *kill* me."

He avoids her eyes. "I told you I thought there was something we had to do to atone. That we would have to give up something we didn't want to lose." He shrugs, helpless. "At the very end—I thought it was you."

Thora puts her hand to her head. "Let me get this straight. You stabbed me in the heart because you thought God wanted you to?"

Santi has the grace to look ashamed. "Tests are supposed to be hard," he points out.

Thora gestures emphatically around them. "Well, we're still here. Obviously you didn't pass."

A heavy silence falls between them. Thora turns back to the portrait of the man in the blue coat. "You're looking for him," she says. "Why?"

Santi walks hesitantly closer. "Everyone else who comes back— they belong to you or they belong to me. But this man knows us both. I think he might be able to tell us what's really happening." He looks at her sideways, reading her silence. "What?"

Sometimes, she wishes he didn't know her so well. "Nothing," she says. "It's a good idea. It's just very—you. Find the man in charge and ask him to explain what it all means."

She sees him resist a smile. "What were you doing on the bridge?"

Thora explains her plan. He listens with his usual careful attention. "Trying to find a miracle that will break the world," he muses when she's finished.

Thora rolls her eyes. "Of course you'd find a way to make me hate my own idea." She watches his face. "Go on then. Tell me what's wrong with it."

"You're assuming that if we crash the simulation, we get out," he says. "What if we don't? What if it just—takes away the only reality we have?"

Thora gnaws her lip. Why does he always have to see the weakness in her plans? "It's possible. But right now, I don't have any better ideas."

Another silence: an opening for them to keep talking, to find a way to work this out together. But what happened last time is still an open wound between them. "I should go," Thora says. "World's not going to break itself, is it?"

"Keep me posted." Santi leans back against the painting of the man in the blue coat. "If I'm not out looking for him, I'll be here."

Thora pauses at the top of the stairs. "Why?" she asks, gesturing at the rest of his gallery. "What's this all for?"

"Last time, you told me none of this was real." Thora hears the pain that hides under the words: Jules standing in the square, her face a mask of confusion; Héloïse's hand vanishing from her grasp. Santi turns back to his paintings. "I don't think that's right. I think there are—pieces of the real, scattered through each life." He brushes dust off a corner of his work. "Those pieces are what I'm trying to find."

"You told me once that was why you started your memory book." The dim-lit kitchen of her and Jules's flat at two in the morning, feeding Oskar while Santi wrote a codex of their deaths. The memory hurts. Was that the last life she got right? That self seems so far away, overwritten by all the mistakes she's made. "And if we find out what's real?" she asks. "How does that help us get out?"

Santi closes his eyes. "The life where we met in the hostel. I thought if I could find out who I was, then I would know where I was going." His eyes open, meeting hers. "If we find what's real, we find the way out."

Thora looks away. She's not sure she wants to know who she truly is. However much she dislikes her current self, she can still find comfort in the lives where she made different choices. What if her real self has made a choice she can't take back: a choice she can't live with? If she stops moving, if she tries to confront who they really are, she thinks she might fall to pieces.

She nods tightly. "Good luck," she says. "If I see your guy, I'll let you know."

Santi watches her leave as if he doesn't expect her to come back.

Thora sits on the grass, a spray bottle of water in her left hand and a blanket in her right. In front of her is a plate of millet. Behind her is a cage filled with parakeets.

The next bird lands in a flurry of bright green. Thora stays as still as death until it starts pecking at the millet. She moves like a closing trap, soaking the bird with her spray bottle. As it struggles to take off, she throws the blanket over it, bundles it up, opens the cage, and releases it inside.

She closes the cage door and counts the birds. Enough for a morning's work. She gathers her tools and starts walking backward across the park toward Ehrenfeld. She hefts the cage at an old woman following her down the path. "Never seen someone walking backward with a cage full of parakeets before?" she yells, in a nonsense pidgin of bad Czech and Icelandic.

The old woman shakes her head and takes another path. Thora laughs out loud in the illusory sunshine, feeling herself teeter on the brink of madness.

At the foot of the lighthouse, she sets the cage down. She pushes each wriggling bird through the solid concrete and lets it go. When the cage is empty, she picks up her bag of seed and pokes her head through the wall. Inside, the air is a whirling mess of birds. She scatters a few good handfuls, tops up the water feeder, then backs out onto the street.

Trying to break the world is hungry work. She heads to the old town and grabs a miracle currywurst from the van outside the cathedral, although she's not sure it will help. For the last few lives, food has been sitting hollow in her stomach. She doesn't plan to tell Santi. He would only say it's a metaphor for her spiritual starvation, or something equally profound.

She's leaning against the glass wall of the Hauptbahnhof when she sees him on the cathedral steps, sketching in his book. She finds herself thinking of the house, empty and waiting, filled with their memories. Before she's conscious of what she's doing, she finds herself on the next train to Fühlingen. She doesn't understand why until she walks through the house's empty doorway and her feet take her straight to Jules.

She looks down from the wall, vivid as life, eyes crinkling in a frank smile. Thora thinks of all the versions of Jules she has known: each, if Santi is right, an echo of the real one. She remembers the conviction that crystallized in her over time, that she could only be with Jules if she gave up the idea of elsewhere. Is that a choice she has already made? Or one she is still making?

Before she leaves, she pauses under the painting of the man in the blue coat. There's something she needs to remember: a word, lurking at the tip of her tongue. She closes her eyes to try and hear it better. Brightness flares at the corner of her vision, the smell of smoke sudden in her throat. Sand under her fingers, and a flash of blue.

The beach. The man in the blue coat lying on the sand, telling her something had happened. She asked his name, and he told her. *Peregrine.*

She writes the name on the wall under the painting. Let Santi find it, next time he comes. No doubt he'll decide it means something.

*   *   *

The next day, she's up a ladder in the planetarium of the Odysseum, patiently unscrewing the bulbs that stand for the stars, when her phone buzzes with a message.

It's from Santi. She considers deleting it unread. Damning her curiosity, her constant need to know, she opens it.

I found him. We're in the house.

It's not an invitation. Thora doesn't care. She slides down the ladder and runs.

When she comes up the stairs of the memory house, Peregrine is standing in the center of the room. Santi sits against the wall, head in his hands.

The man in the blue coat looks at Thora, quietly lost. She turns to Santi. "Where did you find him?"

"I called him here." He points to Thora's scribbled addition to his painting. "I said his name aloud, and he walked in."

Trust Santi to try what amounted to a prayer: a leap of faith she would never have dreamt of making. "And?" she prompts.

Santi shakes his head. For the first time, she sees the despair in his eyes. "It's no use. He's not making any sense."

She can't bear it: she has never seen him so hopeless. She strides up to Peregrine. "Okay," she says. "Tell me what's happening."

Peregrine frowns. "You're here," he says.

"We'd figured out that much, thanks." Thora's anger surges. "Where. Is. Here?"

"I—" His mouth falls open. "I can't tell."

"Yes, you can." She feels her rage closing in on her, narrowing her to a single point of fury. Easier to accept her nature than to fight it. Easier to lash out, to break him like she's trying to break the world. She paces away from him, grabs a broken spar of timber from the floor. "You can and you will."

Santi stands up. "What are you doing?"

"Getting answers." Thora advances on Peregrine. "He's about to tell us what's going on."

"Thora," Santi says in warning.

"He knows something." She hears herself pleading, without knowing what she's asking for. "He knows something and he's hiding it from us."

Santi comes to stand beside her. "Look at him," he says. "He's confused. He can't—"

"*He's* confused?" Thora slams the spar against the floor. Santi jumps. Peregrine doesn't move. She hates him for that, as she hates him for what he is, an empty cipher, promising answers and delivering nothing.

Santi turns to face her. Only someone who knows him as well as she does would see the tension in his shoulders. "This isn't you," he says.

"Are you sure?" She laughs. After all this time, how little he knows her. "We killed each other, Santi. I annihilated your wife and made you watch. We don't know who we really are. And I don't think we want to." She gestures wildly at the walls, his beautiful visions of the lives he chooses to remember. "You say you're trying to find the truth of us. But how do you know you're not just finding what we wish was true? You can't just—collect all the bits of yourself you like and say, that's me, everything else is an aberration. We've both done terrible things. That's part of us, and we have to own it."

"We do," he says, and she sees how deeply he means it, how the scar of her murder has sunk into him. "But it can't be all we are."

His words vibrate through her. She wants to believe him, desperately, but all she can feel is Héloïse's fingers disappearing, her own hand driving the knife into Santi's chest. "Who cares?" she says, her voice breaking. "If I've been a murderer, does it matter if I've been anything else?"

"Yes," he says, fire in his voice. "Thora, *yes*. It's not one choice. It's a hundred choices, every single day, and all of them matter." He holds her gaze steadily as he says, "I learned that from you."

All the fight goes out of Thora. She hangs her head with a breathless laugh. She drops the spar. "I'm sorry," she says to Peregrine. "You can go."

Peregrine looks at Santi, as if he needs his permission. Santi nods. The man in the blue coat wanders away down the stairs. Thora exhales and sits down, feeling like she has won and lost at the same time. Santi comes to sit beside her. They watch, together, as their only real lead disappears from view. It hurts like it hurt when she was eleven years old and her parakeet flew away.

"Well done," Santi says, like he's congratulating her on passing a test.

Thora laughs under her breath. "I thought you decided we weren't being tested," she says. "After you stabbed me in the heart and it failed to magically get us out of here."

Santi looks at her wryly. "You think I act the way I do because I'm being tested?" He shakes his head. "I act the way I do because it is the only choice I have left."

Thora smiles at the echo of her own thought, coming back to her changed by Santi's mind. She watches him as he turns to the window. Lifetime after lifetime has made him translucent, until she can see through his varying exterior to the constant thing within. She was wrong a hundred lives ago, when she laughed at him for saying two people are forever a mystery to each other. She knows Santi as well as one person can know another, all his facets and sides and angles. But his heart is further from her understanding than ever. The shadows she's seen it cast make up an impossible object, bigger and stranger than he should be able to contain. The same isn't true of her. World by world, she's felt herself becoming smaller, diminishing into an obvious, snarling thing whose only desire is escape. Perhaps that's all she was, even back at the beginning she can't remember; the rest was fragile dress-up, like her orange pinafore and her sharp comebacks, sloughed off by the hurricane of what they've been through. Or perhaps Santi is right. Perhaps she still gets to choose who she wants to be.

"His name," she says, looking up at the mural of Peregrine. "It means wanderer."

"Pilgrim," Santi corrects her softly.

He meets her eyes. She sees the grief there, deeper than hers: he really believed Peregrine would lead them to the truth. "I'm sorry he didn't have the answers," she says.

He half-smiles. "It doesn't mean the answers aren't there. It just means we have to keep looking."

Thora looks down at her fingers, the rope-like tendons controlling the poor puppet of her body. "I wish I was more like you. I wish I could see a meaning."

"I don't see it. I look for it." His voice is quiet. "You think it's easy. You think it—comes naturally to me. But it doesn't. I choose it. Every single time."

They keep looking. Thora sticks her fingers into the live sockets of the world, trying to raise a spark that will burn down the lies and leave the truth behind. Santi draws together threads from each of their lives, seeking a color that glitters through them all.

In a strange way, Thora is happier than she has been in life-times. She has a mission, the possibility of a way out, and she is not alone: Santi is searching beside her. Still, it doesn't surprise her that the same goal manifests differently when filtered through their two minds. He's still reading the world for meaning, as he has always done. She is trying to break it apart from the inside. Either way, this strange work suits their natures. In their different ways, they have always been explorers.

After a morning spent stripping padlocks from the rest of the bridge, she heads for Fühlingen under strange gathering clouds. She makes it to the house before the rain starts. Lounging on the sill of one of the front windows, she waits for Santi to arrive. Something odd is happening outside. Rain is falling, but not only rain: something else, heavy and flopping, splattering messily on the overgrown driveway. Thora leans out of the window and watches in delight.

A few minutes later she sees Santi running across the garden, pulling up the back of his coat to shield his head. He appears on the stairs, panting and shaking himself off. "Thora," he asks patiently, "why is it raining fish?"

"Because my approach is working." She jumps down from the windowsill and comes to see what he was painting last time. A vague, impressionistic portrait of a man she doesn't recognize: bearded, with long dark hair, veiled in shadows. "Who's this?"

Santi steps back from the wall, tilting his head. "After we fell from the tower." Thora notices he doesn't say *jumped*. "I saw this face."

Thora stares at him. "Really? I saw a face too."

"The same one?" This version of Santi goes so swiftly from vague artist to laser-focused investigator. Thora supposes he's had enough practice at being both.

She shakes her head. "The one I saw was definitely a woman.

Also way less—Jesusy." She wrinkles her nose. "Maybe we both just saw what we expected to see."

"Why did you expect to see a woman?"

Thora shrugs. "Because whoever's masterminding all this has to be pretty smart?"

Santi laughs, then closes his eyes, catching himself on the wall.

Thora frowns. "What's wrong?"

Slowly, he opens his eyes. "Dizzy spell. I've been having them for a few lifetimes now."

Thora watches him warily. "I'm hungry all the time," she says. "No matter what I eat. I would have mentioned it before, but I was worried you'd tell me it meant something."

Santi dips his paintbrush, giving her a tired smile. "Probably nothing good."

Pushing down her disquiet, Thora moves past him to examine the walls. "You're running out of space." Almost every brick is covered. "Did you find your answer? Do you know who we are yet?"

He pauses, brush in midair. "I think so," he says. "But you tell me."

Thora takes in the gallery of their lives. Her eight-year-old self, wrapped in her father's scarf, looking up at the false stars in the Odysseum. The two of them hunched over their computers in the astronomy lab, faces lit by the glow of their invented worlds. Santi, lost and homeless, searching a maze of streets for a sign that says WE ARE HERE. She looks back at him now: younger than he was then, but older, too, in a way only she can see.

"So?" he asks her with a fond smile. "What's the heart of us, every time?"

"We always go looking," Thora says. "We always want else-where." She glances across at Jules, smiling down at her from another reality. "Even when it means leaving the ones we love behind."

Santi nods. "I think you're right."

"Are you sure?" Thora's voice catches. "Maybe that's just who we wish we were."

In lieu of an answer, he points with his paintbrush to a corner of the room she hasn't seen yet. Painted down the wall are miniature tableaux of her explorations in this life, Santi's graphic shorthand so practiced he can evoke her in a few lines. Thora on the bridge, hurling padlocks down through water clogged with space helmets and skeletons. Thora holding a flock of parakeets on strings, thorns and diacritics spilling from her mouth. Thora walking endlessly backward, like he's calling her home. "It's who we are right now," he says. "You in your way, me in mine. We chose it, and we'll keep choosing it."

She swallows, too moved for a moment to speak. "Do you think it means we'll get out of here?" she asks him when she can.

He looks up into the eyes of the face he saw when he fell. "It means we're not going to stop trying."

Thora shakes herself and heads for the window. "I have to go."

"Me too," Santi says dryly. "I have to wash the fish out of my hair."

Thora pauses as she straddles the windowsill. "If the simulation shuts down, what do you think it'll look like? I imagine the air sort of—dissolving."

Santi shrugs. "A bright light, I guess."

Thora gives him a look of disdain. "My God. The originality. It kills me." She points out of the window, mock-amazed. "Santi, look! A bright light!"

"That's the sun."

"For now. Give me another couple of days," she says, and climbs out.

She wakes to the knowledge that something is wrong.

Not wrong like waking to a baby crying, or to the smell of gas. Cosmically wrong, like going to sleep under the stars and waking buried alive.

She gasps, clutching at her throat. The air is heavy, then light, gravity and pressure pulsing like a clock out of time. Bracing against the wall, she pulls herself out of bed and hunches over, wincing. Time and space are streaming between her ears. Her nose itches, but she gets the feeling that if she tried to scratch it, her hand would go right through. She straightens up, sidesteps, lunges forward through the black, roaring space. Sounds slice through her, gibberish words made up of German and Russian and English. Visions of parakeets flying through stone, of Santi's face in countless fracturing facets, oscillate before her eyes.

She doesn't know how she gets to the window. Santi stands below her in what used to be the street, now a mosaic of fragments grouted with void. With one step, she is with him in no-place. He stands with his back to her, his outline vibrating.

"Santi." She shakes his shoulder, feeling the buzz of conducted strangeness. Visions tear through her: mushrooms, pale and looming, Jules's face, the skeleton of the clock tower, glassy and made of bones. A lighthouse made of crochet billows wildly across the sky. "I did it," she says, hearing her words echo and split, come back to her as a buzzing whine.

Santi looks up at the swirling sky, fragments of Cologne funneling into chaos. "You did something."

She follows his gaze upward. Twin stars, blinding her as they fall. She recognizes them too late as the lights on a subway train, hurtling down with a sound like claws on glass. She yelps in half-laughing terror and pulls Santi out of the way. She keeps hold of his hand as she runs, leading him in tripping leaps over swathes of nothing, down the floating fragments of what used to be the road into the city. A distorted chittering swoops above her. She looks up into a flock of tiny green birds, flying in a backward loop around their heads.

"Where are we going?" Santi yells.

"Out," Thora yells back over her shoulder. "There are holes in everything now. There has to be one we can escape through."

"Are you sure?" Santi shouts.

"No," she yells back, closing her hand firmly around his. Even if they're going nowhere, they are going together.

They stagger, sometimes crushed by a grinding force, sometimes floating above the shrapnel of the road. They run until the fragments under their feet coalesce into cobblestones. They are in the old town, or what's left of it, a mess of shards like the moment of an explosion. Thora sees herself in the sky, a flash of blue and a beckoning arm. She and Santi are painted on the stars, where they have always belonged. At the base of the clock tower, the words she finally wrote there—WHO WE ARE—stretch and yaw, eddying out to surround them. The tower splits and expands in a spinning helix, a drill boring into the sky. A feeling roots itself in Thora's heart, blossoms into a revelation.

"The stars." Thora points. "They're our way out."

"Yes." Santi laughs, looking at her in joy. "We finally know where we're going."

His hand tightens on hers as their feet leave the flickering ground. They are rising, toward the point where the sky tatters away, a palimpsest universe coming undone. The wind rises so high they have to shout to hear each other.

"There," says Santi in her ear, close enough to drown out the storm. "There, do you see?"

Thora can barely open her eyes. She squints upward where he's pointing, but the light fades, the stars sucked into the maw of the city below, pulling them with it. The square is massing with shapes, a crowd of people staring up. Something is wrong. They're not going to make it.

"We're falling," she tries to say, but the words come out garbled. Her breath pushes out, sucks in again, her body a bellows worked by something outside herself. The hands of the tower clock spin widdershins toward midnight. Time is running backward, unraveling them down to the ground. She holds on to Santi, even as she struggles to push time forward again, to reach the hole the tower is boring into the sky. They spiral down like the linked wings of a sycamore seed into the heart of the crowd. Time judders, resets, restarts.

"Dr. Lišková?" The Santi who was her patient, old and care-worn, an endless sorrow in his eyes.

"Thora, what's happening?"

She turns. He looks up at her, eight years old, lost: the Santi who needed her too much, who held her hand as they leapt from the tower.

Thora spins, looking for the real Santi, her Santi, but she has lost him in a crowd made entirely of himself. She pushes through, uselessly yelling his name, but there are too many of him and they all remember her, they all have a claim on her. They clutch at her, pulling her down until all she can hear is her name, repeated again and again in a hundred voices. A shudder, a crack splitting her into fragments, and everything stops.

IN THE STARS

Santi dreams of a message written on the sky.

He's so close to it—Thora's hand in his, the stars flickering all around them like candles in the dark—that he can't make out what it says. As they start to fall, he stares upward, trying to resolve the pattern, to read the truth he missed. But the message won't come clear. His vision blurs, the stars expanding to globes of light, merging with the flames that always wait at the corner of his eye.

He wakes in sunlight, uncertain who he is. Once, this feeling would have panicked him. Now, he flicks through selves like he's flicking through transparencies, light superimposing them all into one. Thora lies in bed next to him, which narrows down the possibilities. It's rare that they are both attracted to each other in the same life, but it still happens. He reaches out and strokes her cheek. She makes an inarticulate noise, burrowing into the sheets.

"Time to wake up," he says, kissing her frown.

Her voice is muffled. "What do you mean, wake up? This whole thing is probably a dream."

He smiles. "Oh, so you're dreaming about me?"

"Who said this is my dream?" She rolls over, sighing. "Anyway, it can't be a dream. It makes too much sense. If it was a dream, you'd be yourself but also my old physics teacher, and you'd be giving a surprise test I haven't prepared for while an army of goats tries to break the door down."

"I was your old physics teacher," he reminds her.

She makes a face. "If you think that turns me on, you still have a lot of lives to get to know me." She slides out of bed, pulling on a long cardigan and padding across the floorboards to the kitchen. He reaches for her, protesting, but she's gone, the sound of the filling kettle presaging coffee. A meow and a clatter echo from the kitchen. "Jesus, Félicette!"

He smiles. "Is she disrupting the space-time continuum again?"

"No more than usual." Thora pauses in a patch of sunlight, biting her nails. In that moment, she dazzles him, as though she is a window through which comes some rare and incandescent light. Thoughts move across her face like storm clouds. He wants to draw her, to collect this moment in his memory book. He wonders sometimes if his search for meaning has driven him crazy, if he is nothing but a mad old man filling his pockets with bright pebbles from the gutter. He hears the voice of another Thora. *Don't go raking through broken glass looking for diamonds.*

"I had that dream again," he says.

Thora's face changes. There are parts of her he will never see, his presence irrevocably altering how she is at rest. She turns as she pours the coffee. "The one where we're in the stars?"

He nods, looking up at the ceiling. "I really thought we'd found the answer." He returns to the idea he has clung to since his time on the streets, like a talisman worn smooth with rubbing. *The key is to know who you are. Only then will you know where you're going.* Does it feel true because it is, or because he wants it to be? He rubs his eyes, trying to dispel the blur from his dream. "I've been so sure, so many times, and it's always ended the same way." The same way, or worse. He looks down at his hands, remembering where his certainty once led him. A knife in Thora's heart.

She comes back to bed, a mug in each hand. "This time, I was sure too." A ghost of a smile crosses her face. "Both of us sure of the same thing. When has that happened before?"

Santi ponders the strange convergence of their perspectives: the moment they looked at each other and knew absolutely where they had to go. It felt like it meant something. But he's had that feeling too many times to trust it.

Thora tilts her head back against the wall. "I don't know why I thought it would work. It's literally the same thing I tried before, just in a different direction. If we can't escape by walking out of the city, why did I think we could escape by making it to the stars?"

Santi hears the bitterness of failure in her voice. Even though he feels it too, he doesn't want her to blame herself. "We don't know for sure it wouldn't have worked," he points out. "We fell before we actually made it."

She snorts. "Santi, we can't catch a train to Düsseldorf. How do you suggest we try and leave the planet? Build a very large ladder?" Her face changes, as if her words have struck against something in her memory. She clutches his arm. "Unless."

"Unless?"

Thora looks at him, her face alight. "You think everything in here means something. Stands for something."

"I did," he admits. His own use of the past tense jolts him. Is he really letting go of his long-held conviction? How could all of this be meaningless, after everything they've been through?

Thora's fingers tighten on his arm. "Here, in the city. What stands for the stars?"

Santi thinks about what the stars mean to him. Elsewhere; transcendence; the hope of discovery, of revelation. "The cathedral?" Thora shakes her head. "The university? The top of the clock tower?"

Thora's face screws up in amusement. "You're really overthinking this."

In a rush, he understands. How could he not have seen it before? "The planetarium."

A laugh escapes her, bright and joyous: a Thora he hasn't seen for lifetimes. In seconds, she's out of bed and on her feet. "Come on then," she says, pulling on her jeans. "What are we waiting for?"

He dresses quickly. As he follows her to the door, a wave of weakness runs through him. He catches himself on the wall.

Thora frowns. "What's wrong?"

"The usual," Santi says with effort. He pinches his forehead until it passes.

Thora bites her lip. "Maybe you need to cut back on the coffee."

He smiles. They both know his dizziness has nothing to do with what he drinks, any more than food can satisfy Thora's hunger. She gives him a look of pained understanding. "Let's go," she says, taking his arm.

It's Monday: the Odysseum is closed. The doors are chained shut, held by a simple padlock.

"This is where my skills come in handy," Santi says, unfolding his knife, as Thora picks up a rock and hurls it at the glass.

Santi braces for a siren that doesn't sound. "No alarm," he observes as he ducks through the shattered door.

"Who would break into a children's museum?" Thora asks, boots crunching on broken glass.

As Santi follows her past the ticket booths, his vision blurs. He stops, rubbing his eyes.

Thora comes back, touches his shoulder. "Dizzy again?"

He shakes his head. "Something new."

"How exciting." The worry on her face belies her sarcasm. "You'd better not die on me again. I'm starting to take it personally."

They pass through into the planetarium under the mirror gazes of empty spacesuits. Together, they stand looking up at the softly twinkling lights. Santi feels a sinking sense of anticlimax.

"We've been here a hundred times," Thora mutters. "What could there be that we haven't seen already?"

At the same moment, they realize. Without saying a word, they cut left into the hallway where the image from the Kepler telescope paints infinity on the wall. Ahead of them is a boarded-up door with a sign reading "im Bau/Under Construction."

"How many worlds?" Thora asks in a whisper.

"Every one I remember."

They look at each other. They step forward and grab the board from both sides.

"Three, two, one," Thora says. Santi heaves with her, and they use their combined strength to wrench the board away from the door.

The room beyond is dark. Santi hears a deep, whooshing hum as he gropes for a light switch. A glow from the ceiling falls on a series of display panels. At the other end of the room, where the sound is coming from, an image flickers on the wall. They split up: Thora heads for the wall, and Santi for the exhibit. He's ready for revelation, for truth no matter how terrible, for anything except what he sees.

This can't be right. He runs to the next panel, then the next, clutching at them like a drowning man. "They're blank," he says, choking. "All of them."

Thora doesn't answer. Santi stares at the terrible vacancy, embodying his worst fear: that the world is an empty cipher, that the message he has been waiting to hear for so long is nothing but white noise.

Dizziness rushes through him. The floor seems to move under his feet. He falls onto his back, staring up at the ceiling. The soft lights scatter randomly across the dark like chance constellations. No: not randomly. He raises himself up on his elbows, squinting through the blur. He's not imagining it: the lights form a star map. At one edge of the room, he recognizes the solar system. A course charted from Earth cuts across the ceiling in blue light. He follows it through swathes of darkness to the other side of the room, where it ends at a planet orbiting a small, pale star. There, a green light pulses, soft and expectant like a silent alarm.

"Santi."

In all their lifetimes, he has never heard Thora's voice sound like this.

He scrambles to his feet and runs to where she stands, facing the wall. Santi stares up at the giant image, trying to understand what he's seeing. A man and a woman in loose blue jumpsuits, tied up in tubes and wires, their eyes closed. He thinks he's looking at a still picture until he sees a green light moving infinitesimally along a small black screen. Over the minute and a half that he and Thora stand silent, it draws a crawling peak and subsides. A heart monitor in slow motion. In a flash of insight, he understands the humming sound: breathing, slowed down a hundredfold.

The man's hair is long, his beard untrimmed. The tips of the woman's hair are dyed blue. Santi's eyes flicker across the image, landing on the tattoo of a constellation on the woman's wrist.

"I don't understand," Thora whispers.

Santi looks into her eyes. "Thora," he says. "That's us. That's where we really are."

Thora stares at him in desperation. "Where?"

Santi steps back, looking for the final piece. A glass case under the video wall. He and Thora head for it at the same time. He leans over to see a model spacecraft, the top cut away so they can look inside. Fuel tanks, oxygen, water, supplies. And two tiny figures in separate compartments, the simulacra of the people on the screen.

He becomes aware of a sound, a ticking like an irregular clock. It hypnotizes him until he realizes it's Thora, tapping a silver plaque on the front of the case. *Peregrine*, it says. Below is a smaller version of the star map on the ceiling. Santi traces a course from Earth to an exoplanet orbiting Proxima Centauri.

For a long time, Thora doesn't speak. Finally, she looks up at him. "You're telling me we've spent lifetime after lifetime struggling and striving and longing to go to the stars, and we're *already fucking there?*"

It's such a Thora response that he laughs aloud. His laugh breaks through some wall in her. She laughs too, throwing her head back. "Santi, this is absurd. How could we—we can't be . . ." She's faltering, his endlessly argumentative Thora finally running out of words. "It doesn't make sense."

"It does." Santi taps the plaque. "Remember his name?"

Thora traces the letters. "Peregrine," she says softly. She straightens up, turns it into a summons. "Peregrine!"

He walks in as if he has been waiting outside. As the man in the blue coat limps toward them, Santi meets his eyes. Sad eyes, anxious eyes, like someone carrying a great burden.

"This is you?" Santi asks, pointing to the model ship in the glass case.

"Yes." Peregrine looks at Thora, his expression flickering from awe to tenderness to grief.

"He's an interface," Thora says. "Between us and the ship."

Santi was sure the man meant something, that he stood for something greater. It was true, but not in the way he imagined. He is a construct, built to turn a mind-melting complexity of matter into a form they can speak to.

Thora's voice trembles. "What is our mission? Why are we going to Proxima?"

"You . . ." Peregrine's eyes close, his face twitching. "First," he says finally. "To see, to seek, to know."

Joy bursts through Santi's heart, filling his veins with light. He was right all along, to believe there was a meaning. "Exploration," he says. "The first crewed mission to a planet outside the solar system."

"Yes."

Santi meets Thora's eyes. "What no one else has ever seen," he forces out through his rapture. "We're going to be the ones to see it."

Thora shakes her head, a violent, repetitive motion. "I can't believe it. I want to believe it too much—I—"

He takes her in his arms. "Believe it."

He feels the moment she succumbs, lets the knowledge become her reality. She gasps, her rib cage expanding against his like she is taking her first breath. "We fucking made it," she says fiercely in his ear.

"We'd always made it." He takes her hand, draws her back to look up at the two of them. He laughs hoarsely. "It's us. Look at us. There we are."

He can feel her shaking. "You're really rocking the Jesus look."

"Your hair *is* blue," he says. "Well, part of it."

"I would never dye my tips," Thora says scornfully. "That's short hair that's grown out."

At the same time, they realize what it means. Santi turns to Peregrine. "How long have we been in there?"

"For you—" Peregrine stutters, begins again. "Fifteen point three years."

"Fifteen—" Thora's eyes widen. "We've been in that box for fifteen years?"

Santi hallucinates the metal enclosing him, his body inert and powerless. He flexes his hands into fists. "How much longer until we arrive?"

Peregrine blinks, harrowed then calm in the space of a second. "Minus four point nine years."

Santi looks at Thora. "I'm sorry. Did you say—minus?"

Thora's face goes pale in the ghost-light. "He means we already arrived."

"What?"

"He told us. Don't you remember? He's been telling us, and telling us. *You're here.* Since that first time by the clock tower, worlds and worlds ago." Thora gazes into nothing. "The stars changed, and they stopped changing. We were traveling, and then we arrived."

"Almost five years ago." Santi feels the beginnings of panic, dizziness rushing over him. "So why haven't we woken up?"

Thora's voice is a command. "Peregrine. Wake us up."

Confusion crosses Peregrine's face. "Crew—cannot wake. In transit phase."

"We're not in fucking transit phase. We're here." Thora steps so close to Peregrine that a real person would reflexively step back. "Wake us up."

Santi thinks of the memory house, a jagged spar clutched in Thora's hand. He touches her shoulder. "Maybe we just need to ask him in the right way."

"We shouldn't have to ask him. He's supposed to initiate it." Thora spins, gesturing wildly to the blank panels at the other end of the room. "This room—it should be full of information about our mission. But it's not ready, because Peregrine thinks we're still traveling. That's why it's under construction." Thora laughs, bitter and knowing, like she's appreciating a clever joke at her own expense. "Listen to how he talks. Do you think they'd design an interface to work like that? He's fucking broken. Peregrine, are you functioning normally?"

Peregrine looks at Santi, lost. "Something happened."

"Something happened." Thora steps closer again. "That's what you said to me on the beach, when you collapsed. I thought you were having a stroke. But—you're not a person. How could you be having a stroke?"

"Not a stroke," Santi says. "A catastrophic error." He remembers the beach, the way the ground shook like the city was coming apart. He looks at Thora. "There was a collision. I felt it. You felt it. Peregrine—the computer systems must have been damaged." Dread is building in him, a claustrophobia that has nothing to do with the walls of this half-darkened room. "He knows we're here, but he can't shift out of transit phase. He can't wake us up."

Thora stares into Peregrine's eyes. "So what, you're just going to let us starve?" She points at the video screen, her hand shaking. "Look at us. I thought the jumpsuits were baggy. But we're fucking skeletal."

Santi follows her gaze. His unkempt beard hides it, but now he sees it in Thora's face: the unnatural prominence of her cheekbones, the pallor of her skin. It's an uncanny contrast to the version of her that stands in front of the screen, vibrant and alive.

"The supplies," he says to Peregrine. "Oxygen, food, water. There must have been more than we needed for the journey here, or we'd already be dead. How much do we have? Enough for the journey back?" *Five years gone, so at least five years more. We'd be stranded until we found a way to replace them, but maybe we could figure it out—*

Peregrine shakes his head. "Fuel and supplies for return—sent ahead. To planet. Crew—pick up—on arrival."

Santi exhales. "All right. But there was a safety margin?"

Peregrine nods.

Thora snorts. "A safety margin we've been burning through for four point nine years."

Santi ignores her. "How long do we have left?"

Peregrine's face flickers. "One month."

"In real time?"

"Yes."

Santi turns to the crawling green line of the heart monitor. "How long is that in here?"

"Eight years."

Silence settles in the darkened room. Santi thinks of the days, the months in the city that stretch between them and annihilation. It feels like forever and less than a heartbeat.

Thora shakes her head, marching past Santi toward the door.

"Where are you going?" he asks her.

She doesn't turn. "I don't know about you, but I need a fucking drink."

They walk back across the river, the skyline a dark smear against the morning sky. The strangest thing is how real it still seems. Santi can know intellectually that he is walking through an illusion, and still believe in the breeze on his face, the gray roll of the water, the sounds of the city waking as they reach the bank and turn left toward the old town.

When they get to Der Zentaur, it's still closed. Thora inverts one of the upended chairs outside and sits down. Inside, Santi sees Brigitta setting up. He waves at her. She taps her watch and shakes her head.

"The clock," Thora says. "It was a countdown."

Santi follows her gaze to the tower, hands stuck at midnight for so many worlds. Four years eleven months of compressed time. Four years eleven months of supplies gone. He tries to summon the trained professional he doesn't remember being. "We need to assess the situation and come up with a plan."

Thora hiccups with laughter. "All right. Here's the situation. We're exactly where we've always wanted to be, but we can't see or touch it. And if we don't find a way out, we're going to starve to death inside a metal box without ever waking up." She darts a glance through the window of Der Zentaur. "Where's my wine?"

"Brigitta's still opening up."

"Brigitta's not fucking real." Thora gets to her feet and hammers on the door. After a brief, tense conversation Santi can't hear, Thora comes back to the table with a wine and a lager. She raises her glass. "To achieving our dreams," she says bitterly.

Santi clinks with feeling.

Thora puts her glass down, making a face. "It's not the same now thatI know the real me is getting all my fluids intravenously."

Santi takes a sip of his lager. "Still tastes real to me."

"But it's not. None of this is. What we just saw is definitive proof." Thora shakes her head. "I get that it makes sense to put us under for the journey. To make a fake world to keep us entertained. But why not let us remember where we really are?"

Santi shivers, thinking of the close metal walls surrounding his real body. "Maybe it's important for us to accept the reality of this place. I guess that's why they put copies of our loved ones in here. Héloïse. Jaime. Lily."

"Jules." Thora toys with her glass, a strange tenderness on her face. "I want to see her. I mean, the real her."

"Maybe you will," he says. "When we get back."

She looks at him as if she's afraid to hope. "Ten years out, ten years back, plus however long we're going to spend on the planet? Not to mention five years' unscheduled delay? No one would wait that long."

"You don't know that."

Thora takes a morose swallow of wine. "No wonder she kept breaking up with me. *I'd* break up with me. Can you imagine? *Hey babe, I signed up for a twenty-plus-year mission across the far reaches of space, no hard feelings, see you when I get back!*"

Santi smiles sadly, thinking of Héloïse, of the look in her eyes he has seen again and again: anxious, expectant, waiting for the moment he would leave. "We may know them, but we only know them from one side," he reminds her. "You think Jules would want you to stay, so that's how you imagine her. But the real Jules might not want what you think she does." He taps Thora's hand. "Think about it. Everything here was by design. They must have agreed to the use of their likenesses, their personalities. It means Jules wanted to send part of herself with you."

Thora gives him a pained smile. Santi tries to imagine it: coming back to Earth, stepping out into the eyes of the waiting crowd. "On the video," he says. "How old did we look?"

"I don't know. Late thirties? Hard to tell when we're half-starved." Thora gnaws on her nail. "It's so weird to think about being one age. At this point, I feel like every age I've ever been." Watching him, her face changes. "You're thinking about your parents."

He nods.

"They'll be fine," she says. "Healthy Mediterranean lifestyle, all that olive oil. Mine, on the other hand . . ." She throws her wine back in illustration. "I suppose they might have pickled themselves," she mutters.

Santi knows it's her way of coping, but he can't smile. He imagines the version of himself that left his mother and father, knowing he would likely never see them again. The real version. He wishes he could say it feels impossible. A sudden pain pulses between his eyes. He presses on his temples, inhaling until it passes.

"Shit," Thora says. "It's worse than that."

Santi tries to focus on her. "What do you mean?"

"Relativity." She moves her glass of wine aside. "Proxima Centauri is four point two light-years from Earth. If it only took us ten years to get here, we must have been traveling at a reasonable fraction of the speed of light."

Santi nods. "More time will pass back home."

"How much more?" Thora unfolds her napkin and holds out

her hand for Santi's pen. "Subjective journey time, ten point four years," she mutters. "So, twenty point eight years round trip. Assuming constant acceleration . . ." She scribbles down the formula.

Santi leans over, fascinated. "You can calculate hyperbolic sines in your head?"

"To an approximation." Thora frowns. "Time passed on Earth should be . . . around twenty-three years. Compared to twenty-one for us." She laughs.

Santi gives her a puzzled look. "Why is that funny?"

"Jules will finally get her wish. When we get back, she'll be a year older than me." She stops, correcting herself. "If we get back."

"We'll get back."

Thora meets his eyes. After a long moment, she drains the last of her wine. "Okay. Situation assessed. I'm ready to come up with a plan."

Santi rubs his temples. "Here's how I see it. We have an interface with the ship. I suggest we use it."

"Peregrine?" Thora snorts. "He's about as much use as a broken toaster. I already asked him to wake us up. Twice."

"You only asked him one way."

Thora rolls her eyes. "So we should say please?"

"That's not what I mean." Santi leans across the table. Something is wrong: Thora is getting further and further away. "The error has affected his language, right? Maybe if we ask the right way, we can get around his mental block."

"You're suggesting we try and *argue* our way out of here?"

"God knows we've had enough practice." He can't see Thora clearly, but he can still tell she's giving him a look. "Let me guess," he says wearily. "You propose a different approach."

Thora's voice comes out of the blur. "I want to go back to the Odysseum. Watch the video, go over every inch of that model ship. There has to be something we can—Santi?"

He goes to rub his eyes, but his hand won't obey. He tries to stand, but his feet won't support his weight. He collapses.

"Santi." Thora's voice, urgent in the darkness. The cobbles press against his back.

"Thora." *Did you break the world again?* She's shouting for help, and he's floating, free of the cobbles, free of the restraints around his real body, on his way to the stars.

He wakes in a hospital bed. Thora sits in a chair by the window, biting her nails.

"It's cancer. Again," she says when his eyes open. "Brain tumor this time. Inoperable. They're giving you less than a month."

A month in the simulation; a matter of hours in real time. Santi hallucinates himself in his body, half-starved and feather-light, and feels a thrill of claustrophobic reality. He rubs his eyes. "Thanks for breaking it to me gently."

"Don't worry." Thora shakes a bottle of pills. "Remember, I'm a pro at thwarting destiny. I'll follow you. We can try again next time."

Santi sits up, fighting the fog in his mind. A dawning horror breaks through. "No."

Thora crosses her arms. "If you're seriously going to try and argue me out of killing myself—"

"It's not that." He grips the thin hospital sheet with sweating hands. "We only have eight years left. If we die—yes, we come back, but there's no guarantee we'll come back together. Sometimes we've arrived in the city ten, twenty years apart."

Realization spreads across Thora's face. "I guess it's part of the design," she says. "To give each of us periodic breaks from the simulation. But if the clock starts as soon as one of us gets back—"

"By the time we both arrive, we could already be dead." Terror transfixes Santi, worse than the fear he felt when he saw the blank panels in the museum. He could die between lives and it would mean nothing. All their striving, everything they have learned from each other, all for them to end as two corpses in a box, cut off from an elsewhere they will never see.

"Fuck." Thora gets to her feet, paces across the room. "Fuck! I don't believe this. What, are they trying to keep things interesting?" She punches the wall.

"Thora." He needs her to stop, to damp down her anger and give his own room to blaze.

She doesn't understand. "Of course. This is where you tell me there's a reason." Her voice drips with bitterness. "Go on. Tell me what it all means."

He screams it at her. "I can't!"

Thora stares at him without recognition. He waits for her to fight back, to demand the argument he's denying her. Another Thora might have done that, long ago. But this one closes her eyes and nods. When she leaves, she shuts the door quietly behind her.

Santi stares at the hospital ceiling, gray tiles spidered with meaningless faultlines. He has tried so hard, all his long lives, to understand. What he saw in the darkened exhibit hall felt like the ultimate vindication: there is a meaning, a purpose to their existence, and it is the one he has dreamt of since before he can remember. For that to be destroyed, by something so senseless, so arbitrary as a randomly programmed death, feels like the root of his world being torn out.

Thora isn't here to see. He doesn't have to be strong for her. He weeps in rage until he falls into an exhausted, furious sleep.

When he wakes, a curtain has been drawn around his bed. He feels vague, groggy, half-there. Symptoms of his imaginary illness, or his real starvation? It doesn't matter. There is only one question in his mind now, and only one person who can answer it.

"Peregrine," he says.

The door opens. The man in the blue coat ducks through the curtain and stands by the end of the bed. Santi remembers how it felt when he tried this the first time: when he spoke a name to the air and the answer walked in. There in the memory house, he took Peregrine for a channel to God, a mouthpiece of the universe. But he was only another hollow revelation, a puzzle box with nothing inside. Santi takes him in, his lank hair, his bewildered face. He has freckles. Who thought to give an anthropomorphic construct freckles? "Peregrine," Santi says. "Why do we have to die?"

Peregrine frowns. "I—I don't . . ." He trails off.

Santi draws in a breath. However long it takes, he has to understand. "This is a simulation," he says. "Whoever designed it could have chosen to compress time differently. To have us live one long life. Why not?"

Peregrine tilts his head. "Transit phase."

We're not in transit phase. A Thora response, jumping to the front of Santi's mind as naturally as if it were his own. He closes his eyes, searching for the calm that used to come so easily, but it's as impossible as grasping a flame. "What does dying over and over have to do with transit phase?" he snaps.

Peregrine's face flickers from anguish to serenity. "Part—part of the plan."

"Wow," Santi says, scratching his chin. "Thora's right. That *is* annoying." Peregrine looks at him with open curiosity. "Why?"

Santi asks, his voice thick with all they have been through. "Even if you have to kill us, why not kill us at the same time? Why do we come back the same but different, again and again? What plan is it part of?"

Peregrine's mouth opens, then closes. He tries again. "Not enough. Two people. Need—every one. Of you, of him. That was—" His brow furrows. "Sorry. Something—"

"Happened. We know." Thora pulls back the curtain. How long has she been listening? She looks at Santi, and what he sees in her face breaks his heart. "They're discharging you," she says. "We're going home."

She takes him back to their apartment in the Belgian Quarter. As she lowers him onto the sofa, Santi stares past her at the raindrops dotting the gray square of the window. His rage has subsided, leaving behind a quiet despair. "How do you do it?" he asks her.

She looks down at him with a pity he can't bear. "Do what?"

"Go on. Live." His voice sticks in his throat. "When you don't know if there's a meaning."

Thora sits down next to him. "Spite?" When he gives her a look, she smiles. "I guess—I make my own meaning. From my life, the world, the people I love." She brushes his hair back from his forehead. "That's probably not enough for you, is it? You want Meaning with a capital M. A message written by God in the stars, telling you the way you should go."

Tears spring to his eyes. He can't look at her. "You don't believe that exists."

He doesn't know how many thoughts she lets pass unspoken. "I don't know," she finally answers. "But if it does exist, I'm okay with not knowing what it says." She looks at him seriously. "Maybe that's the only way to survive this. To be okay with not knowing." She stands, patting her pocket for the keys.

"Where are you going?"

"To find a way to wake us up."

Santi tries to lift himself. "I'll come with you."

"Santi, you can't stand up for more than five minutes without fainting. Sorry, but you're not the most useful person to have around right now." She pauses in the doorway. "I'll come back."

A memory, half-imagined: Thora in the life where she helped raise him, disentangling herself from his childish, clutching hands. *I always come back*, she told him then. This time, she doesn't promise so much.

He lies on the sofa, Félicette purring under one hand while he slowly slips away. Thora comes and goes, but it seems to Santi that she is there more often than not: sitting with him, helping him to the bathroom, feeding him miracle food scavenged from the void. He watches her bring home a haul of identical bread buns, apples, cans of soup, and marvels at her: a survival expert adapted to the strangest of environments. She has always been stronger than him. Even when she was a seven-year-old child and he was her teacher, full of misapprehensions and doubts: perhaps especially then.

He's suddenly angry with her. "Why are you wasting time looking after me?" he protests.

Thora looks over her shoulder at him as she opens a can of soup. "Because if you were me and I was you, you wouldn't leave me to die alone."

It's true, but Santi doesn't care. "This isn't fair." He tries to sit up. "It shouldn't be happening."

"You're absolutely right," Thora says in a calm voice.

He lies back, fuming silently. When she brings him the soup, he sniffs it suspiciously. "What kind is this?"

"The miracle kind. Why, does it smell weird?" Thora pulls the bowl back. "Maybe you shouldn't eat it."

He rolls his eyes at her. "What, in case it gives me some kind of incurable disease?"

She glares at him. "Stop trying to be me. It's not cute."

"I'm not trying." He takes a shallow sip. "We've both collected plenty of pieces of each other by now."

Thora frowns. Then she laughs.

"What?" he asks.

She smiles ruefully. "I was about to say that's bullshit. But look at me. Patiently feeding you soup while you rail against the injustice of the universe." She looks away, holding out her fist for Félicette to rub up against. "I spent so long defining myself in opposition to you. At first it was subconscious, but later—I guess I was scared. Of how much I'd taken from you."

Santi looks at her, remembering a letter he once wrote. *I don't know how much of me is me anymore and how much of me is you.* It's almost a comfort. When he goes, part of him will remain, as long as Thora is alive.

"Don't follow me," he says, on impulse.

"What?"

"Stay." He takes her hand. "Use the time you have. Don't risk it just for the chance I'll come back."

"Would that be enough meaning for you? Sacrificing yourself so I could get out?" She shakes her head. "You really should have been a martyr. How you would have enjoyed being eaten by lions." She takes the soup bowl from him. "Thanks for the offer, but I'll decline, if it's all the same to you. We don't tend to do well when we stop talking to each other."

He shifts away from her. "I don't know what you mean."

"I'm referring to the time I decided to throw your cat and your wife into a void and you decided to stab me." She smiles. "Besides. What if I get out, and then I still can't wake you up?" Her brow furrows. "Both of us, or neither of us. Okay?"

It's not okay, but he's too tired to argue. He sinks back into the sofa, eyes closing.

When he wakes, Thora is there. "How are you feeling?" she asks.

"I don't know," he says honestly. "How am I alive? How are you here?"

She pokes his arm gently. "That was not a philosophical question. Can I get a serious answer?"

Santi feels his grip on this world loosening. The Thora in front of him seems more and more like a mirage. "The serious answer is that it's serious." He swallows. "I don't think I have much time left."

She nods. "Okay," she says, her voice hoarse. He understands. They have lost each other so many times, but this is different: neither of them knows for sure if they are coming back.

Santi decides it doesn't matter if he knows. He chooses to hope. A fragile, tentative hope, compared to the deep faith of his old, sure self, but all the more precious for that. "In real life," he says. "Do you think we're friends?"

"No. We probably hate each other." She looks down at him fondly. "As soon as I wake up, I'll remember how much. Then I'll throw you out of the airlock."

He laughs. "This may shock you, but I disagree."

"Well," she sighs, "it wouldn't be the first time."

"I look forward to continuing this argument in our next life." He wants to keep his eyes open, to keep the sight of her as long as he can, but he's so tired, so ready for an ending. He lets them drift closed. In the darkness, points of light hover unreachably far away. There's a pattern here: one he may never understand, at least not while he is alive. But he chooses to believe the pattern exists, whether or not he can see it. "Ah," he sighs, something like peace stealing over him. "Thora, I wish you could see this."

Her voice is quiet, getting quieter. "What is it? What are you seeing?"

Through the pain, a smile spreads across his face. "The stars."

ONLY ONE CHOICE

○ ☀ ◉

Thora lives.

In a strange, accelerated place, between somewhere and no-where. She watches her life happen from a distance, like an audi-ence who knows the magician's tricks: sees the secret door in the drowning cabinet, the assistant swimming free. The early move from the Netherlands to the UK that should have fractured her. The chance comment from her father that was supposed to lodge in her mind forever. She floats through it all, a skillful sailor on a sea she knows by heart. At thirty-five, she rides the wave to a crest and leaps, landing on her feet outside the Hauptbahnhof, the cathedral rising above her into the cloudless summer sky. Here she is, back in Cologne again as if she never left.

She takes in a shuddering breath. She's not dead. There may still be time to find a way out. She runs, abandoning the suit-case she brought with her. The staring people fade into the back-ground as she pelts past the cathedral, one goal in her mind. Get to Der Zentaur. Wait for Santi.

It doesn't occur to her that she might not be the first one there until she sees the mural on the building across the street: a blue-haired girl sitting on top of the clock tower, her profile making a gap in the stars.

She stares up at it in mingled joy and dread. Santi is already here. How long has he been in the city without her?

She hurries on past a food truck, the frying smell tugging at the emptiness inside her. She didn't think the hunger could get worse. She forces herself on, into the narrowing streets of the old town. Colors blaze on the white wall of one of the old beer houses. Another mural: a lighthouse, parakeets flying out through the lantern room's shattered glass.

They keep appearing. On the next street corner; above an archway that spans the alley, leaning over her as she walks beneath. Mural after mural in Santi's unmistakable style. The old town turning inside out, the clock tower drilling into the sky. A fox and a wolf, hunting together under the stars. Passing each one, Thora tallies in her head the weeks it must have taken, subtracting precious hours from what's left of their lives. By the time she comes out into the shadow of the tower, her unease is crystallizing into despair.

Santi is waiting for her outside Der Zentaur, drawing in his memory book. Thora stops, taken aback by the intensity of her reaction. For the first time since she remembered him, she wasn't sure if she would ever see him again.

He looks up. When he sees her, his face crumples in what looks like sorrow before it turns to heartfelt delight. He stumbles to his feet as she runs toward him. "I never stopped hoping," he mutters as he catches her in his arms.

His voice is thick. Thora realizes he's crying. She pulls back from him. "How long have you been here?"

He closes his eyes. "Seven years."

"Fuck." She drops into a seat on the other side of the table, feeling savagely vindicated. Of course they're almost out of time before they even start. "One year left to find a way out."

Santi doesn't look worried. Through his tears, he's grinning like God just handed him the keys to heaven. "How are you feeling?"

With effort, Thora looks past her memories and sees him as he is: short-haired, clean-shaven, as if he's trying to look as little like his real self as possible. She notes in passing that this version of her doesn't find him attractive at all. "So hungry I can barely function," she says. "You?"

He grimaces. "Light-headed. Slow. Like I'm thinking through a fog." He runs his hands through his hair. "Not ideal for trying to win a riddle contest with a mad god."

"You mean Peregrine?" He nods. Thora leans back with a smirk. "Of course you would actually put your insane plan into action."

Santi sighs. "I've tried everything. Showing him the clock. Showing him the stars. Telling him in a hundred different ways that we're here. But none of it works."

"He already knows we're here," Thora points out.

"But he can't connect that knowledge to the part of him that's convinced we're still in transit phase." Santi shrugs. "He just— believes. It's hard to argue with that."

"Tell me about it," says Thora dryly. Her hands itch. She wants to smoke, but she resolved last time to quit forever. She hates the idea of spiraling down into the worst version of herself. "Have you got anything useful out of him?"

"He has total control over the ship and its operations," Santi says. "So even if we can't get him to wake us up, we could get him to do something."

"Like what?" Thora says sourly, stealing a sip of his lager. "Fix himself?"

Santi shakes his head. "He can't even diagnose himself. He knows something's wrong, but he can't find out exactly what, let alone fix it."

"Just like the rest of us, then." Thora's head drops onto her arms. "God, Santi. I really, really wanted us to get out. And not just so we could see what we came here to see. I wanted to get home again afterward. I wanted us to get back to Earth and be big fucking heroes and go on stupid TV shows and inspire kids to be astronauts. All that wonderful, wonderful bullshit. And I wanted to see the people I love. The real versions, not their echoes."

He looks at her curiously. "Why are you talking in the past tense?"

"I just—" She shakes her head. "We have to be realistic about our chances. We're running out of time. In real life, we have days."

"But in here, we have a year." Unbelievably, Santi is smiling. "Now you're with me, we'll find a way. I know we will."

"I see," she says with a bitter laugh. "I can't believe, after everything we've seen, you're still talking about a miracle."

He gives her his most serene expression, the one she hates. "We see them every day."

"Oh, yes. I'm sure a magically refilling cup of coffee is going to end up being the key to everything." She stands. "Come on then. Let's go and check on how your beard's growing."

"So how does this work?" she asks as they weave through the crowded lobby of the Odysseum. "Do you have to break in again every time, or does the room stay open?"

Santi shrugs. "I haven't tried since we broke in together last time." To her incredulous look, he answers, "I was waiting for you."

"At what point were you going to accept that I wasn't coming?"

He looks at her as if that's an irrelevant question. "You're here, aren't you?"

"That's not an answer!" They're at the "Under Construction" barrier. Curious museumgoers stop to watch as they brace to pull it away from the wall. "I can't believe—"

"Hey!"

Thora looks over her shoulder. A man in an Odysseum polo shirt stands watching them, arms crossed. "What are you doing?"

She sighs. "We are orbiting an exoplanet four point two light-years from Earth. We have lived more lives than we can count, and we are tired, and we are hungry. We do not have time for this."

The man stares, lost. "I don't know what to say."

"You people never do." Thora looks back at Santi. "Three, two, one—"

No one follows them inside. It's as if the darkened mission hall is invisible to everyone else. Thora goes straight to the video wall, starved for a glimpse of reality. Are the two of them thinner than she remembers, or is she imagining it? The last time she stood here, Santi was dying twice over: on the video before her eyes, and back in their flat, sinking into a programmed oblivion. She blamed that illusory death for distracting her from finding a way out of the real one. She thought what she needed was a new self, a new perspective. But she stands here now the same old Thora, without any new ideas.

"It's not easy." Santi looks up in mingled awe and terror, like a worshipper witnessing saints in the flesh. "Seeing what we've come to."

"But it's real." Thora watches the crawling green line of their hearts, listens to the deep, slow hum of their breathing. She knows she should be grateful that time in the simulation passes a hundredfold slower than time on the ship, stretching and magnifying their last days. But it's tortuous too, a slow starvation made almost endless.

The image changes, showing a dim metal room. The only light comes from two glass panels, a face visible through each one.

"There's another camera?" Santi asks.

Thora still can't understand why he has spent all these years hiding in the simulation instead of confronting their real selves. "Outside our compartments."

He steps closer. "What's that?"

"What?"

"That dark patch on the wall." He points. "Looks like a scorch mark."

Thora lifts her hand as if she can touch the cold metal. "I think there was a fire. After the collision."

Santi inhales sharply. "We're lucky to be alive."

"I guess good old P put it out before it could cause too much damage." Thora fixates on their shadowed faces through the glass.

"Nice of them to give us windows to look out of," Santi remarks.

"Not like we'd see much except our own reflections." Thora stares at the video as it switches back to a close-up of their dying bodies. "It's hopeless," she says. "All we can do is watch."

"So stop watching." Santi touches her back. "Come on. Let's get out of here."

*   *   *

Thora is expecting him to show her a particularly poignant mural, or, worst-case, a church. She isn't expecting to find herself in his flat in the Belgian Quarter—a flat that, with its dark blue sofa and crochet blanket, could belong to almost any of the Santis she has known—while he makes her a cup of tea. As the kettle boils, she stares at the star map on the wall, willing it to dissolve, to reveal the wall of her compartment and the real stars beyond.

Félicette meows and rubs up against her ankle. Thora leans down absently to pet her, using her free hand to sort through the uncharacteristic mess on the table. A copy of *The Last Days of Socrates*, annotated in Santi's neat hand. Sketches for murals in his usual dreamlike style. Other papers, less familiar: diagrams, schematics, logical flowcharts. Visual aids for his attempts to argue with Peregrine.

She looks up at him as he deposits the tea in front of her. "Nice place," she says. "Anyone would think you actually lived here."

Santi sits down. "I've been here seven years," he reminds her. "Did you think I'd be sleeping in the gutter just to prove a point?"

"I didn't think you'd be sleeping at all. I thought you'd be spending every second trying to find a way out." She stares at him accusingly. "All this talk about waiting for me, about how you're so sure we'll figure it out now I'm here. It's just another way of saying you've given up."

"I haven't given up," he protests.

Thora points at Félicette. "You have a cat. Universal symbol for *I'm not going anywhere.*"

"I'm still trying." Santi holds up a bundle of drawings and ideas. "I've been trying, all this time. I just don't think we're going to come up with a solution by constantly staring our deaths in the face." Thora looks away. He taps her hand gently. "Remember the times we were scientists? The answer wouldn't always come when we were looking for it. It would come in the gaps, when we were busy doing something else."

"We're not *for* anything else." Thora gestures at the flat, at Félicette, at his mother's crochet blanket, so familiar she could remake it from scratch. "We left all this behind, Santi. Everything we knew. Everyone who loved us. Because we cared about being explorers, about touching the unknown, more than we cared about anything else. Maybe that's selfish, but it's who we are. It's what we did. We can't run away from that."

"You're right," he says. "But there's another way of looking at it." He sorts through the papers until he finds the drawing he's looking for. He turns it toward Thora. It shows the two of them tied back-to-back blindfolded, their hands and feet bound. But where a bright light casts their shadows, they are free, and they run.

He meets her eyes. "We gave up the prime of our lives to spend them sleeping in a metal box. We made that sacrifice willingly, for the sake of the journey. But a lot of people put in a lot of work to make sure that wasn't all we would experience." He picks up Félicette, sits her in his lap while he strokes her chin. "And I think they made that decision for a reason. This world may be an illusion, but it's given us the space to grow, to learn. To think beyond the bounds we're trapped in."

Thora crosses her arms. "What's your point?"

"This—this life, this world—is a gift. I think we should start treating it like one."

"And I think that sounds dangerously close to treating it like reality. We can't forget for a second where we really are." She picks up a sheaf of his sketches, brandishing them at him. "Why are you still making these? Pictures of our imaginary lives? We already know who we are. How is this helping us find a way out?" She feels her anger surging, but she doesn't resist it. This is part of who she needs to be: the person who challenges him, who jolts him out of his complacency. She sweeps a pile of drawings to the floor. "Wake up, Santi. Or we're both going to die in our sleep."

He sets Félicette gently down and kneels to put his drawings in order. "I'm not sleeping," he says. "I'm wide awake. You're the one who's closing your eyes to everything that brought us this far."

Thora stares. "Stop."

He looks up at her, frustrated. "What?"

She grabs at the drawing in his hand. Baffled, he lets her take it. She looks down at the cross-hatched scribble of a familiar face: long-haired, bearded, wreathed in shadows. "You painted this in the memory house."

He nods, getting warily to his feet. "The face I saw when I fell from the tower."

She looks up at him. "It's you."

"What?"

"I don't know why I didn't recognize it before." She holds it up. "I guess when I saw your painting, I hadn't seen the video. I didn't know what you look like in real life."

Santi smiles. "En un mal espejo, confusamente," he murmurs. His gaze becomes urgent. "Thora. When you fell. You said you saw a woman."

The face is burned into Thora's memory. Long-haired, shadowed, framed in blazing light. She was looking so hard for an enemy that she didn't recognize herself.

"Our reflections," she says. "In the glass panels of our compartments." Her eyes meet Santi's. "We must have woken up."

They head for the door. Neither of them speaks until they

stand in the shadow of the tower. Thora watches Santi climb through the gap that leads inside.

"Wait," she says.

He turns, framed in the dark. "What's wrong?"

Thora faces him, old bloodstains under her feet. Too much has happened between them in this place. She bites her lip. "We both think this is the right thing to do."

Santi tilts his head, almost laughing. "If we agree for once, isn't that a good thing?"

Thora's eyes travel up the tower, the clock face unreadable at this angle. "This could be our last chance. If we're doing this, I don't want us to just agree. I want us to agree on why."

Santi spreads his arms as if it's obvious. "We know it worked before."

"For a second," Thora says. "But then the simulation just reset. What makes you think it'll be different this time?"

"Back then, we didn't know what we were seeing. This time, we'll know it's reality. We'll recognize ourselves, and we'll be able to hold on."

"How can you know that?"

He shrugs. "I can't. But I'm willing to hope." Thora's heart sinks. Santi steps out of the tower. "I don't understand. If you're not sure, why do you think we should do it?"

She leans back against the stones, feeling like a cornered animal. "Because we're not going to think of anything else. This is all we've got."

Santi comes to face her. "That's the wrong reason."

"So is yours," she argues. "We can't just try the same thing again out of misguided hope it'll turn out differently."

"We can't do it out of desperation either."

Dread settles in Thora's stomach. An easy solution gone, and nothing to replace it. She sits down against the tower, picking at the grass that grows between the cobbles. "It's all right for you," she says sourly. "You probably believe you're going somewhere else after you starve to death inside a tin can."

"I do," Santi admits, sitting down next to her. "But I don't want to die without seeing what we came here to see." Thora follows his gaze across the square to the hanging sign of Der Zentaur. "Last time," he says. "When I was dying. It was hard for me to accept that we might not make it. But in the end, I chose to believe that we will. I chose hope."

"But hope isn't always a good thing," Thora argues. "Hope can paralyze you. Make you wait around for salvation instead of seeking it yourself." She looks at him, pleading. "We might not make it, Santi. We have to accept that."

He shakes his head, stubborn as always. "And if we're sure we won't make it, then we won't be able to see a way out. Even if it's right in front of us."

Thora feels the void in her belly spreading out through the rest of her. "You're right," she admits.

"So are you."

Even after all this time, he can still surprise her. She laughs, her head knocking back against the stones. "How can we both be right?"

"Because of who we are." He bumps her shoulder. "Think about it. To make it here—to be the people who set out on this mission—we had to have both. Hope and despair. We had to hold them in our minds at the same time."

"Know the difference between an acceptable risk and an act of desperation," Thora says, not sure if she's inventing or remembering. "Be willing to lose everything, but ready to fight to keep it."

Santi nods. "Hold on with one hand, and let go with the other."

She looks sideways at him. "Are you saying you can do all that?"

"Not yet." He gets to his feet. "But I can try to learn."

Thora sighs deeply, taking his hand and rising. "Maybe we both can."

Balancing hope and despair. It sounds easy enough until you try it. A week later, Thora sits in front of the annihilation portal, throwing glow-in-the-dark stars stolen from the Odysseum gift shop one by one into the void. There's an odd, bitter satisfaction in watching a fake representation of her dream dissolve into nothingness, over and over. She's aiming the last star in her stack when she hears a familiar voice. "Are you okay?"

Thora's heart turns over. Of course. Lovely Jules, who can't stumble upon a stranger looking upset without trying to help.

She looks over her shoulder, considering her possible answers. *Yes, I'm fine. No, I'm trapped inside a lie while my body whirls around a distant planet a few short days from starvation.* "Hi," she says.

"Hi." Jules frowns as she climbs the fence. "So was that a yes or a no?"

Thora turns and shifts backward, putting herself between Jules and the portal. "It's complicated."

Jules sits down cross-legged in front of her. "Why not tell me about it?"

Thora laughs. "Because you'd think I'm crazy?"

"I like crazy."

"Then you're going to love me."

"Am I now?" Jules smiles, and her dimples break Thora's heart. "Why don't we start with a coffee and see how it goes?"

Thora thinks about it. Maybe it doesn't matter that Jules isn't really here. Maybe there is enough of her in this simulacrum for Thora to love, to love Thora back. She knows now which version of her Jules likes best. She knows how to make her happy, how to make her stay. She could spend the last year of her life in a glorious dream, loved into oblivion.

She wants it so much it hurts. But this isn't Jules, not really. This is her own idea of Jules: a partial, one-sided portrait that could never measure up to her reality. The real Jules loved her enough to know what she wanted more than anything, to send this echo of herself along for the ride. Santi was right: it's a generous gift. But it's not enough, not for the version of herself that Thora wants to be.

She shakes her head. "I don't think so."

Jules looks hurt. "I guess I got the wrong idea."

"You didn't. You got exactly the right idea."

Jules laughs in frustration, the way she always laughs at Thora's strange moods. "Then why not get a coffee with me?"

Because you're an echo of someone real I left behind. Echoes aren't enough to keep a person alive. "I just—can't," she says. "Not right now."

"Okay," Jules says. "Does that mean maybe later?"

Later. There might not be a later for Thora. But then again, there might. In the moment Jules smiles at her, both possibilities exist at the same time. The hope of seeing her again; the risk of losing her forever.

"How about—" The thought makes her laugh before she says it. "How about I look you up when I'm back on Earth?"

Jules smiles, getting to her feet. "All right, space girl. I'll be waiting."

*　*　*

They keep trying. Thora drags Santi with her to the Odysseum to watch the grainy video of their real selves, poring over the feed for any detail they might have missed. In return, she sits by his side and listens to him argue with Peregrine until words lose all meaning. A hundred times, one of them comes up with a plan; a hundred times, the other one dismisses it. One day, they will find the possibility that lies between hope and despair, and be the right people to grasp it.

Until then, Thora lives a half-life in the city, in it but not of it. She thought by now she had seen all of time's tricks: the elastic summers of childhood, the speeding-up sight of a beautiful girl, the way years, in hindsight, can seem to have flashed past like seconds. But she has never experienced anything like this. Now, she is painfully aware of time passing, the days that are minutes to their sleeping selves. On the afternoons when she walks the river path back from the Odysseum, she watches her shadow lengthen, imagining a heartbeat that lasts a hundred seconds. Sometimes, she thinks she can hear it.

Santi keeps painting his murals, until they spread all across the city from Deutz to Ehrenfeld. At night, Thora ventures out to embroider them with words: fragments of conversations, point and counterpoint in what she now recognizes as one long argument. Finally, she stands under the clock tower, facing its broken wall. Painted over the layers of graffiti is a mural of Peregrine as they know him, the ship that bears his name cradled in his upturned hand. Thora adds a speech bubble coming out from the window. *Help*, it reads. *We're trapped inside this bird*.

Santi laughs when he sees it. "Perfect." He touches up the paint, never quite finished, never quite satisfied. Thora watches him working, frowning in concentration, until he stops. "What?"

"Nothing," she says. "Just—if I have to be temporarily stuck in a broken simulation with someone, I'm glad it's you."

He pulls her close and kisses her cheek. "Me too."

Following his lead, Thora tries to pay attention to the beauties of this place. It's easier now that she can see it as something created, something built with love. The light reflecting from the ripples on the water; the quiet hum of repeated conversations in the background of Der Zentaur; the flights of the parakeets from tree to tree and back. Even the mistakes have a sweetness to them, like familiar imperfections on a beloved face. Because, she realizes, she does love it: a painful, tired love, like the love you feel for a friend who has let you down, but who is so much a part of you that you cannot imagine yourself without them. Still, that's all she does. Imagine a way out, built of the tiny revelations she and Santi offer each other day by day.

"I figured out what that sound was," she says, sipping tea at his kitchen table. "The one we heard on the video the other day."

Santi raises an eyebrow. "The one you described as 'fucked-up whale song'?"

She nods enthusiastically. "I recorded it on my phone and sped it up." She plays it to him, watches his face as he listens. "You were singing in your sleep." The song she sang to him as a baby, the tune he used to hum in the astronomy lab.

His brow furrows. "Did you come up with that, or did I?"

"I don't remember." She finishes her tea and gets up to leave.

"Oh. Your question for Peregrine," Santi says. "I finally got an answer."

Thora stares at him, heart in her mouth. "Oh?"

He looks away, mumbling. "You're in command."

"I knew it!" Thora slaps the table in triumph.

Santi shakes his head. "Took me three hours to get that out of him. *Who's in command, me or Thora?* didn't work. He just stared at me like I was crazy. *López or Lišková*, though, that was fine."

Thora smiles. "You told me I was the captain. When you were my teacher." To Santi's puzzled look, she says, "Don't you remember? We were in the Odysseum, playing the navigation game. We had to decide whether to take the long way around or go through the debris field—" Her hand goes to her mouth.

"Peregrine made us play the game. Because it wasn't a game." Santi stares at her. "He had a decision to make, and he needed our input without waking us up."

"So the collision was our fault."

Santi nods.

"Fuck." Thora punches the table. "One decision. One stupid fucking wrong choice." She laughs bitterly. "All the chances we've had to live our lives again, to do things differently. And now the one thing that really matters, we can't take back."

Santi meets her eyes. "I guess that's how we know it's reality."

Thora holds up her hand. "All right, Mr. *there's-no-wrong-choice, there's-just-what-happens*." She drops back into her chair. "Do you think we would ever have chosen differently?"

She thinks she knows what he'll say: *No, never. We are who we are.* But he shrugs. "Maybe in a different universe." He gives her a sad smile. "But we're in this one. We have to live with it, and make the best next choice we can."

The last leaves fall from the trees. The city takes on a wintry beauty, the cobbles gleaming with frost. Thora's breath puffs in the stairwell as she makes her slow way up to Santi's flat. It takes him a long time to open the door.

"Sorry." He rubs his eyes. "I keep falling asleep."

"Look at us," she says, breaking into laughter as she lowers herself onto his sofa. "I was in better shape when I was eighty years old and dying of cancer."

"Thora," he says. "What do we do?"

Thora feels a churning in her stomach, a last refusal. But it's futile, like screaming *no* into a hurricane as it tears your house apart. "Go to the Odysseum, while we can still get there. Keep trying. If we don't make it—at least we'll see how it ends."

He nods, a terrible peace in his eyes. She knows him. The one thing he's never been afraid of facing is death.

At the door, he casts about as if he's forgetting something. He laughs. "What am I doing? It's not like we can take anything with us." Félicette rubs up against his legs, then spasms, hissing at something that isn't there.

"We're not bringing your defective cat," Thora says, guessing what he's thinking. She watches him scratch Félicette's ears, make her promise to be good.

At the Odysseum, they sit in front of the video, looking up into the faces of their dreaming selves. Thora shakes with hunger. "So where are we now?" she asks Santi. "Hope or despair?"

"Both," he says.

"Both," she agrees. She lets her head fall onto his shoulder.

They watch and wait: for the end, for an answer, for a revelation. Time stretches and compresses like the beating of a slow heart. Thora is not sure if they sleep. She only knows she is aware of something new: a noise from the video, impossibly low, rattling like a train coming down the track toward them.

She lifts her head. "What is that?"

Santi sits up. "Do—do your trick," he says, searching for words. "What you did with my song. Speed it up."

Thora fumbles with her phone, the controls baroque and unwieldy to her clumsy fingers. On the third try, she manages. She presses play and hears a chime, soft and insistent. "Must be an alarm, warning us of our imminent demise. How considerate."

"I've heard that before." Santi turns to her, a spark shining through his exhaustion. "At the beach. Remember?"

Thora closes her eyes, reaching back through her myriad lives. Once, she was a teenage girl crouching on shaking sand. After the collision, after Peregrine collapsed beside her, she heard it, coming from everywhere and nowhere. "I could smell smoke," she says. "But there wasn't a fire."

"There was," Santi says. "But not in the simulation. On the ship."

Thora understands. Flames too bright for this world, blazing at the corner of her eye in odd moments ever since. The smell of smoke. The alarm. Fragments of reality bleeding through.

She opens her eyes. Santi's face is a mirror of her own: excitement, fear, and a trace of strange regret. "We were starting to wake up."

"Fuck," Thora says, and then, "Peregrine!"

"Yes?"

They both jump. He's standing behind them, manifested from nowhere.

"Jesus." Thora stands up, leaning on Santi for support. "Peregrine, this is important. Remember the collision? There was a fire on the ship. Whatever you did to stop it—could you reverse it?"

Peregrine stares at her like she's speaking in tongues.

Santi gets to his feet. "Let me talk to him. I've had seven years of practice, remember?"

Thora bites her nails as Santi takes Peregrine aside. She watches him as he talks, as he listens, coaxing fragments of truth from a broken machine. Peregrine stutters, blinks, speaks. As Thora watches, something happens to Santi's face.

"What?" she says when he comes back. "What did he say?"

He shakes his head, quick and tight. "We can't do it."

"Why?" He avoids her eyes. "Santi, I'll ask him myself, even if it takes all the time we have left to get an answer. What, would it destroy the ship?"

"Not the ship." He takes in a shuddering breath. "Your compartment. The fire—it started to melt the wires that control the outflow valve. It got stuck half-open. Air was leaking out."

Thora inhales, each breath feeling like it escapes through a hole in her. She's back in the Odysseum, looking up at an empty spacesuit, at her distorted seven-year-old reflection in the visor. She hears Mr. López's reassuring voice. *If it was a small hole, the suit would decompress slowly. You'd just run out of air and fall asleep.* On the beach, after the chime and the smell of smoke faded, she felt light-headed, as if she had been holding her breath. "Okay," she says. "But Peregrine obviously fixed it before."

Santi looks at her in anguish. "Because he'd stopped the fire. If he let the fire keep burning long enough to wake us—"

"The valve would stay open longer. I could suffocate before we wake up." Thora hears the echo of her own voice, as if she is listening to this conversation from somewhere far away. "What are my chances?"

"Six percent," Santi says. "So we're not—"

She talks over him. "What about you? What's the chance you'd survive?" He bites his lip, looking away. "Come on," Thora says. "If it was low, you'd just tell me."

He gives her a grimace of a smile. "Ninety-two percent."

Their lives, reduced to two numbers. Thora bows her head, thinking about the numbers that make up this whole world: the trees, the parakeets, Santi's murals. A calculation, a gamble. An equation with one solution.

"Can you make him do it?" She sees what he's about to say and holds up a hand, forestalling him. "I'm not asking right now if you're willing to. I'm asking if you're able."

"He would do it, if I asked. But we both—we'd both need—"

"We both have to agree," Thora says, feeling light and heavy at the same time. "Of course." For an instant, she's angry, so angry she could set the world on fire. Then she laughs, surprising herself as much as Santi. He is looking at her, stricken. "What, you don't see how funny this is?" She laughs again, throwing her head back to the starry ceiling. "It's enough to make you believe in a plan."

"We're not doing it," Santi says.

Thora blinks at him. "I'm sorry. Who's in command again?"

"That doesn't mean anything. You can't order me to let you die."

Thora crosses her arms. "Go on, then. What's your alternative?"

Santi's mouth opens. "We stay. We—take our time, we find a safe way for us both to get out."

Thora laughs. "Take *what* time? Last I checked, we had less than six months left. And we'd already decided we were too far gone to do anything but sit and watch ourselves die."

"We were wrong. We just need to try harder. We could do a

lot in six months." He advances on her, angry. "You said it last time. Both of us or neither of us."

"I was wrong. You know I was wrong. If one of us can get out, we take that chance. No question."

Santi shakes his head. "We got this far by working together."

She laughs at him. "Got where? Got *where*, Santi?" She sweeps her arm wide in answer. "Here. Always here."

He walks away. She watches him stand with his back to her, silhouetted by the video wall.

"Be honest," she says. "If our positions were reversed, you wouldn't hesitate for a second. You'd sign your life away before the question was even asked."

He turns. "And you'd be happy to let me?"

"Of course not. But it wouldn't make any difference. You'd insist anyway. And so will I."

He sets his jaw. "I'm not going to let you do it."

Thora gazes at him. "Hope and despair, Santi. Who did we realize we had to become to make it out of here?" She shrugs. "This is it. This is the risk that's worth taking. This is the everything we had to be willing to lose."

Santi sits down, head in his hands. "This isn't how it's supposed to be."

Thora joins him on the floor. "You're just upset to have been denied your chance at martyrdom. Sorry, pal, the lions get to gnaw on me this time." She is in awe of how she feels: joy, almost euphoria, coursing through her like she is made of it. Sometime soon, this rush will be over, and she will have to confront what she has agreed to do. But for now, she rides the certainty like a chariot through the sky. For so long, she has been obsessed with making the right choice. Now, at what might be the end of her, she doesn't feel like she's choosing. There is one path, and she walks it with a glad heart. She marvels at the paradox: this constraint, this inevitability, feels like the freedom she has been kicking and screaming for her whole long existence.

Santi runs his hand through his hair. "God knows how to test me. And always, always in a different way from what I was prepared for." A shallow laugh escapes him. "You'd think I'd be prepared for *that* by now."

Thora looks at him fondly. "Of course you still see God in this. Why am I surprised? You saw God in a coffee cup." A laugh rocks him like a tremor. Thora moves to sit opposite him, takes his hands in hers. "You would do this for me, yes?"

He meets her eyes. "In a heartbeat. I can't imagine a better reason to lay down my life."

"Then why won't you let me do it for you?"

His mouth moves, struggling to let something out. "It's not fair," he says finally. "It's not fair to compare how I would act in this situation to how you should act. My beliefs—I—"

Thora smiles. "Oh, I get it. You mean because I'm a godless heathen? You think it's harder for me to risk myself because my life and death are meaningless anyway?"

"I didn't mean—"

"I told you. I make my own meaning. No, I don't think I'm going anywhere after this. I don't think God is watching, and I don't think there's a cosmic plan that my death is designed to fulfill." She looks up into her own sleeping face. "Honestly, I'm angry about it. I'm angry that I might never meet Jules—the real Jules. I'm angry that there's an entire new world out there, just— right there"—she reaches out, as if the planet is hovering on the other side of the darkness "and I may never get to see it." She meets Santi's eyes, warm and bright and terrified for her. "But if it means you live, and see it for both of us—that's meaning enough."

"No." He shakes his head. "No, I won't do it. I won't let you go."

Thora's heart beats like a fly trapped in a glass. She traces the lines of Santi's face, wipes the tears that are already starting to fall. "Do you know why I'm smiling?" she asks.

He chokes, shaking his head.

"Because I have a knock-down argument, and it's going to destroy you." She looks into his eyes. "Who are we, Santi?"

He understands. He turns his head, tries to pull his hands away, but she holds on. "You know who we are. We're explorers. Both of us, always and forever." She squeezes his hands, rests her forehead against his. "We gave up everything for this. Our loved ones, our futures, our whole lives. All for the possibility of a new world. Are you telling me either of us would draw the line here? Say, no, this is too much, it's not worth it?"

He stares at her, across the space that contains only them. Versions of them spiral out from this moment, and Thora finally understands: they all exist, every one of them, no matter what happens next.

"No," Santi says, his voice broken.

She shakes her head against his. "This is what we were always for. To touch the unknown, or die trying." She smiles. "Even if I never see it, I'm glad I got to make it this far."

They walk slowly back across the night-lit bridge, through the small-hours quiet of the old town.

"We don't have to do this now," Santi says. "We have a few more months. We could live them, first."

"You really think I could live like that? With my death hanging over me?" Thora looks at him. "I know what you'd want, if you were me. A farewell tour of your favourite haunts. A heart-to-heart with Héloïse and your parents. A series of murals summing up the meaning of your existence." She looks away from his rueful smile. "But that's not me. I'm taking one last look at the city, and then we're doing this." *One last look.* Thora pushes down what she's really afraid of: if she has time to think about it, time to slow down and look her decision in the face, she might change her mind.

They take their time climbing the tower. Thora tells herself they're being careful. She knows what they're really doing is pushing back the moment when they will have to say goodbye.

At the top, they sit side by side looking over the city: the cathedral, the river, the Hohenzollernbrücke covered in beautiful foolish gestures of love. Thora closes her eyes to a vision, clear as a gift: Santi stepping onto the surface of a new world, its dust rising to welcome his feet.

"Bury me there," she decides. "If I don't make it."

"Where?"

She opens her eyes to Santi's beloved, shattered face. "On the new world."

He takes a long breath before he speaks. "If that's what you want."

She frowns at the implication. "What, would you want your corpse hauled back to Earth? I assume the training we can't remember included briefings on cargo efficiency."

He shakes his head, looking up with a soft smile. "No. No, I'd want to be buried among the stars."

She snorts. "You mean drift forever through space as a human icicle? Whatever floats your boat."

Behind his smile, he's starting to cry again. Thora feels herself buckling like a tin in a vacuum. If she doesn't do this now, she won't have the strength. "Peregrine!" she yells, her voice ringing out.

Nothing happens. She looks uncertainly at Santi.

"Can he even come up here?" he wonders.

"I was kind of expecting him to float down from a cloud, if I'm honest."

A scrabbling from inside the tower. Peregrine climbs up through the opening, dusting off his coat. "Yes?"

Thora clears her throat. "We decided."

Peregrine looks uncertainly at Santi. "Both?"

Santi shudders. Thora knows a moment of terror mixed with relief: he is going to refuse, spare her and doom them both.

"Yes," he says, and it's over, the choice is made.

Thora convulses with her first real jolt of fear. She holds on to the edge of the tower until it passes. "Peregrine," she says. "I was wondering if you could do something for me."

"Yes?"

"I want there to be a copy of me in the city. Built of everything I was in here. Sitting outside Der Zentaur, swearing at the new recruits, drinking Brigitta out of red wine." She makes the mistake of meeting Santi's eyes. She swallows. "Can—can you do that?"

Peregrine nods.

Thora turns to Santi, takes his hands. Her heart is an exploding star, and she wants this to be over, and she never wants it to end. "Remember me," she says. With a choked laugh, she adds, "All of me."

Santi shakes his head. "All of you wouldn't fit in my mind, or in any simulation. Only the universe can hold you."

"I've been lucky, really. Most people only get one life. I've had more than I can count." She squeezes his hands. "They tricked us, by the way. Do you see how they did it?"

"No," he says, heartbroken. "Tell me."

She rests her head against his, looking out over the river. "I used to be so obsessed with making the right choice. Then, after I found out what was happening to us, I thought it proved that none of our choices in here meant anything. But I was wrong. Every single choice we made told us something about ourselves, about each other." She turns back to him, moves his hands in emphasis with her words. "Peregrine tried to tell us, but I didn't understand. I do now. That was the point. For me to know every you. And for you to know every me. Because there's only the two of us here, we needed to be everything to each other. And no one can be that. Not in just one life." Her voice shakes. "But we've lived so many, and I know you, as well as I know myself. And I know that every single version of us would choose the journey. Whatever it costs."

He gazes at her, the tears streaming freely down his face. "Look," she says, mock-frustrated. "I'm giving you this one. Why are you crying?"

A laugh mixes with his sobs. Thora kisses his forehead as a shadow falls across her. Peregrine, standing between her and the stars. "Ready?" he asks.

Thora takes in a deep breath. How could she ever be ready to die? She needs a recapitulation, her life flashing before her eyes, but which life? The one she wants is the one she doesn't have: the real life she'll never remember, shattered into echoes across this imaginary city. *All right, space girl,* Jules says in her mind. *I'll be waiting.*

"One more thing." She looks at Santi, a strange calm settling over her. "I want you to take a message back to Jules. I don't know if we're together, or if we used to be, or if it's just something I wish could have happened. I guess I'll never wake up to find out. But I want you to tell her that if she's half as amazing as her echoes, then I was very lucky to know her."

Santi nods. "I'll tell her." He closes his eyes, getting himself under control. Thora just looks at him: his long eyelashes, his strong nose, the way his mouth moves when he's trying not to cry. Like a childhood home, seen so close and so often that you stop noticing what it looks like, until you leave and ache with missing it. Before she can look away, he opens his eyes. "You can change your mind," he says, almost pleading.

She smiles. "Would you?"

He shakes his head.

"Well, then." A plume of parakeets rises from the fountain. Thora watches them fly over the river toward the edge of the city, imagines she can catch the moment when they disappear. She remembers standing at the top of this tower so many lives ago, sparking a flickering flame. *You never know when you might need to set something on fire.* "I'm ready."

Santi turns to Peregrine, murmurs something. Then he gathers her into his arms.

She feels the warmth first, moving through her chilled limbs. Then she sees the flames, invisibly bright at the corner of her eye, the only light up here besides the stars. Her breath comes short. Santi is gasping in her ear, and she is clinging to him, and she doesn't want to die. *No*, she thinks in desperation, *no, I can't do this, I need to live.* But if she says it aloud, Santi will save her. She focuses on him, thinks of him waking into their shared dream. She relaxes her fingers and willingly, joyfully lets go.

The chime sounds in real time, sharp as the gathering smoke.

She can't feel Santi anymore. Her vision crowds with hallucinations: parakeets bursting through the wall of a spaceship; her and Santi's names written across the stars; bridges crumbling, borne down by the weight of human love. She sees the view from the top of the tower, the square spread below her in impossible daylight. Squinting, she thinks she sees him at a table outside Der Zentaur: Santi as she has known him, head bowed, drawing in his memory book.

A laugh gasps through her stricken body, using the last of her air. Maybe this is what the afterlife will be for her. An endless argument with Santiago López Romero. In this moment, she can think of worse ways to spend eternity.

The visions fade, burned away by a white light that hums as it expands. Thora tries to draw in a final breath, but she is nothing and nowhere, drowning in radiance. *A bright light*, she thinks as it consumes her. *How original.*

○ ✶ ◎

The light hurts Thora's eyes.

A cacophony of sound, resolving into the endless alarm and the delayed humming of Peregrine's extractors. Thora rips her way free of the IVs, the heating pads, clumsy as if she has gained an extra dimension. She is here. She is alive. Gasping, she gropes for the button that unseals her compartment. She claws her way out in weightless delirium, her body remembering her training while her mind lags behind in the simulation, clinging to Santi at the top of the clock tower. She palms her way down the scorched wall to his compartment, believing for the first time in a miracle. *Both of us. Both of us made it out.*

Then she sees his body through the glass.

Her breath won't come. She is alive, she made it, but now she is suffocating, staring at him where he floats, frozen and inert. She doesn't understand. "Peregrine," she yells, but there is no one here: only the silence of the ship where she is the only living oc-cupant. Only the marks of the fire on the wall. Only the damaged panel beside Santi's compartment, the melted wires that opened a tiny, fatal window to the stars.

Thora pounds on the wall and screams.

*   *   *

An hour later, she sits in the pilot's chair of the lander, watching the planet turn beneath her. A vastness of blue and gray, speckled with alien clouds: a new world.

The ship creaks, a minuscule adjustment that hits Thora's senses like an earthquake. It's too much, as everything has been since she woke: blisteringly, painfully real, in a way that makes the city seem in retrospect like a shadowed dream. *Through a glass darkly,* she thinks, and wonders where the thought comes from.

She moves her head slowly, tracking across the mementoes taped to the wall. The photo of Jules smiling, the reality she remembers more incandescent than any version she projected: her own fear, her own insecurity muddying the lens. She keeps turning, past the flags of their many allegiances, Spain and Iceland and the Czech Republic and the EU's gold stars on blue, a child's drawing of the immensity she's seeing through her window. Finally, her eyes come to rest on the empty chair beside her.

It doesn't matter why. But she still searched like a madwoman, as if finding the reason would enable her to start again, have another chance to get it right. By the time she found the damage from the collision, Peregrine's clumsy repair that cross-wired her and Santi's compartments, there was a hole in her too, and it was pulling her apart from the inside. *He thought you were me, and I was you.* For a crazed, grief-drunk moment, it was true. She hadn't lost Santi: she had lost herself. She knew, even as she pressed her forehead to the cold metal wall, that it wouldn't have made any difference: he would have insisted, as she did, and she would have let him, because of who they are.

She let him go, as he wanted. Set him loose among the stars. Now, strapped in the seat of the lander, she thinks of him drifting

forever, open-eyed, face-to-face with his God at last. She wonders how she can feel so full of him and so empty at the same
time: a paradox, a trick of physics she will never understand. As
baffling as how she knew all of him and yet there was an infinity
left to discover. She thinks of all the people waiting for him, people she will have to tell if she makes it back alive. Héloïse, his on-
again, off-again girlfriend, who they all knew would marry him
one day. Jaime, who came to visit when she and Santi were doing
their basic training in Cologne, spending a wild evening crawling
the bars of the old town. His parents, who came to see him off,
his father alight with pride and his mother a wreck of premature
grief, as if she already knew what was going to happen. His sister
Aurelia, and Estela, his niece, their borrowed daughter. Félicette,
who won't ever understand why he didn't come home. For some
reason, that is the one that breaks her. Sobs take her over, until
her body is nothing but a channel for her bursting grief. Finally
she's crying for him, and he can't see it.

She has to control herself. She holds her breath until the sobbing stops. "Get it together," she says out loud. Like folding the
universe into a box, she pushes her grief down. She has a mission
to complete, and she has to do it alone.

She sets up the landing sequence. For as long as she can, she
doesn't think of Santi. She thinks instead of her trajectory, of
the thousand variables between her and survival, of what might
await her on the surface of the new world. But she can't keep him
out. He seeps through the cracks in her: his smile, his bowed head
as he carefully draws in his memory book, the look he gets sometimes like God stooped down and kissed him right between the
eyes. The look she loves. It's too late. Though her hands still work
the controls, her thoughts are of nothing but how much she loves
him; how he never knew, because while he was open and flowing

as a stream, she was dammed up, too cold and guarded to tell him what he meant to her. And now she'll never see him again. She hunches over, racked by spasms of grief. "How did this happen?" she gasps, and she knows she's asking him, that she will keep asking him until the day she follows him. But she already knows the answer. She did this, by arguing too well for her own annihilation, and she can't take it back. Worst of all, even if she could, she can't imagine any version of her choosing differently.

There's no wrong choice, Santi says. *There's just what happens.*

She sits up, gasping. Like a gift, like a curse, she remembers him, a flood of him coursing through her: laughing in the park with her and Lily, throwing crumbs to the parakeets; playing table tennis with Joost, the engineer who gave Peregrine his face; painting his mural on the wall of the clock tower, brow furrowed in concentration; in the pool during spacewalk training, giving her an underwater thumbs-up. His real and virtual selves collide into something that's smaller than the truth of him and yet bigger than she can contain. She draws in a shuddering breath, focuses on one image: Santi at a table outside Der Zentaur, raising his glass to her.

I knew what I meant to you. She doesn't know if it's exactly what he would say. He always did know how to surprise her. But the feeling behind it, she's sure of. *Now go. See it for both of us.*

"I will," she says, and starts the countdown.

ACKNOWLEDGMENTS

Huge thanks and appreciation are due to the following people:

To my brilliant, determined agent, Bryony Woods, without whom this book would still be little more than two characters in search of a story.

To Natasha Bardon and Julia Elliott, whose editorial genius and deep understanding of the characters made the book into a much stronger version of itself.

To the teams at Harper Voyager and William Morrow, whose enthusiasm for the book carried me through the increasingly uncertain times of its editing and production.

To Anna Burkey and Barbara Melville for giving me my first professional opportunities as a writer. To David D. Levine, David J. Schwartz, and the participants of the 2016 and 2017 WisCon writers' workshops, for offering helpful critique at a crucial time. More broadly, to everyone who has ever given me much-appreciated feedback on my writing: Christos Christodoulopoulos, Laura Gavin, Kit Holland, Peter Kendell, Hazel Lee, Carla Sayer, and Lynette Talbot. Special thanks go to Hannah Little and Ariana Olsen, who have read pretty much every complete manuscript I have ever written, and have been shining lights of encouragement and joy since 2010. Nice Times forever.

To my friends, who have been possibly more excited for me than I even was for myself (special shout-out to Emily Smale for the amazing book cover cake). To my family in Scotland, the United States, and Greece, for their love, enthusiasm, and support.

Finally, with all my love, to Christos, my favorite determinist, who may find some of our arguments echoed in these pages. I'm so glad I exist in the universe where we met. And to Alistair Orpheas, who has only been around for a few months at this writing, but has already been a surprise and a delight I could never have imagined.